Praise for the Ivy N

OLIVER 1

"Brown mixes laugh out loud observations about the acting life with a witty and intriguing mystery. Consider yourself warned. *Oliver Twisted* is a fast-paced addictive read impossible to put down until Ivy has caught the killer."

– D.E. Ireland,
Agatha Award-Nominated Author of *Move Your Blooming Corpse*

"A fun and rollicking mystery at sea with a delightfully twisty plot and a heartfelt heroine who is as entertaining as she is soulful. I highly recommend this series. More please!"

– John Clement,
Author of the Dixie Hemingway Mysteries

THE SOUND OF MURDER (#2)

"The setting is irresistible, the mystery is twisty, and Ivy is as beguiling as ever, but what I really loved was the depth and complexity of painful human relationships right there in the middle of a sparkly caper. Roll on Ivy #3!"

– Catriona McPherson,
Anthony and Agatha Award Winning Author of *The Day She Died*

"It is not easy to combine humor and murder, but Cindy Brown does it effortlessly. Who else would think of combining *The Sound of Music* with *Cabaret* with a serial killer? The result is such fun."

– Rhys Bowen,
New York Times Bestselling Author of *Malice at the Palace*

"The author blends theater lore with a deeper psychological layer, and always on stage is her delightful sense of humor. The concept of a mash-up of *The Sound of Music* and *Cabaret* is as brilliant as it is ripe for absurdity, and readers will thoroughly enjoy this extremely fun mystery that entertains until the final curtain call."

— *Kings River Life Magazine*

"The mystery kept me glued to the pages and I enjoyed all facets as each clue got me closer to the killer's identity...had me roaring with laughter...A delightful read and I can't wait to see what happens next in this amusingly entertaining series."

— *Dru's Book Musings*

MACDEATH (#1)

"This gut-splitting mystery is a hilarious riff on an avant-garde production of 'the Scottish play'...Combining humor and pathos can be risky in a whodunit, but gifted author Brown makes it work."

— *Mystery Scene Magazine*

"An easy read that will have you hooked from the first page...Brown uses what she knows from the theater life to give us an exciting mystery with all the suspense that keeps you holding on."

— *Fresh Fiction*

"Vivid characters, a wacky circus production of *Macbeth*, and a plot full of surprises make this a perfect read for a quiet evening. Pour a glass of wine, put your feet up, and enjoy! Bonus: it's really funny."

— Ann Littlewood,
Award-Winning Author of the Iris Oakley "Zoo-dunnit" Mysteries

"This gripping mystery is both satisfyingly clever and rich with unerring comedic timing. Without a doubt, *Macdeath* is one of the most entertaining debuts I've read in a very long time."

— Bill Cameron,
Spotted Owl Award-Winning Author of *County Line*

OLIVER TWISTED

**The Ivy Meadows Mystery Series
by Cindy Brown**

MACDEATH (#1)
THE SOUND OF MURDER (#2)
OLIVER TWISTED (#3)

OLIVER TWISTED

AN IVY MEADOWS MYSTERY

Cindy Brown

HENERY PRESS

OLIVER TWISTED
An Ivy Meadows Mystery
Part of the Henery Press Mystery Collection

First Edition | June 2016

Henery Press
www.henerypress.com

Trade Paperback ISBN-13: 978-1-63511-041-8
Digital epub ISBN-13: 978-1-63511-042-5
Kindle ISBN-13: 978-1-63511-043-2
Hardcover Paperback ISBN-13: 978-1-63511-044-9

Printed in the United States of America

To Judy Hricko

For her insight, friendship, and boundless enthusiasm

ACKNOWLEDGMENTS

After I began writing this book, I thought, "Am I crazy? I may be a Dickens fan, but I'm certainly not a Dickens scholar. Plus, I went on one cruise ten years ago, have no Eastern European friends, know very little about epilepsy, and next to nothing about aerial dancing." Luckily my friends—old and new—came through and provided me with information, feedback, and support. I am enormously and happily indebted to:

Luis Torres Barragan, a wonderful aerial dancer and teacher who taught me the basics of aerial dancing from a nice safe vantage point on the ground.

Cyndi Wright, Director of the SUDEP Institute at the Epilepsy Foundation of America, who is a great resource for information about SUDEP and epilepsy in general.

Veronica Nett at Holland America, who gave me a tour of the Westerdam. Thanks also to the lovely mystery author Cathy Ace, who checked all my cruise ship details, and to Josh Ferrer and Ada Harrison, who helped me see cruises through crewmembers' eyes (BTW, Ada is very nice, unlike the Ada in this book).

Kristina Brendel, co-founder of the nonprofit "New Thing," the largest humanitarian organization in Belarus. If my characters' Eastern European dialogue sounds realistic, it is thanks to her.

Christopher Lord, a Dickens scholar and mystery author—how did I get so lucky?

Fellow mystery authors Bruce Cantwell and Gretchen Archer for their help with marketing (and a bunch of other things). I'd also like to thank my mentor and friend, *NY Times* bestselling author April Henry for the incredible support she's given me over the years.

My writing and reading friends who caught the plot holes and typos, and made this book so much better: Lisa Alber, Delia Booth, Holly Franko, Mary Sue Evers, Doug Levin, Ann Littlewood, Janice Maxson, Marilyn McFarlane, Erin Pawlus, Shauna Petchel, and Angela M. Sanders.

The outstanding team at Henery Press: Kendel Lynn, Erin George, Art C. Molinares, Stephanie Chontos, Anna L. Davis, and Rachel Jackson. I couldn't ask for better editing, book design, and all-around support. And speaking of support, I want to thank my fellow Hens, who must be the most generous group of authors ever.

And as always, Hal. My books—and I—owe more to him than anyone could possibly imagine.

CHAPTER 1

Summoned into Another World

"You okay, Olive...er, Ivy, or uh, should I call you Nancy?" said my uncle, sticking his foot further and further in his mouth.

I should have known Uncle Bob would be the one to blow our cover. After all, he was just a private investigator, while I was a professional actor. But I didn't think he'd blow it so quickly. We'd been undercover on the *S.S. David Copperfield* for less than six hours and weren't supposed to know each other. Luckily, the security guard didn't notice that my uncle called me by my real name instead of what was printed on my nametag.

Probably because there was a dead body in the room.

Our adventure on the high seas began early that morning on dry land (very dry land: Uncle Bob and I lived in Phoenix).

"OMG," I texted my uncle, who stood in line in front of me at the airline gate at Phoenix Sky Harbor. "Is that a Rolex?"

He chuckled as he read my message, then my cell announced his reply: "Nice fake, huh?"

Uncle Bob had ditched his usual Hawaiian shirt and cargo shorts in favor of Wranglers, a pearl-snap-buttoned Western shirt, a big silver belt buckle, the fake Rolex, and a gold bolo tie with a steer in the center, fashioned out of what looked like diamonds. I couldn't compliment him on his stunning ensemble because we were already undercover, and I had to act like I didn't know him. We'd been hired to investigate a string of thefts aboard a cruise line. Uncle Bob was pretending to be a guest—a wealthy rancher— and I was posing as one of the actors in the onboard show. That's right, we were getting paid to cruise to Hawaii (Hawaii!), plus we'd each get a ten-thousand-dollar bonus if we found evidence that would stand up in court. Nice work if you can get it.

On the plane, I settled into an aisle seat across from my uncle. Even though I couldn't talk to him, I still liked being near him. As I buckled myself in, the elderly man who had the window seat in my row tapped me on the shoulder. "I'll probably fall asleep," he said, leaning over the open seat between us. "I might sound like I'm choking, but don't worry. It's just the way I sleep."

I nodded, pulled out a copy of the script the cruise line had sent me, and began to reread it. I'd only had a few days to prep, but would've jumped on a plane right away for a chance like this. Working part-time at my uncle's PI firm kept me financially afloat, but just barely. My car had recently failed emissions, so I was in desperate need of funds and had no acting work lined up. When I learned about the cruise, the money, and the fact that I'd play Nancy in the onboard musical version of *Oliver Twist*, I felt like I'd died and gone to Broadway.

"SNOrkLER!" said my now-asleep seatmate. Wow. Good thing he warned me.

"And what takes you to San Francisco?" The fortyish blonde sitting next to Uncle Bob drew out her words in the manner of a Western rural-dweller.

"I'm goin' on a cruise, ma'am."

Ma'am? And was that a drawl? Maybe acting ran in the family.

"I am too. Which cruise line are you on?"

"*Get Lit!* Cruises."

"Me too." The woman sounded delighted. "Thought it'd be a hoot to learn something new."

Get Lit! was a high-end literature-themed cruise line designed to appeal to readers, to families who wanted their kids to take an interest in the classics, and to cruisers who wanted to feel like they were getting an education *and* a buffet. There were Shakespeare cruises and Jane Austen cruises and Mark Twain riverboat cruises, and...

"Did you hear about the *Jack London* incident?" she asked.

On the Alaskan cruise in question, a pack of huskies got loose and ran rampant through the dining room. The dogs were rounded up, but not before eating five hundred pounds of steak dinners, several Baked Alaskas, and a mink coat.

"Yeah, but the dogs were—" Uncle Bob stopped. Pretty sure he was about to say "framed," which was what *Get Lit!* thought. Seven thousand dollars' worth of goods were stolen during the doggie dinner, both off guests and from their in-room safes.

"The dogs?" The woman's voice cracked with concern. "They were...?"

"Adopted," my uncle said with authority. "All to good homes."

"I'm so glad. I'm Bette Foxberry, by the way," said the woman, whose tousled, layered, subtly streaked hair swung perfectly as she turned to Uncle Bob.

My uncle stuck out a hand. "Bob Stalwart."

I snickered. I couldn't help myself.

"So which ship are you on?" Bette said to the fake Mr. Stalwart. "Not that awful Poe ship, with the pendulum and all the ravens, I hope."

"NeRRmoRR," snored my seatmate. I had the sneaking suspicion he might not really be asleep.

"I'm on the Dickens ship, the *S.S. David Copperfield*."

"Me too!" she said again.

A flight attendant hovered over me, his eyes on the snoring man who had drooled a bit on the window. "Is he all right?"

"Just sleeping," I said as he dropped little bags of peanuts on our trays.

"I love Dickens," Bette said. "Have you read *Oliver Twist*?"

"Please, sir, I want some—" I tried to flag down the flight attendant to get a few extra snacks for the road.

"SMmorRRRR," said my seatmate, and slid his bag of peanuts toward me without opening his eyes.

CHAPTER 2

The Expedition Begun

On the ground at San Francisco International, I hauled my luggage out to the shuttle area and headed toward a van with "Uriah's Heap" painted on the side. Uncle Bob stood on the sidewalk with Bette, looking confused, so I texted him: "Uriah Heep, a character in *David Copperfield*. Guess who knows her Dickens?" I'd watched a bunch of BBC miniseries and was feeling a little smug.

But my unfounded sense of literary superiority waned as the van wound its way through the mist-shrouded, Victorian, vaguely Dickensian city. I really should have *read* more Dickens. Then the shuttle pulled into the parking lot of the cruise terminal. All remaining smugness evaporated at the sight in front of me.

Behind the glass-housed cruise terminal, the *S.S. David Copperfield* rose out of the fog like Miss Havisham's wedding cake, the near-distant Golden Gate Bridge looming from the mist to frame the entire picture. And under the bridge, and the ship, and stretching out into the bay on the other side of the terminal, was water. Fathoms and fathoms of it, with hungry sharks and stinging jellyfish and seaweed that wrapped around your legs and pulled you down, down, down into the cold black...

"Ladies and gents," said the van driver. "We have arrived. Welcome to the world of Dickens and the *S.S. David Copperfield*."

Uncle Bob turned to the blonde woman. "Did you know, ma'am, that S.S. stands for steamship?" He was a big trivia buff.

"Pretty sure we're not traveling under steam power, so it must be a Dickens thing."

"I love it," said Bette. "I'm learning things even before I get onboard."

The driver parked and jumped out of the van, then slid open the door, letting cool salt-drenched air rush in. Uncle Bob passed by me on the way out of the shuttle. "You okay?" he whispered.

I nodded and sat in my seat as everyone got off the van.

Then I sat some more.

I lied to my uncle. Both right then and earlier, before we took the job, when he asked me if I was over my fear of...

My breath caught in my chest. I beat down my rising panic and pulled out my cell. "Help," I said when Matt picked up. "There's water. Lots and lots of water."

"And you're good with that now, remember?" Matt's calm groundedness made him a favorite with the guys at my brother's group home where he worked, and with me. In fact, since my friend Candy had moved to L.A., he was probably my best friend in Phoenix. "Think about that picnic at Saguaro Lake," he said. "You even waded in a little."

I had been afraid of water since I was eleven years old. A successful swimming pool standoff last spring had cured me. Or so I'd thought. I'd begun taking baths again. I'd dipped my feet in the shallow end of a pool. And fueled with hotdogs (and with Matt and my brother Cody on either side of me), I'd ventured into Saguaro Lake as far as my ankles.

But this. This. This water was dark and deep and...

"Ivy?" said Matt. "Just close your eyes and breathe."

I did.

"Just for a minute," he said. "Think about—"

"Hey!"

My eyes shot open as someone rapped on the van window.

"Is this you?" A young man with a cigarette dangling from his lip held up a sign with "Ivy Meadows" scrawled in black marker.

"Matt, I gotta go."

"Call me later?"

"Not sure how my phone will work at sea." I'd hopped online to look at the FAQs for my carrier, but it seemed the customers of CHEEP cellular didn't cruise much.

"Hello?" The guy stuck his head inside the van, the smell of his cigarette overpowering the salt air. "You okay?"

I waved at him. He stepped back to give me space, maybe because he saw how I clutched my phone. It felt like a literal lifeline, anchoring me to solid ground. A lifeline I had to leave behind for now. "Take care and tell Cody bye," I said. "And Matt, thank you."

"Anytime. And Ivy..." He paused and took a breath, like what he was going to say next was difficult or important. But he just said, "Call anytime. We'll miss you."

I grabbed my bags. I'd told Uncle Bob I was over my phobia, and so I would be. Or at least I'd act like it. I swallowed and stepped out of the van.

The sign holder grinned. "Hello, Ivy Meadows." Though my uncle called me by my real name, Olive Ziegwart, I mostly used my stage name, for what should be obvious reasons. The guy, lanky and beetle-browed with skin the color of Cream of Wheat, held out a hand to help me as I climbed out of the shuttle. Up close, I saw that one of his eyes was light blue and one was half blue, half dark brown. Cool, in a creepy sort of way.

"I am Val Boyko, here to take you to ship, because I won," he said in a thickly accented voice—Russian? Polish? "We see your photo and all the men want to greet you and I won. But..." He cocked his head. "You do not look like your headshot."

"I know." I'd had a little hair dye accident. Since the store was out of my usual brand, I'd picked another one. It *said* "light ash blonde," but my roots were now bright orange.

"I like it. You are like sexy Creamsicle." Val grabbed my suitcase and shepherded me around the hordes of embarking passengers toward an entrance reserved for crew. A big-bellied security man checked our IDs. "Welcome aboard," he said, popping open my suitcases. He nodded at Val's cigarette. "Better put that out."

"Crew can't be seen smoking?" I asked as the guard rifled through my unmentionables.

"Tsk, tsk, tsk," chided the security guard. "Looks like someone didn't read her employee handbook."

Yeah, probably should have asked *Get Lit!* for one.

"Is non-smoking cruise." Val stubbed out his cigarette and dropped it into a large standing ashtray. "Vaping is permitted on outdoor decks, and cigars and pipes in cigar bar only."

"Yeah, thank God for Dickens," said the security guy. "They wouldn't even have that bar if passengers hadn't complained that people smoked in Victorian times." He shut my suitcases and handed me a crew member badge. "Smooth sailing."

"Let us go, Ivy Meadows," Val said as he hefted my suitcases once more. He led me to the gangplank, where I took a deep breath, focused on the ship in front of me, and walked out over the water.

CHAPTER 3

Something More than Usual in the Wind

"You are lucky." Val walked quickly through throngs of crew members, leading me down a passageway and up a staircase. "You room with Harley. She is Madame Defarge."

Though the current onboard show was a takeoff on *Oliver Twist*, *Get Lit!*'s brochure mentioned that major characters from Dickens's other books would be onboard, greeting people and posing for photos, like Snow White at Disneyland.

"I'm lucky there's no guillotine on the ship if I'm rooming with her," I said as we exited onto a deck filled with excited passengers. Val's heavy brows drew together in confusion. "She's playing Madame Defarge from *A Tale of Two Cities*, right?" I spoke loudly to be heard over the din. "The hateful, awful one who likes seeing people's heads cut off?" I followed Val and my suitcases down a passageway.

"No need for guillotine when you can throw people in sea." Val stopped in front of a cabin door, slipped a keycard in the lock slot, and opened the door. Me, I tried to just breathe normally. Val turned and caught sight of my face. "Is joke." He laughed. "No one falls off ship. If you did, I would save you, my Creamsicle. You are lucky to stay with Harley." He stepped aside to let me enter the cabin. "You get best room."

"Wow," I said.

"Nice, yes?"

"Wow, this is the best room?" was what I meant, but Val seemed sincere in his appreciation, so I kept my mouth shut. The windowless cabin held two twin beds, two small closets, and a built-in desk at the far end of the cabin. The far end wasn't very far: the entire space was about eight feet long by six feet wide. Not bad if you were on just one cruise, but I knew most crew member contracts lasted at least six months.

"You are even on passenger deck," Val said. "With paintings." There was a large reproduction of an illustration from one of Dickens's books mounted above the desk. Still.

Val set my bags on one of the beds, then closed the door behind us. "You play Nancy," he said. "I am Bill Sikes."

I whipped around. Val's Eastern European accent was gone, replaced by a crass Cockney twang with an undertone of menace. "I kill you," Val continued in that creepy voice, his unsettling two-colored eyes roaming my body. Then, in his own voice, "So it is good we are friends, yes?"

"Yes," I managed to say.

"I see you are impressed by my big talent." He grinned, showing snaggledy teeth. "I have other big things."

Actors.

A knock. "Has Fagin's newest girl arrived?" said a familiar voice.

"Timothy," I said, opening the door with a flourish. "Please do come in."

Timothy played Fagin, *Oliver Twist*'s king of petty crime, and was the reason Uncle Bob and I were hired. A semi-regular on *Get Lit!* ships, he'd recommended us to the cruise line after hearing about the thefts. Timothy and I met last spring when he played opposite me in an original musical, *The Sound of Cabaret*. He was a great dancer, a big flaming queen, and the hairiest man I'd ever met. I adored him.

Timothy gave me a big wet one right on the smacker and hugged me with furry arms. "Omigod." He stepped back to look at me. "Your hair."

"I like it," said my new friend and murderer, Val a.k.a. Bill Sikes. "Is sexy hair."

"I'll fix it for the Set Sail party," Timothy said.

"Is it really that bad?"

"*Honey.*"

"Okay, okay." I smoothed my obviously awful hair. "What's this about setting sail?"

Timothy shot me a look. "Don't you think this room's a bit tight for the three of us?"

"Not if one sits on the bed. Or maybe two, Ivy baby." Val sat and patted the mattress next to him.

Timothy arched a manicured eyebrow.

"Okey-dokey." Val got up. "I see you at party." He left.

"Should I be scared of him?" I said to Timothy, whispering in case Val stood outside the door.

"Only that he'll upstage you," said Timothy. "His Bill Sikes is crazy good. I mean crazy evil. You know."

I plonked down on the bed. This undercover thing was going to be tougher than I thought. I needed to be extra careful, to suspect everyone I met, and to vet everything I said before it came out of my mouth.

Thank heavens Timothy knew the real situation. I could relax around him.

He took Val's place on the bed. "Didn't they tell you you'd work as an ambient character too? Like for the Set Sail party?"

"Not specifically, but if I'd thought about it..." Of course. If Madame Defarge was available for a chat with travelers, my character would be too.

So even though the ambient character thing hadn't been mentioned in my PI/actor contract, I should have known. I also should have read *Oliver Twist* all the way through. But hey, I watched the miniseries.

"You okay with that?"

"Sure." I would be. Tonight I'd skim the rest of the book for the parts where Nancy appeared.

"Good." Timothy got up and opened the door. "I'll come back to pick you up for the Set Sail party in," he checked the time on his phone, "fifteen minutes."

Guess I'd wing it.

Timothy blew me a kiss and shut the door. I began unpacking, then stopped. Maybe I should plan my next investigative steps. Or read *Oliver Twist*. Or find the costume I was supposed to wear for the party in fifteen minutes. Yeah, that.

The door opened behind my back. "Timothy," I said, "do I need to go somewhere to get my costume?"

"No," said a new, female voice. "No, no, no."

I turned around to find a short brunette staring at me. Must be Harley.

"No, no, no."

I knew my hair was bad, but this was an overreaction.

"I am not supposed to have a roommate." The woman yanked open her closet, pulled out a long, full, brick red skirt, and stepped into it. "Ever. They promised." Was that anger or fear on her face?

"I'm a great roommate." I gave Harley a winning smile. She was already buttoning a brown vest over a white full-sleeved blouse. She'd be great at quick changes backstage. "I don't snore or hog the bathroom, and I've been known to make midnight snack runs."

"Doesn't matter. No. No way." Harley jammed on a mobcap, grabbed knitting needles and a scarf knitted of gray yarn, and threw a shawl over her shoulders. "Don't unpack."

CHAPTER 4

Something Dangerous Too

Why was Harley so adamant about not having a roommate? Sure, the room was small, but it had two beds, two nightstands, and two closets. Obviously meant to be shared. She could see from my two small suitcases that I didn't have a ton of stuff. And she didn't know me, so it couldn't have been that I lied a little bit about my excellent roommate qualities. (I may snore a teensy bit.)

Maybe Harley had something to hide.

I started my search with her desk. Nothing on the desktop but a pen, a small tube of hand lotion, and a few hairclips. I was just about to open the top drawer when my phone buzzed. A text from Timothy: "Five minutes 'til places." Yikes—had ten minutes passed already? This whole working-as-an-actor-and-an-undercover-PI thing was going to be tough time-wise. And I still didn't know where to find my costume.

I threw open my closet. Phew. Two identical costumes hung there. I yanked a petticoat off a hanger and stepped into it, praying to God that its stains were part of the costume and not leftover yuck. I wrangled myself into Nancy's red and green dress, tightened the green laces that cinched in my waist, and...wow. Between the lacing and the square low-cut neckline, my modest C-cups looked positively voluptuous.

I finished my makeup just in time. "C'mon, girl," Timothy said from out in the hall. "Time to be one of Fagin's minions."

I opened the door. "Ready."

"You are not." Timothy was nearly unrecognizable under a broad-brimmed black hat, a wig of stringy red hair, and a beard to match. He pushed me back into the cabin, sighed exaggeratedly, and held out his hands, ensconced in fingerless gloves. "Ponytail holder, bobby pins, and hairspray, stat."

Right. My hair. I scrambled through my duffle bag and found the tools Timothy needed. He arranged my shoulder-length hair in an updo that mostly hid my orange roots and we were off.

"Hey," I asked as we trotted up the stairs, "what's up with Harley? She really does not want a roommate."

"Less space in the bathroom, shorter showers, someone else's hair in the sink—who does want a roommate?" Timothy smoothed down his long green Fagin coat. I was relieved to see the stains on it matched the ones on my costume. Definitely on purpose, then.

"Yeah, but her reaction was over the top. Even for an actor."

Timothy shrugged. "Probably shagging someone."

Duh, Ivy.

We arrived at the main deck, the Pickwick Promenade. "Wow," I said. This time I meant it.

The Victorian-style lobby was resplendent with columns and cornices and framed niches, all painted in shades of green and cream with gilded edges. A massive crystal chandelier hung above our heads, while sconces with fake candles threw pools of flickering light on the oriental carpets. The lobby's open atrium spanned several decks, which were united by a grand staircase with intricately wrought bronze handrails. The whole thing was like a movie set, but a sturdy one that floated.

"No time to gawk." Timothy grabbed my hand and led me up the staircase, which circled an enormous statue of Charles Dickens. "The party's four decks up."

We left the elevator for the paying guests and hoofed it up the stairs to the London Lido deck. Loud laughter and music poured in through the open door. "Party time," said Timothy. "Remember, no drinking while on duty. Though you'll want to."

Fifteen minutes, ten pickup lines, and three marriage proposals later, I knew what he meant. So when I heard, "Can I buy you a drink?" for the umpteenth time, I felt the urge to smack my latest suitor. Luckily I didn't, as my admirer turned out to be a portly rancher with a glint in his eye. "Bob Stalwart at your service, ma'am." Uncle Bob wore a Western-cut suit jacket over his jeans. "How's the day treating you?"

I smiled a good actor smile and said under my breath, "I can't figure out how I'm going to investigate and work as an actor at the same time, my roommate hates me, and every male over twelve is way too interested in me."

Timothy had sidled up beside us. "It's the girls." He pointed at my breasts, which threatened to spill out of my costume. "They're irresistible to the common man."

Uncle Bob glanced at my chest, blushed, then kept his eyes on my face. "Could be." He turned to Timothy. "Have we met?"

"When Ivy was in *The Sound of Cabaret*."

"Timothy?" Uncle Bob peered at him.

"I know," Timothy said. "It's hard to see my hot young body under this costume."

I was anxious to talk to my uncle while we had the chance. "You found anything yet?"

"Just listening and watching right now. Big party like this is a good opportunity for a thief. Hey, you looked a little green earlier today on the van. You okay with—"

"There you are." The blonde woman—Bette—approached us, wobbling a bit, whether from her heels or the enormous drink in her hand, I couldn't tell. "And who in the Dickens do you have here?" she asked Uncle Bob, laughing at her own joke.

"Fagin and his number two protégé at your service, madam," said Timothy in a broad London accent.

"Number *two*? Off with you!" I playfully hit Timothy and a cloud of dust rose from his greatcoat. It smelled like baby powder. I curtsied awkwardly to Bette. "Charmed to make the honor of your acquaintance. They call me Nancy."

She looked at the nametag pinned just above my bosom. "Hello, Nancy-slash-Ivy. You look familiar." She caught sight of something over my shoulder and her eyes grew wide. "Lord almighty, did you know he was onboard?" She grabbed my uncle's arm, pointed at a tall man with black hair, and teetered off her heels and onto me, spilling her entire gin and tonic down my top.

"I am so sorry," Bette said. She did not look sorry. She looked like she wanted my uncle all to herself.

"Here, my dear," Timothy withdrew a handkerchief with a Fagin-y flourish. I patted my wet bosom with it, but my costume had soaked up the gin like an old alcoholic. "Nance, love, we're being summoned." Timothy nodded at a square-jawed blonde man who was waving at us. "That's Jonas, our director."

Jonas, a good-looking guy in his thirties, stood stiffly next to the black-haired object of Bette's interest, who had his arm around a willowy blonde.

"Who is that dark-haired guy?" I asked Timothy as we waltzed over. Literally waltzed: Timothy had taken me in his arms and hummed a tune as we wove though the crowd.

"No idea."

No surprise. Timothy was up to speed on the newest musicals, hair products, and trendy cocktails, but that was about it.

"Fagin and Nancy, at your service," Timothy said as we halted in front of the trio. Up close, the tall man looked vaguely familiar, the slender twenty-something blonde looked like a supermodel, and our director looked like his tie was slowly cutting off his air supply.

Jonas smiled formally and said, "I'd like to introduce you both to my stepfather and—" He sniffed the air, then pulled me aside. "Why do you smell like gin?" he whispered.

"Authenticity?" I said hopefully.

My new director set his jaw and said, "Please go." He pulled out his phone and checked the time. "Don't bother coming back to the party. Just be ready for rehearsal at ten."

"Ten o'clock tonight?" I knew this wasn't a union gig, but still.

"Tonight." He turned back to the group.

I slunk out of the party and back to my room. I got out of my stinking costume and dropped it on the floor. The discarded gown and petticoats took up most of the available floor space, but Harley was still at the party, so I had the place to myself. Or so I thought.

Then I opened my closet.

CHAPTER 5

Under Very Suspicious and Disreputable Circumstances

"I thought we were dealing with thieves, not murderers," I whispered fiercely into my phone.

"What happened?" said my uncle.

"Harley is dead, to begin with."

"What? Dead?" he said again, over loud music and laughter.

I really didn't want to shout about the corpse in my room, so instead I yelled, "Go someplace where you can hear me."

"Gotcha." He hung up.

I glanced at my closet. My roommate was not at the party. She was in there. Or at least I thought it was Harley. I had slammed the door before I saw much more than a contorted body dressed in Victorian clothes. As a regular person who felt squeamish about dead things and sad about people dying, I didn't want to open the closet door again. As an investigator, I knew I had to.

I eased the door open a crack. The young woman just fit inside, so she was small like my roommate. She was also a brunette, but missing the Madame Defarge mobcap Harley had put on right before leaving. A shawl covered most of the clothes that I could see, but her skirt was rusty red. It was almost certainly Harley. I leaned in to get a better view of her face. Her face...

I shut the door again, and leaned against it, breathing hard. There was nothing wrong with Harley's face, except that it was pretty and young and it reminded me that she was recently a living breathing person who might have eventually been my friend and—

My cell rang. Uncle Bob.

I picked up. "There's a dead body in my closet."

"I thought you said 'dead.' Anyone else in the room? Could you be in danger?"

No one in the bedroom for sure, but I looked inside the minuscule bathroom and pulled aside the shower curtain, just in case. "No."

"Then why are you whispering?"

"I don't know. Respect for the dead?"

"Do you know who it is?"

"I think it's my roommate, Harley."

"Are you sure she's dead?"

I thought of Harley's contorted body and her still pale face. "I'm sure."

"Okay. Gimme your room number and I'll be there in a minute. In the meantime, find out as much as you can without disturbing the scene. You pack your gloves?"

"Yeah."

"Good. Wear 'em. And don't open the door to anyone but me."

"Got it." I hung up. Uncle Bob had taught me to always carry a few tricks of the PI trade, including latex gloves to avoid messing up other fingerprints. I grabbed them out of my bag, along with a short robe so I'd be semi-decent when Uncle Bob arrived. I put on the robe and gloves, turned on the recorder app on my phone, and went into the bathroom. "Makeup on the counter, drugstore variety," I said into my phone. "Shampoo and conditioner for curly hair in the shower." I opened the medicine cabinet. Lotions and potions and serums, all for "the first signs of aging." As I catalogued them into the recorder, I upped my estimation of Harley's age from early twenties to somewhere around thirty and filed a mental note about her skincare line for future use.

I may have been in my twenties, but I did live in Arizona, an environment not conducive to great skin.

Besides the skincare products, there was a hair pick, a brush and toothpaste, a couple bottles of cologne, a collection of Band-Aids, some gauze and medical tape, a packet of birth control pills, and two prescription bottles: one for Amoxicillin, half full, and one for Keppra, empty. Amoxicillin was an antibiotic. "What is Keppra?" I said into my phone—a note for later.

Back in the bedroom, I began with the small desk built into the far end of the cabin. Nothing on the desktop that wasn't there earlier. A shelf above the desk held a few travel books, a dog-eared romance, and a copy of *Great Expectations*. I riffled the pages. Nothing but a bookmark in *Great Expectations*. Harley had highlighted a passage on the bookmarked page: "In a word, I was too cowardly to do what I knew to be right, as I had been too cowardly to avoid doing what I knew to be wrong." Huh. Did that mean something to her for personal reasons or professional actor reasons?

I put the book back on the shelf and opened the top desk drawer. "Harley's personal papers include her *Get Lit!* contract," I said, flipping through the standard-looking contract. No mention of a guaranteed private room. I sorted through a short stack of papers. "Written prescriptions for Keppra and birth control pills, and a letter signed," my throat swelled up, but I croaked out the last words, "'Love, Mom.'" Soon, a mother would know she didn't have a daughter anymore.

Swallowing hard, I put myself back to the task at hand. I opened the second drawer, which was filled with undies and socks. The bottom drawer held t-shirts and shorts. "Clothes, nothing unusual," I said.

A knock. "It's me, Bob."

I let him in, shutting the door quickly before anyone could see, since we weren't supposed to know each other.

"Find anything?"

"No clues, and no jewelry or anything that looked like stolen goods."

"Look like anyone else went through her stuff?"

"Not unless they were really neat when they put it all back in place."

Uncle Bob pulled his own pair of gloves out of a pocket inside his suit coat. "Which closet?"

I pointed.

"You got your tape recorder on?"

I nodded and he opened the closet door.

Whoa. The ship rolled and we both nearly pitched into Harley. Uncle Bob braced his hands on the edges of the wardrobe. I stood next to him.

If I was going to learn to be a PI, I'd better learn to look at things objectively. Even dead roommates.

"No marks as far as I can see." Uncle Bob peered at Harley's face. "No bruising, no blood. Eyes beginning to film over. I can only see her right hand." It was crossed over her chest, like she was saying the pledge of allegiance. "But no defense wounds or scratches."

"Wait, what's that?" I reached above my uncle and grabbed a lone book from a shelf at the top of the closet. "*Positively Powerful* by Theo Pushwright," I read out loud. "Why isn't this book with the others?" I turned it over. The black-haired man at the Set Sail party gazed at me from the book's back cover photo. "I knew I recognized him at the party earlier. He's that positive thinking guy. He's on all the talk shows." I flipped through it. "Hey, he signed the book: 'To my dear Harley. You are positively perfect. Theo.'"

A knock. "Ship security."

My uncle and I looked at each other. "I didn't call," I whispered.

"Me neither." He shut the closet door.

Another knock, more insistent. "Ship security. Open up. I have a report of a disturbance."

The security officer let himself in just as the ship rolled again, throwing me firmly into Uncle Bob's arms.

"What's going on here?" said the security guy. We hurriedly separated. "Ahh." He smiled lasciviously. "Into that, are you?"

"Into what?" I said, then followed his glance. Oh. I still wore just a robe, and both of us had on our latex gloves. Ick.

He smirked. "You theater people."

"Nothing's going on," said Uncle Bob. "I...heard a scream, so I came in to see if everything was all right."

"Must have been some scream." The guy sounded like he was talking about a porn film.

I raised my chin. "Yes. I found a dead body in my closet and I screamed."

"A dead body. Right. Well," the security guy leered at me, "you just keep your screams to a dull roar, and everybody will be happy." He winked at Uncle Bob.

He also pushed one of my buttons. Actually, two of them: the "since-you're-an-actress-you-must-be-a-slut" button, and the "since-you're-a-cute-blonde-I-don't-take-you-seriously" button. I especially hated the second. Being dismissed pissed me off royally.

So I flung open the closet door in a grand dramatic gesture just as the ship hit a big wave. "See for yourself!" I said, and dead Harley tumbled out of the closet and into my arms.

CHAPTER 6

Surprises, Like Misfortunes, Seldom Come Alone

After the stunned security officer got Harley off of me, and after Uncle Bob asked me if Olive/Ivy/Nancy was okay (blowing our cover if anyone had been listening), and after a more serious-acting security guy came and asked us a bunch of questions, they let us go with a promise not to say anything to anyone.

Harley's death had to be connected to the crimes onboard—too coincidental otherwise. And she was an actor. Did that mean theater people were part of the theft ring? I needed to be careful. I scrambled to get ready for rehearsal, raced up to the Pickwick Promenade, and yanked open the door to The Royal Victoria Theater just as a Big Ben-sounding clock struck ten.

Jonas stood between the front row and the stage, talking to a redhead with a gymnast's body. I trotted down the aisle to join them. "Pee-yew," Red said in a five-hundred-seat-theater voice. "What's that smell?"

Harley's body hadn't smelled at all, since she hadn't been dead very long. I, on the other hand, stank. After the security detail left my cabin, I realized I had five minutes to get to rehearsal. No time to shower off the fear sweat, so I spritzed myself with something Harley had in the bathroom, only to realize as I ran to the theater that it was men's cologne.

In my rushed state, I'd covered it up with the coconut perfume that had been rolling around in the bottom of my bag. I now smelled like an old man on a Hawaiian vacation. Who hadn't bathed in three days.

Jonas wrinkled his nose. "I liked the gin better." Then, in a quieter voice, "By the way, I'm sorry if I was a little harsh earlier. My stepfather—the man I was with—was stressing me out."

Up close I saw that Jonas's eyes were a deep blue, almost indigo.

He continued, "And when I realized he might be able to smell liquor on you, I panicked."

Harley's eyes had been blue too. I could see them—open, staring, beginning to cloud over...

"Ivy," said Jonas. "Are you with me?"

I pushed the image of Harley's face out of my head. I couldn't tell him what had happened. The security guys had sworn us to secrecy until they'd notified her family. Plus, Jonas might be a suspect. The redhead too.

"Sorry about the smell," I said. "And I'm sorry about earlier tonight too. With Theo."

"You know my stepfather?"

The redhead tittered. "C'mon, everyone knows Theo. The real question is: who's the blonde with him?"

"Madalina is helping him write his memoir." Jonas's square jaw somehow got squarer. Was that a clue? Harley had that signed book from Theo. Maybe she and Theo and Madalina had a love triangle. Maybe Theo tried to dump Harley and she fought him. Maybe I'd been watching too many telenovelas.

"Ada, why don't you prep the stage?" Jonas said to the redhead. "I need a few minutes with Ivy."

Ada muttered something under her breath and hopped onstage.

Jonas sat and patted the seat next to him. I sat, glad for a moment to take in my surroundings.

The Royal Victoria Theater looked like the photos I'd seen of European opera houses: shaped like a U with ornately carved wooden boxes on either side. Tasseled gold velvet drapes framed the boxes and swaths of burgundy velvet cloaked the proscenium. Dark green walls bore a faint gilt pattern that caught the light.

Ahh. The theater. My shoulders relaxed, the sight of Harley's dead eyes faded away, and I sighed with relief. I loved theaters in general—the plush seats and high ceilings and sense of expectation they all held. This one was all that on steroids.

"Let's start over." Jonas smiled at me with teeth that looked like they belonged in a toothpaste commercial. "I'm Jonas, your director. Glad to have you on board, so to speak." He looked at me more closely and his smile faltered. "Uh, your hair..."

"I've been told it's sexy hair."

"It's something. We'll get it fixed first thing in the morning. Right now we need to get you up to speed. It's going to be crazy. That's the other thing stressing me out. I've never known anyone to...never mind." He ran a hand through his blonde hair, which was long on the top and short on the sides. "You got the script I emailed?"

"Yeah. Thanks."

Oliver! At Sea! was a reworked, condensed version of the famous musical *Oliver!* Wasn't sure if the new title was a wink at the original's strangely upbeat title or if *Get Lit!* just liked exclamation marks. Our show followed the musical's basic plot line, with song lyrics revised to emulate life onboard the *S.S. David Copperfield* (and probably to avoid copyright issues). As Nancy, I didn't have many lines, but I did have a great death scene and two songs: a bouncy number with Oliver and the Dodger called "Consider Yourself Onboard" and a mash-up ballad "Where is Food?/As Long as He Feeds Me."

"Great script," I lied.

Onstage, the redhead tugged on a rope, and a length of red fabric fell in a waterfall to the stage floor.

"I've memorized all my lines and songs," I said. "I rehearsed the dances too, as much as I could." Two of the show's numbers had dance breaks, which I saw via links to YouTube videos.

"Good. Timothy said you're a strong dancer. You'll need to be."

Huh. The dances didn't look that difficult. Ada released another red cloth from where it was looped up in the fly space. She was about my age, with the strong back and shoulder muscles of a swimmer.

"Tonight we're going to rehearse *Fagin's Magic Handkerchief.*"

I nodded. That explained the lack of cast members. My contract did mention this magic act, though I didn't get a script for it. I hoped the show's benign-sounding name meant I wouldn't be sawn in half. Didn't want to put myself in harm's way any more than necessary, especially now I knew there was a murderer onboard.

"Ada's our choreographer." Jonas nodded at the red-haired woman hauling a mat onto the stage from one of the wings. "Let's get going." He jumped onstage. "I wish we didn't have to work this late, but you'll need every bit of rehearsal you can get. Be extra careful tonight. I know you're probably tired, but at least you can learn the silk basics."

"The what basics?" I followed him onstage.

"The silks. The aerial silks?" Jonas motioned to the two lengths of red cloth suspended from the catwalk forty feet above our heads. "You're going to be an aerial dancer during the magic show. Didn't they tell you anything?"

"Umm." Another thing left off my contract. A pretty important thing.

"Please tell me you're not afraid of heights," said Jonas.

"I'm not."

It wasn't a lie. I wasn't afraid of heights. I was afraid of dangling forty feet above a hard wooden stage with only a piece of cloth for support. I was afraid of whoever shoved Harley in my closet. I was afraid of the fathoms of water underneath us too.

Ada hauled herself up one of the silks, like she was climbing a rope but way more elegantly. She wound the fabric around one leg, pulled herself up with her arms, then put her other foot on the silk and pushed herself into a standing position.

"See that?" said Jonas. "Ada's using her legs so it's not just her arms supporting her."

She's using magic and muscles I don't have, is what I thought. I watched her climb all the way to the edge of the proscenium, where she somehow wound the fabric around her, then turned and did the splits, hands-free. Upside down.

Never, never would I be able to do that.

"Ada? Let's get going." The miracle dancer shimmied down the silk and landed lightly on the stage. "Your silk is the one with the mat," Jonas said to me. I walked over and stood on the mat. No way this little bit of padding would break any fall.

"Of course, you won't have a mat during performance," said Ada.

Great.

I grasped the silk fabric, which wasn't actually silk, but some kind of slightly stretchy cloth. I pulled on it and it gave a few inches.

"It's Lycra," Jonas said as I tested the fabric. "It has a bit of stretch so it's not so hard on your body. Okay, then." He smiled encouragingly. "We'll begin by teaching you to climb."

He should have said, "by *trying* to teach you to climb." After fifteen minutes I'd managed to climb just two steps. Now I knew how Ada got her figure. Climbing a silk took an enormous amount of upper body strength. I had strong dancer's legs, but my arms...Let's just say the experience was humbling.

"God bless us," Jonas said, implying the opposite. He ran his hands through his hair. "I was afraid of this."

I started to apologize but was distracted by the fact that my arms were on fire.

"I don't think your muscles will be in shape in time for the show, so we won't have you climb like Ada."

Phew. Maybe I'd just wind the fabric around me while I danced or...

"We'll just have a pulley haul you up." Jonas pointed at a spot far above the stage. "And you can dance from there."

CHAPTER 7
A Decided Propensity for Bullying

"Can you die from falling forty feet?" I asked my uncle over the phone as I walked back to my cabin.

"Sure. Hey, can I call you later? I'm in the middle of something." This was uncle code for "Olive, I asked you not to call unless it was absolutely necessary." I knew I shouldn't have used the phone, but after my debacle of a rehearsal I wanted to hear a reassuring voice.

After determining that we could do the routine with a minimum of climbing, Ada had taught me another basic, a single foot tie-in, which was basically using my feet and legs to tie a knot around one foot in the silk. A footlock, she called it. Thank heavens I learned that one pretty quickly. But I performed just four feet off the ground. For now.

My phone buzzed. A text from Uncle Bob: "Forty feet? Depends on how you land. Do you think H. fell?"

"No. Maybe I will," I texted back.

"?"

"Never mind. Good night."

As I neared my cabin, yellow "do not enter" tape crisscrossed over the door reminded me I had bigger things to worry about than aerial dancing. An envelope addressed to me was taped to the door. I opened it. "Due to the earlier unfortunate circumstance, you will need to change rooms," read the note inside. "Your things have been moved to Cabin 234 on Deck B2. Please pick up a new keycard at the front desk. Sorry for the inconvenience." Good thing I hadn't unpacked. And good thing they'd moved my luggage for me. My arms were already so sore it hurt just to text.

After picking up my keycard, I headed down the stairs. My new accommodations were on a different deck, one for crew members. I opened the stairwell door. A different deck indeed. Now I knew why Val was enamored with my previous floor. The passenger part of the ship was luxurious, with tufted velvet furniture, thick carpets, and stained glass lamps. The crew section looked like the ship had taken off its makeup and was older and more tired than it first appeared. Fluorescent lighting did no favors to the stark white hall, instead highlighting the plumbing pipes overhead and the scuffed linoleum underfoot.

I unlocked the door to Cabin 234 and stepped into an empty room the size of a Kleenex box. A set of bunk beds took up less space than the twins in my former room. My suitcases sat on the lower bunk. There wouldn't have been room for them anywhere else. The beds, a small desk/dresser, and two mini wardrobes took up the entire space, leaving just a three-by-six space to maneuver in. I took two steps, opened a door, and peeked into the bathroom. If I wanted to, I could shower my feet while sitting on the pot.

"What the hell?"

I backed into the bedroom to see Ada staring at my bag, hand on her hips, her face nearly the color of her hennaed hair.

"They moved me," I said. "Sorry."

"Whatever. But no way do you get the bottom bunk." She heaved my suitcases onto the top bunk, then flung herself onto the bottom. "I thought you had the fancy room with Madame De-fart. Or did she scare you away?"

She sorta did, but I suspected Ada wasn't talking about her being dead. "What do you mean?"

Ada snorted. "Harley's freaky. Makes weird noises when she sleeps. That's what her last roommate said."

"Is that why she gets a whole room to herself?"

"She has the room to herself because she has a 'special arrangement' with management. They must be making a lot of money off her."

I put on my ditz face. I'd found it helpful for investigating. "A lot of money?"

"Omigod, are you really going to pretend you don't know? They're pimping her out."

I'd only had a minute or two with Harley alive, but she didn't seem the type. That said, prostitution could provide another explanation for her death. Maybe someone got too rough with her. Maybe she knew too much about a client's sexual predilections. Or maybe she was blackmailing someone. Hmm. But if management was Harley's pimp..."Why did they put me in with her?"

"We all thought you had a special arrangement too."

I kinda did. Was Harley also in on the investigation?

Ada flounced up off the bed, pushed past me in the tight space, and yanked a short dress off a hanger in the closet. "Isn't that why you're playing my role?" She pulled the dress over her head.

"What?"

"They promised me Nancy. I had the lines memorized and everything. Then out of nowhere, it was you. Now I have to play Whore Number Two in the magic show and Little Dorrit the rest of the time."

"Who?"

Ada laughed. "Someone said you might have gotten the job because you really knew your Dickens. Others said it was because you were a great dancer. I thought you must be sleeping with somebody important. Looks like I won the bet." She swiped on some red lipstick. "I'm going to the bar." She opened the cabin door, then stopped. "Listen up, girlie." She spoke without facing me. "You got my role. You screwed up my living arrangements. Don't come to the bar. It's my territory, and I don't want any fresh meat there." She looked at me over her shoulder, eyes glittering like broken ice. "Got it?"

"Got it."

CHAPTER 8

In the Dead Time of the Night

Ada was right. I wasn't a great dancer and I didn't know my Dickens. Not much I could do about my lack of upper body strength at the moment, but I could remedy the other problem—and maybe find a clue to Harley's murder at the same time.

Though I was exhausted, I dragged myself to one of the onboard internet cafés. No. Too many people and too public. I tried the others—same deal. Finally, I hauled my tired ass to the ship's library, hoping it would still be open. I was in luck: a sign on the door said, "Open twenty-four hours for your reading pleasure." I pushed open the door and...wow. I walked in, my footsteps muffled by thick carpet. No fluorescent lights or banks of computers here. Instead mahogany-paneled walls gleamed with reflected light from a gas fire. Two leather wingback chairs flanked the fireplace, and a heavily carved antique desk occupied a corner of the room.

The rest of the room was filled with books. They lined the walls and filled several standalone shelves that looked like library stacks. Hundreds of books, maybe thousands. Brass plaques mounted above each of the built-in bookshelves announced their contents. "Nonfiction" filled one wall, "Contemporary fiction" lined another, and "Victorian fiction" and "Dickens-themed fiction" occupied the two niches on either side of the fire.

All the other books were by Dickens. The stacks, built of the same warm wood that paneled the walls, held his books in a variety of shapes and sizes, including paperbacks. And the longest wall in the library was filled with gorgeous books with leather covers in deep blues, browns, and burgundies. The plaque above these shelves simply read, "The Inimitable Boz."

It made sense. Since *Get Lit!* was a literature-themed cruise line, of course they went all out with the library. And since this was the *S.S. David Copperfield*, they went overboard (pun intended) with the English manor house theme. Still, I felt as if I'd truly been transported to a Victorian home, complete with flickering fire and the heady smell of books and old leather. Wow again.

But the no-computers thing threw me a little. I'd intended to do my research online. Now I needed a different plan. I dropped into one of the leather chairs, just to think for a minute. Ahh.

I stood up right away. Too comfy. I slapped my cheeks lightly to wake myself up and sat in the hard wooden chair at the desk. A sheet of paper on the desktop said, "Back in the morning. Help yourself to a book, but be sure to sign it out." I picked up the pen next to the sign-out sheet and found an extra sheet of paper. I pulled out my phone, played back the notes I'd made while searching Harley's room, and wrote down what I'd found:

1. An underlined passage in *Great Expectations*.
2. An empty bottle of Keppra.
3. A personally signed book from Theo Pushwright.

Where to begin? Maybe I could find a medical book where I could look up Keppra. I went to the nonfiction section. Oh. The books stuck with the ship's theme, with titles like *Gin and Juice: The Victorian Guide to Parenting*, and *Daily Life in Victorian England,* and hey, a medical book: *Dying for Victorian Medicine.* Pretty sure it wouldn't mention Keppra, but it might be useful somehow, and besides, I was curious. I slid it out of its place anyway—and immediately wished I hadn't. A half-dissected corpse accosted me from the cover of the book, under the subtitle: *English Anatomy and its Trade in the Dead Poor*. I turned the book over, partly to hide the body on the front and partly out of a grim curiosity. "A detailed analysis of the body-trafficking networks of the dead poor that underpinned the expansion of medical education from Victorian times" read the back cover copy.

Body trafficking. Death. Autopsies. I shivered and deposited the book back in its place, but not before my brain served up a vision of dead Harley on a slab, waiting for the coroner to...

Wait. A noise from behind one of the stacks—a quiet rustle of paper. Was someone in the room with me? I crept around the stacks. No one. So where did the noise come from? Did ships have mice?

I went back to the nonfiction section, listening hard. It was so quiet in the library, so hushed and insulated and isolated. If I screamed, would anyone be able to hear me? Had Harley screamed?

I shook my head. There was work to be done. I forced my eyes back to the titles in front of me. *Dickens and the Workhouse: Oliver Twist and the London Poor.* Then *Fagin's Children: Criminal Children in Victorian England.* Next, *Dickens and The Business of Death.* Not helping my mood. I started to turn away when I saw *Dickens for Dummies.* I took it off the shelf and searched through the index. Oh. Little Dorrit wasn't just the name of a character; it was also the title of a book. Yeah, really didn't know my Dickens. That was something else I needed to do, brush up my Dickens, so I would know when people were acting as characters as opposed to being themselves.

I went to the "Inimitable Boz" section (I did know "Boz" was Dickens's pseudonym) and ran my finger over the gold-lettered spines until I found a burgundy leather-bound copy of *Little Dorrit*, and then a blue copy of *A Tale of Two Cities.* Maybe the character of Madame Defarge could tell me something about Harley or why she was murdered. A long shot, I knew. Harley's murder was probably connected to the theft ring. I mean, what other reason...

Oh. The room felt cold in spite of the fire. If the thieves killed Harley, they might not look kindly on two undercover detectives either. Maybe this job was more dangerous than I thought. *Get Lit!* was paying us awfully well for just finding a few thieves.

Stop it, Ivy, I told myself. That kind of thinking is not going to help you solve anything. Right. I carried the books back to the fireplace. This time I couldn't resist the siren's call of the leather chairs. I sank down into the deep comfort of one, tucked my notes inside *Little Dorrit*, and opened *A Tale of Two Cities*. I flipped to a random page, trying to keep my eyes open. "Death is Nature's remedy for all things," I read. Not helpful in terms of Harley, and not making me feel any better. I flipped again. "The time was to come, when that wine too would be spilled on the street-stones, and when the stain of it would be red upon many there!"

Bloody cobblestones. I shut that page but quick. One more try: "Liberty, equality, fraternity..." So far, so good. "...or death—the last, much the easiest to bestow, O Guillotine!"

Gee, thanks, Boz. I slammed the book closed and shut my eyes tight, but the firelight penetrated my closed eyes, dancing blood red behind my lids.

CHAPTER 9

A Prophetic Misgiving

A few minutes later, I felt a tap on my shoulder. "Miss?" said a voice. I opened my eyes to see a kindly looking woman in a black dress with a high Victorian collar. She smiled at me. "I'm the librarian. I wasn't sure if I should let you sleep."

I stretched. Wow. And I thought my arms were sore earlier.

"But I thought you might like to know it's morning."

"Morning?" I yelped, propelling myself out of the chair. "What time in the morning?"

The windowless room held no clues.

"Seven."

"Thank you!" I grabbed my books, started for the door, then stopped. I ran the few steps to the desk, where the librarian was fanning out a sheaf of papers that highlighted the ship's *Daily Dickensian Delights*. "Last night I thought I heard—" A listing on the day's events page distracted me. "Wait. Theo Pushwright is speaking today?"

"At ten this morning. I'd go early if you want to see him. He's very popular." She said "popular" like some people say poop. "You said something about last night?"

"I heard a noise. Do you have...mice?"

The librarian looked me up and down. "You're a crew member?"

I nodded

"Then you'll understand that *officially*, we don't have mice onboard."

"Thanks." I pushed open the door.

"No bats on the lower decks either," she said. "Officially."

I dashed down the deck, books under my arm. Jonas had told me to be at the ship's hair salon by seven so they could take care of me before they opened for passengers. I race-walked to the salon, hoping there would be coffee. Not only did I need the caffeine boost, I hoped it might cover up what I suspected was pretty bad morning breath.

Coffee might also help my Dickens hangover. Bloody images from *Two Cities* flickered in the back of my mind, like scenes on a big screen TV in a bar, with Harley's imagined autopsied body interspersed between reels like an especially gruesome commercial. I wished I had time to talk to Uncle Bob. He always made me feel better.

I shoved open the door to Sweedlepipe's Salon at five past seven. Just one stylist at work this early, dressed like a Victorian barber in a white coat over a vest and tie.

I felt an unwarranted sense of relief. It could have been the genteel normality of the scene, or it could have been the coffee. He was drinking *coffee*.

It smelled better than anything ever.

"Coffee," I croaked.

The stylist opened his mouth as if to say something, then thought better of it. He poured me a cup from a coffeemaker and carried it over to a barber-style chair. I took the hint and sat in the chair, where I was rewarded with the elixir of life.

"Jonas sent me."

"Ah, the new girl. I'm Martin. Welcome aboard...I guess."

"What?" I craned my head to look at him.

Martin leaned toward me conspiratorially, even though there was no one else in the salon. "I mean, maybe this isn't the luckiest ship to be on right now. You did hear the news? About the dead body?"

Oh no. Just when I'd banished those horrible images. But maybe I could learn something. "No," I lied. "Who died?"

"A crew member named Kawasaki."

"Really? How did he die?"

"Someone found him locked inside a freezer."

I froze too. Could we have a serial murderer on our hands?

"I heard he was stuffed inside it, dressed in costume like a girl."

Stuffed inside...dressed in costume...wait. "Kawasaki," I said. "Like the motorcycle?"

"I think so."

"You know him?"

"Nah. You know how many crew members are onboard?"

"Anyone you know a personal friend of his?"

"No, but it was all anyone talked about in the canteen this morning: Kawasaki stuffed in the freezer."

Phew. I was pretty sure it wasn't a serial murder, just a bad case of got-the-info-wrong gossip-itis, where Harley stuffed in a closet turned into another motorcycle-named guy crammed into a freezer. Like that Telephone game we played as kids. Still, now I *really* wanted to talk to Uncle Bob, to see if any news was circulating among the guests. I checked my phone. No reception.

A weird noise behind me, like someone zipping up a tent flap over and over. I turned. Martin grinned at me as he ran a straight razor up and down a leather strap clipped to the counter. "You're an actor, right?" He stopped sharpening the razor and lifted it to the light, eyeing its edge. "I always wanted to be an actor. I'd be a great Sweeney Todd." He regarded the gleaming razor with a rapt expression. "The demon barber of Fleet Street," he sang.

So much for genteel normality.

"Just kidding," Martin said. Of course. Still, I was relieved when he put down the razor. "I don't actually like straight razors, and I really can't sing." He couldn't. "So what are we going to do with you today?" He lifted my orange and blonde hair by the ends. "Oh, honey. Were you *trying* to look like a cantaloupe?"

"I do not look like a cantaloupe," I said. "I look like a sexy Creamsicle."

"You were nearly a Bald-sicle. What in the world did you do to yourself?"

After a bit more scolding about home hair products, Martin pronounced my hair unsalvageable.

"What do you mean?"

"Let's just say it's a good thing you have nice little ears."

An hour and a half later, I walked out of the salon with strawberry blonde hair. What was left of it, I mean. The whole inch and a half. Besides the near-buzz cut, Martin also gave me a wig he had in the back room, a rat's nest of mouse-brown synthetic hair. "Nancy is supposed to be a mess," he said when I looked at it doubtfully. Okay, I could be a mess.

I grabbed a piece of toast with marmalade on the way back to my cabin, then hid my borrowed books under my pillow next to my copy of *Oliver Twist*. Didn't want Ada to know I was reading up.

Tried my phone again. No service. I was supposed to check in with Uncle Bob morning, noon, and night so we could share information and suspicions and PI stuff like that, but we had planned to text. Now how were we going to connect?

I was due to be an ambient character from nine 'til noon, so I dressed in my one non-gin-smelling costume, affixed the wig onto my head, dashed out the door, ran up the stairs, and made it to the Pickwick Promenade just as Big Ben struck nine. As an ambient character, I could pretty much do as I pleased as long as I stayed in character. I wanted to catch Theo's talk, but that wasn't for another hour, and it was a bit early for drinking and dancing, Nancy's typical activities, so I used the time to look for my uncle. I went to every dining area serving breakfast. I even went to the Solitary Oyster Bar, just in case. Didn't see him anywhere.

All the while I was looking for him, I had the feeling I was being watched. Never saw or heard anything concrete, just had a fleeting image of...a man's hat? And though I couldn't put my finger on exactly why I was nervous, my body was on alert. Uncle Bob had taught me never to ignore that feeling. "Might be some leftover warning system from when humans were prey," he said. "If your hackles are raised, look around for the wolf."

I knew there were wolves about. Harley didn't end up in her closet all by herself.

CHAPTER 10

His Oratorical Powers and His Importance

I paced the outdoor Pickwick Promenade, thinking. Who put Harley in the closet? How was she connected to the theft ring? How was I ever going to solve her murder, catch the thieves, and get that ten-thousand-dollar bonus when I couldn't reach my best investigative tool (my uncle)? And, I thought, as I saw a black hat out of the corner of my eye, who was following me?

I thought the hatted person had disappeared indoors, so I scurried inside to the atrium just as Big Ben struck ten. Time for Theo's talk, but...a man in a black Victorian top hat headed toward the casino. My stalker? I hurried after him. I could catch Theo later.

The man, who carried a brass-tipped walking stick, went past the Golden Hall Gambling Establishment and maneuvered around the throng of people streaming into the theater for Theo's lecture. I followed him, careful to keep a tourist or two in front of me at all times. And I followed him. And followed him. He showed not the slightest nervousness or interest in me, not one nervous tic or backwards glance.

By the time he sat down to watch a tennis match at the onboard court, I was pretty sure I had the wrong guy. Then I caught a glimpse of a different black hat behind me to the side. I whirled around, but whoever it was had disappeared into a crowd.

Great. I'd been followed while tailing Mr. Top Hat. Uncle Bob had taught me how to shadow someone, but not what to do when I was the one being followed. I checked my phone again. Still no reception. No chance to talk to my uncle. At least I could follow up on my other clue: Theo. I headed back to the theater and slipped inside. The librarian was right. Theo Pushwright was a draw. Almost every seat in the house was full, and all heads were turned toward the handsome dark-haired man onstage.

Timothy, dressed as Fagin, stood near the back of the theater. I slid up next to him. "Good morning...Ow!" I rubbed my arm where he'd pinched me.

"I can't believe you found a dead body and didn't tell me."

"It was supposed to be hush-hush," I whispered.

"Well, it was all anyone talked about in the crew canteen this morning."

"Did they mention Kawasaki in the freezer?"

"What? Another one?"

"No, someone mixed up Harley and—"

"Shhh," said a woman in front of us. We shushed and turned our attention to the stage.

"It's simple." Theo's voice was both warm and powerful. He may have been twenty years older than Harley, but I could see the attraction. "You don't have to stay stuck in a low-paying job. You don't have to be a slave to addiction. You don't have to be crippled by your insecurities. All together now," he said to the audience. "If you think it, it will happen." Other voices in the audience chanted along with him. "If you believe it, it will be."

The crowd clapped and cheered. I'd never heard applause like that, not even after my costume malfunction during a performance of *Chicago*. Theo hushed the audience.

"I have time for a few questions." Dozens of hands went up immediately. He pointed at one. An older man with wispy white hair stood up. "So glad you're here," he said in a voice that sounded like it belonged in a boardroom. "But why a Dickens cruise?"

"This is a Dickens cruise?" said Theo. "I'm just here to sail to Hawaii." Laughter from the crowd, way more than his remark earned. "Seriously, I have always felt a kinship with Charles

Dickens," said Theo. "As you may know, he was very poor as a child. When his parents went to debtors' prison, he was sent to work in a shoe-blacking factory. Can you imagine? He was alone in the world, living and working in horrible conditions with complete strangers at the tender age of eleven. From that challenging beginning came one of the world's most successful novelists. Dickens epitomizes the power of positive thinking. I too grew up in poverty. Like Dickens, I had no advantages other than my mind and my will. But I worked hard, and now I stand before you a successful man."

"A billionaire," whispered Timothy.

"Shhh," said the lady in front of us.

"What did that hard work consist of?" asked a familiar voice with a rural twang. Bette stood up. Ah, there was Uncle Bob, sitting beside her. "How exactly did you become a success story?"

"I worked hard from the time I was twelve, doing everything from hauling rocks to writing books." Theo's words had a scripted quality. "Most importantly, I believed in myself. I saw what I wanted and set my mind to taking the actions that would get me there." He cleared his throat, a signal to listen up. "'I never could have done what I have done without the habits of punctuality, order, and diligence, without the determination to concentrate myself on one object at a time.' That's Dickens, from *David Copperfield*. And that's the power of positive thinking."

Bette persevered. "But what about—"

"Unlike Scrooge, I understand that mankind is my business."

"You can say that again," Bette said. "In fact—"

Theo pointed to another raised hand. "Next question, please." Bette sat down.

The gorgeous blonde who'd accompanied Theo the night before approached and spoke quietly to Timothy and me. "You want book from Theo, you get in line now." She had a thick accent that sounded a little like Val's, jade green eyes that tipped up at the edges, and cheekbones that could cut glass. I had never seen such a beautiful woman in person. "Books are twenty dollars."

"I don't think—" Timothy began.

I nudged him. "Great," I said to the blonde beauty. "Stand in line with me?" I asked Timothy. He got up and followed me to the line that was beginning to form down the aisle. I had two reasons for being there. The first was that I wanted Theo to sign a book for me, to see if what he had written to Harley was typical fan-speak or indicative of a closer relationship. I kept that reason to myself, but I needed Timothy's help for my second goal. "No reception on my cell."

"Welcome to life at sea."

"I can't get ahold of Uncle Bob." I tipped my chin to indicate my uncle's seat in the audience.

Timothy's eyes followed the direction I'd indicated. "Oh, he's sitting next to that woman." He nodded at Bette. "Did you see the look on Theo's face when she first stood up?"

"No." My attention had been on Uncle Bob.

"He knows her, I think. Caught a flash of an 'oh shit' look."

"You'd make a good detective," I said. "Which is good because I need your help. How can I meet with Uncle Bob without it looking like I know him?"

Timothy pondered my dilemma as we edged closer to the folding table where Theo's beautiful assistant took money for books and Theo signed them.

"You need a private place," Timothy said. "The cigar bar. During the first seating for dinner."

"Good." I snuck a look at Uncle Bob, who met my eyes briefly then turned back to Bette. "Now I need to figure out how to get that information to him without it being obvious, and while staying in character."

"This isn't detective work." Timothy pouted. "It's acting. But I am up to the task." Then in a voice so loud that people in line turned around, "Nance, my dear, some of your admirers have complained about the smell of your pipe tobacco."

"Oh they 'ave, 'ave they?" I said in my best Cockney accent. "Dear me."

"Permit me, therefore, to introduce you to a better quality tobacco. Shall we say five o'clock in the Dombey and Son Smoking Establishment?"

I glanced at Uncle Bob, who gave a slight nod. "I'll be there, waiting with Old Stubby," I said. Uncle Bob frowned. "Me pipe, that is."

"Old Stubby?" whispered Timothy.

"It just popped out," I whispered back.

"You shouldn't smoke at all," said the woman in front of us, who obviously didn't get the whole I'm-playing-the-role-of-a-Victorian-prostitute thing. "If you think positive thoughts, you can be free of your nicotine addition," she said. "Right, Mr. Pushwright?"

"Absolutely," said Theo. The woman nearly glowed with adoration. He continued: "Smoking is a weakness. If I were in charge, not even e-cigarettes would be allowed onboard." He looked pointedly at his blonde assistant, who ignored him. I handed her the twenty I stashed in my cleavage for emergencies and she gave me a book.

Theo motioned to me and I passed him my book. "Your name?" he asked, looking me in the eyes with a kind, wise expression.

Which name to give? After all, I had three now, if you counted Nancy. "Ivy," I decided.

"Ivy." Theo's voice was warm. "A beautiful name." Charisma radiated from him like the glow from a fire on a rainy evening. He signed my book with a flourish. "Positive thinking can help you overcome any weakness," he said.

Then he caught sight of Timothy, who stood with his hand on his hip, looking like the gayest Fagin in the world. Theo's voice turned from butter to ice. "Even moral weakness."

CHAPTER 11

Lacking the Niceties of Discrimination

"How in the world did you just stand there?" I corralled Timothy once we were outside the theater. "That was..." I couldn't find the words. My outrage had tangled my tongue.

"Not unusual." Timothy shrugged. "Things are better for us 'friends of Dorothy,' but there are still wicked witches who wish we were dead. The trick is to avoid them."

"Or throw water on them and melt them into oblivion."

"Let me know when you figure out how to do that. I'll see you at rehearsal this afternoon." Timothy kissed me on the cheek. I kissed him back, aiming for the small space not occupied by facial hair, either real or stuck on with spirit gum.

I spent a few more minutes wandering the deck as an ambient character, saying Nancy-ish things like, "Keep the game a-going" and "Never say die!" All the while I kept an eye out for my stalker. No sign of a black hat. I finished my shift and headed back to my cabin.

Ada lay on the bottom bunk, flipping through a *People* magazine.

She glanced at me, then snorted. "Don't tell me you believe that bullshit." She inclined her head toward the copy of *Positively Powerful* in my hand.

"Not sure." I climbed up into my bunk where I could look at Theo's signature in private. I opened the book's flyleaf and read,

"To Ivy, You <u>can</u> stop smoking. Be positively powerful." I tossed it aside. "Oh crap."

"Yeah, it is," Ada said from the bunk below me. "And I hear Theo is an asshole."

"Who'd you hear that from?" I hung my head over the bunk so I could see her face.

"You're going to lose your wig."

Oops. I straightened up and repinned my wig tighter on my head.

"Everyone says that about Theo," said Ada. "Even Jonas thinks so. He's trying to be nice, but he's let a few things slip."

"Like what?"

"Like 'why do you want to know, Miss Busybody?'"

I wasn't giving up that easily, but decided to tread lightly. "Just curious. Theo is Jonas's stepfather, right?"

"Duh."

One more try. "Is he here to see Jonas?"

Another snort. "Theo's here to make money. Jonas asked him to come, even gave him the family discount, but Theo wouldn't come unless he was paid to lecture and allowed to sell books. *Get Lit!* ended up axing the regular Dickens expert so they'd have the money for Theo. Real literature buffs, this cruise line...Hey."

At the change in Ada's voice, I hung my head over the side again, keeping a hand on my wig. "Yeah?"

"Were you the one who found Harley?"

Seemed the dead cat was out of the bag, so I said, "Yeah."

Ada put down her magazine. "How'd she die?"

"Not sure."

"Was she really found stuffed in the freezer?"

"Uh, no."

Ada waited.

"I don't think I'm allowed to say more, but..."

Ada's eyes gleamed with the expectation of some gory detail.

"Do you know if Harley had any medical conditions?"

Ada huffed. "Probably had an STD from one of her customers."

She went back to her magazine.

I couldn't get anything more out of her. I had a couple hours before afternoon rehearsal for *Oliver! At Sea!*, so I finished the last few chapters of *Oliver Twist*, did my regular routine of core exercises on my bunk, and grabbed a late lunch at one of the buffets.

The food was a nice bonus for us actors—we got to eat at the same restaurants as passengers, with the exception of the fancy main dining room, Delmonico's. Other crew members had to eat in their designated dining room, which tried to cater to the tastes of the majority of the workers. I heard they served a lot of cabbage, ghoulash, and borscht.

The line at Food, Glorious Food was too long, so I scurried to The Best of Days, Wurst of Days sausage bar and ate a big portion of Toad in the Hole, which was actually very tasty sausages in some sort of batter. Then I headed to rehearsal. I wanted to be there early.

Jonas was there too, sitting in the front row of the theater. "Hey," I said.

"Hey." Jonas turned to greet me with a smile, which dimmed immediately. "I thought Martin was going to fix your hair."

"He did. He fixed it nice and short and gave me this wig."

Jonas gave me a dubious once-over.

"Nancy is supposed be a mess," I said.

"Not that much of a mess."

"Don't worry, honey." Timothy had come up behind me. "Wig styling is one of my many talents, along with—"

"Good," Jonas cut him off just in time. Timothy had a famously dirty mind. Then Jonas said something else that was drowned out by a tsunami of noise as a pack of boys raced into the theater.

"Ready for rehearsal, Master Bates," said the tow-headed leader of the group.

"Master Bates! Master Bates!" cried his followers.

"Oliver, I asked you not to call me that," said Jonas Bates.

"But it's your name, and besides, the Dick-Meister said it." Oliver looked to be about eleven, with blonde curls and a snub nose.

"Dickens also killed off little children with impunity."

"But only the nice ones," replied Oliver. "I'm safe."

"He did hang the criminals." Jonas said to Oliver. "Onstage, everyone." The boys leapt onstage.

"The new sea urchins," Timothy said, sinking down into a theater seat. He patted the one next to him. "You can relax. This usually takes a while."

Must be why Val wasn't at rehearsal yet. Too bad. I really wanted to see his crazy evil Bill Sikes. Who killed me.

Maybe I could wait.

While Jonas tried to herd the boys onstage, Timothy explained the setup. As I knew, in *Oliver Twist*, the innocent orphaned Oliver ran away from a cruel master. Upon making his way to London, he was befriended by a street boy named the Artful Dodger who took him to the home of Fagin, a villainous but friendly-seeming fellow who headed up a gang of juvenile criminals, all orphans too. The difficulty with mounting any production of *Oliver Twist* was the large percentage of children needed to play Fagin's boys.

"So *Get Lit!* has this genius idea," said Timothy. "They cast professionals for the roles of Oliver and the Dodger—David over there plays the Dodger." He waved to a silent black-haired kid with a battered top hat who stood at the side of the stage, watching the action. "And to families with boys between the ages of nine and fourteen, they offer a deal: The kids get to cruise free if they agree to be in the show. It's brilliant. *Get Lit!* gets a cast for almost nothing, families with boys compete for the few slots available, and their friends and extended families sign up for a paid cruise in order to see their darlings onstage. There's just one problem."

"Boys!" yelled Jonas. "You exit stage left. Stage LEFT."

"They don't have to have any acting experience?" I said as boys ran every which way.

"However did you guess?" said Timothy.

Jonas ran his hand through his hair. "God bless us...Everyone! Let's run it again."

After about an hour, Jonas had worked a small miracle. The boys had made it through their introductory scene and their first musical number, where Fagin taught Oliver how to steal from passersby. "You've got to lift a locket, or two, boy," sang Timothy. "You've got to lift a locket or two."

While waiting, I kept an eye out for suspects in Harley's death, but didn't come up with anything viable. Murder by a pack of marauding orphans seemed unlikely.

Finally, I made my way backstage to get ready for my entrance. My first scene consisted of a song and a few lines to establish my character. Nancy was the original prostitute with a heart of gold who belonged to Fagin's stable and to her brooding criminal boyfriend, Bill Sikes. She was also Oliver's protector, which got her killed in the end. She helped keep Oliver away from Fagin so the boy could have the chance to live a regular, non-criminal life. But her interference infuriated the old villain, who wreaked his revenge by telling Sikes that Nancy had turned informant. Outraged, Sikes beat her to death. Offstage, of course.

In the blackout (quick lights out) before my first scene, Jonas said, "Alright, Nancy. We've changed the blocking from what's in the script. You and Fagin enter from slightly upstage, like you've come in from a different room. Hu's on first."

"Who?

"Yes."

"Who's on first?"

"Yes."

"Which actor?"

"Hu."

"The guy playing..."

The kid playing the Dodger tapped me on the shoulder. "I'm Hu."

And I was really confused. "Okay," I said anyway. The lights came up and the Dodger swaggered onstage followed by a wide-eyed Oliver. Timothy and I moved a few feet upstage in the wings to wait for our entrance.

"Welcome to our 'umble abode," said Hu, doffing his hat to Oliver. "The 'spectable old genelman as lives 'ere will give you lodgings for nothing, as long as I interduces you."

"He must be very kind," said Oliver.

"Enter now, Fagin and Nancy," Jonas shouted over the intro music.

We did, arm in arm and laughing as if we'd just enjoyed a great joke.

"Ah," Fagin said as he spotted Oliver. "And who have we 'ere?"

"A new pal. Oliver Twist," replied the Dodger. Recorded music began to play.

"We are very glad to see you, Oliver, very," said Fagin. "Aren't we, Nance?"

"We are indeed," I said, trying to sound like a Cockney putting on a posh accent.

"Indeed," said the Dodger, whose accent was much more believable than mine. He started off the song. "Consider yourself...onboard." He sang it to the tune of, yep, "Consider Yourself" from *Oliver!* "Consider yourself...one of the barnacles." A smooth-cheeked Asian boy, he had a strong tenor voice and a pitch-perfect Cockney accent.

"You don't have to stow...away," I sang. "It's true, you...have landed a place to stay."

Fagin put his arm around Oliver and sang, "Consider yourself...shipshape. Consider yourself...one of our happy gang."

The blonde boy looked up at Fagin with doe eyes and sang, "It's true that I'm in...your debt."

"Not yet, but, whatever you take, we get," sang Fagin.

I knew this number was about Oliver's introduction to Fagin's stable of young criminals, but still, I wasn't sure it was the smartest choice for a theft-plagued cruise line. We finished the song and Jonas said, "Hold it. Nice job, Ivy. Let's take five. When we come back, we'll put the rest of the orphans into the scene."

"Don't worry, the boys just stand there during our song," said the Dodger as we exited stage left. "By the way," he stuck out a hand, "I'm David Hu."

"Oh."

He grinned.

"Jonas and David like that Hu joke. I don't get it," said the blonde boy. "I'm Oliver. It's my character name and my real name. What's yours?"

"Ivy Meadows."

"Right." The kid laughed.

Jonas joined our group. "Ivy," he said. "I wanted to apologize about yesterday. I wouldn't have pushed you so hard if I'd known about Harley."

"Did you know her well?" I asked.

"I didn't, but..." He glanced at David, who pulled in his bottom lip.

"She was nice," David said.

"What's wrong with Madame De-fart?" Oliver asked.

I wondered who came up with that nickname first, him or Ada.

"She's dead," said Timothy.

"Dead?" said Oliver. "She's dead as a doornail!" he shouted to the orphan actors. Then to me, "It's Dickens."

"It's also Shakespeare," I said. "And not a very nice thing to say when someone's really dead."

"No wonder you were distracted," Jonas said to me. "It had to be horrible, finding her."

"Is she in the morgue now?" asked Oliver. "Hey boys, want to see a dead body?" Before us adults could say anything, he added, "Kids saw dead people in Dickens all the time."

I ignored Oliver. "It was horrible," I said to Jonas, "especially not knowing if her killer was still close by."

"Her killer?" said, oh, the entire cast. "She was murdered?"

Oops.

CHAPTER 12

Troublesome Questions

"They're calling Harley's death natural causes," said Uncle Bob, mumbling around the enormous stogie in his mouth.

"Like people naturally end up in closets when they die?" I waved away the cigar smoke, which smelled like a wet dog eating burnt sausage.

"That would be pretty convenient." He puffed on his cigar thoughtfully. "You could make coffin closets. Just go in when you feel sick, never come out again." He and Timothy and I sat in a back corner booth of the cigar bar, which was similar to the library in decor—dark wood and leather furniture—but done in shades of red, with burgundy leather, scarlet Oriental carpets, and an ornately carved bar lit by lamps with wine-colored shades. "Do you think she fell from somewhere?" Uncle Bob asked me.

"What? Why would you—" Oh. My text after the silk rehearsal. Didn't really want Timothy to know how nervous I was (since he'd recommended me), so I shook my head and snuck a peek at him as I sipped my cream ale (I was off-duty).

He noticed my not-so-subtle glance. "Don't worry about saying anything in front of me. My lips are sealed." He puckered up and blew me a kiss. "They're also really soft, thanks to this new lip balm." He looked at me critically. "You know, Ivy, you could stand a little..."

"Beauty tips later. Investigation first," Uncle Bob said.

"Do you think Harley was poisoned?" I said.

"Maybe. But there are usually signs."

"Maybe there was some drug interaction." It had happened to a friend of mine recently. "Do you know what Keppra is used for?"

Uncle Bob shook his head.

"You can use one of the internet cafes to look it up," said Timothy. "Wi-Fi is spotty, depending on where we are, but if you—"

Uncle Bob cut him off. "Don't think that's wise. Someone could intercept the information, or even just read over your shoulder. Remember, we don't know who is involved here."

Good thing I used the library last night. "Harley wasn't investigating too, was she?" I asked, remembering what Ada said about Harley's "special assignment."

"Not in any official capacity."

"Anyone else know about us? I think someone is following me."

"You sure?" Uncle Bob put down his cigar.

"No, but it feels like it. And I keep seeing a top hat out of the corner of my eye."

"A top hat. Must be a crew member."

"Not necessarily," said Timothy. "A lot of the guests dress up too."

"I'll keep an eye out," said Uncle Bob.

"Wish I had my spy sunglasses."

"Olive." Uncle Bob gave me a stern look. "This is not a game. Be careful, all right?"

I nodded and blew out a stream of smoke.

Yeah, I was smoking. A pipe, which is what I was told Nancy would smoke. What we actors do for art.

"You're not inhaling, right?" Timothy said. "I'd be devastated if I contributed to the ruin of your vocal cords."

"You're safe. I'm not inhaling, and I don't think I'll become a lifelong pipe smoker."

The tobacco I'd bought smelled pleasantly fruity in the air, but tasted like hot ashes in my mouth.

Uncle Bob blew a smoke ring. "Did you know that they sold Pickwick cigars when *The Pickwick Papers* became a hit?" said my trivia-loving uncle. "China tchotchkes too."

"Did you know Dickens studied to be an actor?" asked Timothy.

"I didn't," I said.

"Did you know," Uncle Bob grinned at Timothy, happy to have a fellow trivia buff, "that when Dickens used to read the murder scene in *Oliver Twist*—"

"You mean Nancy's death?" Timothy asked. "Where Sikes beats her to death?"

Uncle Bob nodded. "That scene was so shocking that at one of Dickens's readings, a bunch of ladies," he made finger quotes, "'were borne out, stiff and rigid from its effect.'"

"Never happens to me," said Timothy.

"Can we please get back to the dead girl in the closet?" I turned to my uncle. "Do you think the ship's doctor is covering up what really happened? Maybe he's in on the whole theft ring."

"I had that thought too. I'm looking into it. I've also got a list of regular *Get Lit!* cruisers onboard, people who've been on more than one ship. I'm working on meeting them and questioning them, in a friendly way, of course. Find out if they know anything helpful."

"Or if they're a part of the operation," I said. "Which ships have had thefts?"

"All of 'em. The *Jack London* incident was the kicker, but there have been substantial amounts stolen from all the ships. We don't have a lot to go on. You got anything?"

"Nothing." I took a long drink of my ale. "Except a bad wig, a cranky roommate, and maybe Theo Pushwright."

"Yeah?"

I explained my theory about Theo's book. "I know it's a long shot," I said. "But the fact that Harley kept her copy separate from her other books plus the sort of special signature could imply a relationship."

"You're right about the long shot thing. Plus that guy's got more money than God. I can't see how he'd be involved in any theft ring." Uncle Bob drained the last of his beer. "I got a couple of things. There's a high-end jewelry store onboard. No thefts from it, but several of its customers have had their jewelry stolen a few days afterward."

"Which points to someone with inside knowledge," I said. "Which we kinda already knew."

"Yeah. The thing is, the thieves must stash the stolen goods onboard, but where?"

"Good question," said Timothy. "You know the phrase 'shipshape?' They clean every inch of this ship all the time. They even inspect the crew quarters."

"You said you had a couple of things?" I asked my uncle.

"Yeah. You met any Eastern Europeans yet?"

"Sure. There's Valery and about a hundred others." I wasn't exaggerating. Probably a third of the ship's staff was from Russia or Serbia or Romania or another European country ending with "ia."

"Got a tip that the thefts may be related to some sort of Eastern European gang working the ships. Keep your eye on 'em."

"Isn't that racial profiling?" asked Timothy.

"I don't think Eastern European is a race," I said. "Wouldn't it be 'cultural profiling?' Or 'region-specific profiling?'"

"It would be a tip." Uncle Bob set down his beer glass and got up. "And one that a smart detective would follow up on."

CHAPTER 13

Fresh Discoveries

"Gluhhhhhh," I groaned. "Does anything feel worse than a queasy stomach?"

"Probably lots of things. Torture, surgery without anesthetic, getting your unmentionables waxed."

I smacked Timothy. "It was a rhetorical question. Wait, do you wax...down there?"

"Slick as a whistle."

"Okay, I think you just upped the nausea factor." We sat at a table in Boz's Buffet. We'd gone there after our cigar bar meeting to get some dinner before rehearsal. I had just finished a big plate of sushi, which *Get Lit!* had tried to make more Dickensian by calling it names like Street Urchin's Uni, Oliver's Ono, and Micawber's Mackerel Maki. "Do you think I ate some bad fish?"

Timothy shook his head. "You just ate dinner. Food poisoning takes time. More likely the combination of rough seas, pipe smoke, and beer. Plus sushi."

I could see that. I also knew there were two more things causing my stomach to roil. Harley's dead face still floated in the back of my mind. And as if a dead roommate wasn't enough, there was the idea of dancing forty feet in the air in front of an audience held up by just a piece of fabric. I'd been keeping the thought at bay, but it crept back into my consciousness as tonight's rehearsal neared. I wasn't sure I could do it. Aerial work took a lot of upper body and core strength. I was already sore after just the one rehearsal. Ada had offhandedly remarked that it usually took months to learn the silks. I had just three more rehearsals.

"Omigod, omigod, omigod." Timothy elbowed me so hard I bet I'd have a bruise.

"Ow. What?"

Timothy's furry fake Fagin eyebrows nearly met his hairline. He stared fixedly at the buffet line, where cruisers were lined up, jowl to jowl.

"What?" I said again.

"Val," he whispered. "I just saw him pick that guy's pocket."

"Really?" I followed his line of sight. Sure enough, there was Val chatting with a young brunette who stood in the line for the buffet. He wore his Bill Sikes costume: a ratty hat pulled low, a tattered scarf around his neck, a vest with a few strategically placed moth holes, and a greatcoat. Lots of pockets. Lots of places to hide small stolen goods?

"No way," I said. "Val's not the criminal type." I prided myself on my intuition about people. "What exactly did you see?"

Timothy leaned close. "Val bumped into that guy." He pointed at a large man standing in the buffet line. "And I swear he reached into his back pocket."

Though I was pretty sure Timothy's sighting was the result of an overactive imagination, I did watch Val out of the corner of my eye. He bowed and scraped and flirted outrageously, but I never saw him do anything remotely suspicious.

The big man Timothy had pointed out headed toward a table near us where a woman sat with two kids. They all wore shorts and t-shirts with sayings on them. The man, whose shirt said, "I'd wrap that in bacon," sat down heavily at the table. "When do you think the ship's gonna disappear?" he said to his wife. Her chest read, "I'm not short. I'm fun-size."

"Oh, honey." The guy's wife clucked in sympathy. "I asked, and they said it's not that David Copperfield. I'm so sorry."

"Happens more often than you'd think," Timothy whispered.

"Oh." The guy's face fell. "Well, at least the food's good." He tucked into his dinner.

"There is a magic show though," said his wife. "*Fagin's Magic Handkerchief.*"

"The pressure's on," Timothy said.

And my nausea was back. I pushed myself away from the table and tried to get my mind off silks and audiences and splats of Ivy on the stage floor. My cell buzzed, telling me I had new messages. "Hey, I must have a signal." I took my phone out of my Victorian-style pocket, basically a small muslin bag attached to a cord that tied around my waist underneath my gown. My overskirt had a slit sewn into it that gave me direct access to the pocket underneath. Very handy, so to speak.

"Grab it quick," Timothy said. "Before we go out of range again."

I flipped through a bunch of emails, an old text from Uncle Bob, several missed calls, and one new message. I called voicemail.

"Hi." My brother's voice. "Can you talk to Stu?" A sweet guy with Down Syndrome, Stu was Cody's best friend at the group home. "He's mad about—" He paused. "Stu? Where are you going? Never mind, Olive-y." That was Cody's pet name for me, a combination of Olive and Ivy. He hung up.

The call didn't help the queasy feeling in my gut. Cody never called me. I ran the conversation over in my mind. I was pretty sure I knew what Stu was mad about. When I saw Cody last week, he told me Stu had been put on a diet. Diets made me cranky too. Still, I decided to call.

"Dang." No reception. I held up my phone, trying to find a few bars. Nothing.

"I want to go to the Penny Arcade," said the oldest of the t-shirt family kids, "The World's Okayest Brother" according to his shirt.

Get Lit! cruises tried to appeal to families seeking to further their children's education, so each ship had a few kid-friendly activities onboard. The *S.S. David Copperfield* featured a Curiosity

Shoppe that hosted scavenger hunts, Scrooge's Haunted House (occupied by the three Christmas ghosts plus a pretty spooky Marley), and an arcade that featured Dickens-themed video games, like Betsey Trotwood's Donkey Kong (David Copperfield's great-aunt Betsey hated donkeys).

"I need some cash," said the kid.

"Again?" said his mother.

"I wouldn't, if Dad would let me have a sail-and-sign card."

"Buddy, you're the last person who needs a sail-and-sign card," his dad said.

I stood up from the table and walked a few feet, trying to see if any bars magically appeared on my phone, so I was close enough to see the guy's ruddy face turn pale.

"Damn," he said, standing and patting his pockets. "My wallet's gone."

CHAPTER 14

Still Improving

"So what do you know about Valery?" I asked Timothy as we ran down the stairs to the crew cabin area. My stomach lurched with every step, but we had to move quickly in time for me to grab a change of clothes and get to rehearsal.

"Not much. Russian, good actor, ladies' man."

"Really?" Val was nice in a goofy sort of way, but his ghostly pale skin, muddy-colored dark hair, and creepy-colored eyes put me in mind of an anemic vampire.

"He's got something going for him," Timothy said as he opened the stairwell door to the hall. "Rumor is he's got a big—"

"Heart," I said before Timothy could say more. Didn't really want the image of a naked Val in my head. I mean, maybe all of him was pale, even the nether bits, which would be weird since…Dang. Guess the image was already imprinted on my brain.

"Also, he tends to take his clothes off when he gets drunk. Just a warning."

"I'll keep that in mind. Just a sec." I unlocked my cabin door and went in while Timothy waited in the hall.

I took off my wig and gown and changed into a t-shirt and pair of leggings. I hopped the two steps to the bathroom, popped my last two chewable Tums in my mouth, met Timothy in the hall, ran to the theater, and jumped onstage just a few seconds before Jonas and Ada walked on from the backstage area.

"Hey," said Jonas, "you look great." He sounded surprised and impressed at the same time. "First time I've seen you without a wig since the cut. Short hair really shows off your long neck. I can even see a little Audrey Hepburn in you."

Audrey Hepburn! I stretched my neck like a preening swan.

"Yeah, if Audrey Hepburn had orange hair and a butt like a sack of potatoes." Ada flopped a mat under one of the silks.

I whipped my head around to check out my butt, just in case.

"Ivy has a delicious ass," Jonas said to Ada.

Delicious! It was a pretty nice ass, but no one had ever called it delicious. Was Jonas interested in me? "Start stretching," he said. "The way Ada showed you last time." He turned away. Not interested then.

I dropped to the floor and went into a modified lunge, one leg bent in front with my foot flat on the floor, and the other stretched behind me.

Jonas tugged on a rope, and the second silk fell from its place in the fly space. "Timothy, David," he said to the guys who sat in the front row. "We're going to go over the basic moves with Ivy. You don't have to be here for another hour."

"Moral support," said Timothy.

"Just watching," said David.

"What about Val? Will he be at rehearsal later?" I stayed in the lunge position and put my palms flat on the floor. It felt good to stretch my sore muscles.

"No." Jonas looked at me strangely, probably since Val wasn't in the magic show. I knew that, but wanted to find out what they knew about him.

"He's a great actor." I lowered my front leg to the floor and bent it so that it tucked in front of me. "Sends shivers down my spine when he talks in his Bill Sikes voice."

"He's got a great Cockney accent," Jonas said. "Maybe he could give you a few pointers."

I made a mental note to work on my accent and persevered. "It's crazy that he's so good at acting in English. Did he study here in the U.S.?" I reached back and grabbed my leg, pointing my toe toward the ceiling.

"I don't think he's had any formal training. Do you know, David?"

David shook his head.

"David is his roommate," Jonas said. "Valery used to work onboard as a busboy. He came to me one day after an actor quit. Said he used to act in school and asked if he could audition. Blew me away. I hired him on the spot."

"Did he go to drama school in Russia?" I watched Ada climb up her silk like Jack scaling the beanstalk.

"I didn't ask." Jonas tilted his head, considering me. "Why so interested?"

"Ivy's got a crush," sang Timothy.

I spun around and glared at him. "Do not."

"Do too." He winked at me, unseen by everyone else. I glared at him and he winked again, slower this time, like he was conveying a message. Oh, he was helping me out. I had been sounding a little investigator-ish.

Jonas waved me over to take my place underneath my silk. "Okay. Time to learn some dance moves." He held the silk out to me.

"Tie yourself in, using your left foot," Ada said from above me. I gripped the silk, pulled myself a few feet above the stage and wrapped the silk around my foot, securing my position with a footlock. My arms, still shaky from yesterday's rehearsal, burned with the effort, and my foot felt bruised from my former attempt at climbing. "Now separate the two pieces with your arms, keeping your elbows at head level." The fabric was attached in the middle to a beam above me so that its two tails hung down. I separated them. "Now lean forward through the silk."

"Whoa." I flailed in the air. Must have leaned too far.

"Like this." Ada did exactly what she told me, but leaned forward in a fluid motion, ending up in a position that looked like a figurehead on a ship. I was never going to be able to do that. Never.

But I was an actor and dancer and a stubborn one, so I smiled and persevered. I tried the move again. "Ohhh." I actually got it. Nowhere near performance quality, but a start. "Cool."

"Now bring your right leg up to your knee in a jazz passé."

I did. Now I looked like a figurehead about to leap off the prow of the ship.

"It's called The Ship's Lady," said Jonas.

I performed the move again, more gracefully this time.

"Bravo," Timothy said from the audience.

"Nice," Jonas agreed.

"Please." Ada rolled her eyes.

She whipped through a few more moves. Jonas clapped his hands together, not in applause. "That's great, Ada. Now slow down into teaching mode, all right?"

The look on Ada's face did not say it was all right, but she did stop showing off. She taught me several more moves, mostly dance poses done in mid-air. They took a lot of strength, especially arm strength, but they were familiar moves I'd performed for years, just not in the air. Maybe I could do this.

"Good work," said Jonas as I touched down on the mat. "Just one more piece of business. Let's go up to the catwalk."

Ada began climbing the steel rungs set into the side wall of the theater. I followed. Jonas climbed the ladder behind me. Good thing I had a delicious ass.

I reached the catwalk and walked out on it, the metal grating cool beneath my bare feet. "I'm not going to have to get on the silks from here, am I?" Being hauled up into the air by a pulley was bad enough. Stepping off a catwalk forty feet in the air would feel like walking off a cliff.

"Oh no," said Jonas. "That would be much too dangerous. We're up here so you can see how the silks are rigged. We have certified riggers, like Ada here," he nodded at my roommate, "but you need to check your own equipment too."

"Each silk is secured to a beam by a span set," said Ada, pointing to a black band that wrapped around a metal beam in the fly space. "Then you've got several pieces of hardware connected by carabiners." Those were the little metal hook thingies that climbers used. "First of all, check that all carabiners are locked. There are three. One that connects the span set to the pulley." She pointed at the carabiner and looked to me for confirmation that I understood. I nodded.

"A second one that connects the pulley to the swivel." She indicated a figure-eight-shaped piece of hardware that swiveled in the middle of the eight. "And a third one that connects the swivel to the Rescue Eight." This piece of equipment, the Rescue Eight, was about the same size as the others, but was nearly covered by the silk knotted around it so I couldn't see it well.

"Check your equipment carefully every time you use the silks," Jonas said. "You really don't want to fall from this height."

CHAPTER 15
A Notable Plan

"Thanks so much for doing this," I said to David as I followed him down the hall to the crew cabins. "And thanks to you too," I whispered to Timothy, beside me.

Timothy's white lie about me having a crush on Val was proving useful. After rehearsal, I'd said to David, "You know, I think I should ask Val about helping me with my accent. Do you think he's in your room?" Everyone would think this was an excuse to get close to Val. It was, but not for the reason they thought.

"Either there or the bar," he replied. Ada looked at me when she heard "bar" and pantomimed slitting a throat.

"I'd like to check his room first," I said. "Would you show me where it is?"

David shrugged a slight shoulder. "Sure."

I conferred with Timothy before we left the theater. "Here's the plan. If Val isn't there, I'll say I want to leave a note for him. You offer to buy David a Coke so that I have a few minutes alone in their room."

"A Coke?"

"I don't know. Maybe go to the arcade and challenge him to a game of Donkey Kong? Or a round at George's Shooting Gallery? Whatever you think will keep him away for a few minutes."

"What if Val is in the room?"

"I'll just see what I can. Maybe ask to use the bathroom."

"Be careful. He's a thief, remember?"

I snorted. "I can handle Val."

Luckily, Val wasn't there. I played my "I just need a minute alone so I can write him a note" card.

"I'm not sure—" began David.

"I've known Ivy for years," said Timothy. "She's harmless as a drag queen without heels."

I waved goodbye to Timothy and David and got to work as soon as they shut the door. I went to one of the wardrobes and pulled open the door. Just clothes in the wardrobe, clean ones folded and on hangers, and a few dirty ones on the floor, judging by the mingled smell of detergent, aftershave, and feet. I rifled through the hangers in the closet. Definitely Val's clothes. Though he and David both wore shabby-looking Victorian costumes, David was a good foot shorter and maybe fifty pounds lighter than Val. Nothing interesting in the closet. I shut the door and went into the bathroom. Nothing of interest there either, except for a large box of condoms. Pretty sure they didn't belong to David.

I went through the drawers. Nothing that piqued my interest, and again, pretty easy to see what stuff belonged to who. Or Hu. Ha.

One of the shelves above the desk held a TV and a few books in Russian. The other shelf was bare except for a photo of an Asian family, a serious-faced David tucked in between his two smiling parents.

I'd heard that Oliver stayed with his parents onboard in some sort of family suite. I suspected David's family wasn't here or else he wouldn't be rooming with Val.

I finished my investigation of the room.

I didn't know exactly what I was looking for, but I certainly didn't find it. Oh well. I'd just write the note to Val about helping me with my accent and be off. I grabbed a pen and piece of paper off the desk and sat on the lower bunk.

Huh. A piece of yarn crept out from underneath the pillow. I tipped up the pillow. A gray knitted scarf lay underneath. I felt a tingle of familiarity, but nothing concrete. I picked it up. A subtle pattern was woven into it, using gray yarn just a shade lighter than the rest of the scarf. I peered at it. Was that a bear? Yes. And a name. Val.

Someone dear to him must have knitted the scarf, or why would he have it under his pillow? I carefully tucked it back in its place when it hit me. I knew where I'd seen that gray yarn. In Harley's hands, the last time I saw her alive.

CHAPTER 16

The Intricacies of the Way

"I found something. I'm following up on it." That's what I texted Uncle Bob the next morning as the ship pulled into Ensenada. What I didn't say was that I was going to follow Val. I was pretty sure my uncle would say it was too dangerous. I was also pretty sure I knew how to tail someone (thanks to Uncle Bob and my PI handbooks), and that I wouldn't look too suspicious if I got caught, since I was supposed to have a crush on Val and everything.

The *S.S. David Copperfield* had a four-hour stop in Ensenada, thanks to some maritime law that required a stay-over in a foreign port. We actors were given the time off to explore and blow off steam. Before leaving, I put on big sunglasses and a floppy hat to hide my strawberry blonde buzz cut. It wasn't really a disguise, just something to make me a little less identifiable at a glance. Thus prepared, I pretended to gab with Timothy at the end of the hall so I could keep an eye on Val and David's cabin. We'd only been talking a few minutes when Val emerged, wearing a t-shirt and cargo pants, a canvas messenger bag slung across his body. I waited until he opened the door to the stairwell, then took off after him.

"Be careful," Timothy said after me.

"I won't drink the water," I covered.

I ran quietly up the stairs just in time to see Val exit onto the next deck. I did too. Once there, it was easy to lose myself in the line of employees waiting to get off, and easy to keep sight of Val. His white arms nearly glowed against the sleeves of his black t-shirt. I hoped he was wearing sunscreen.

As soon as he debarked, he lit a cigarette and headed off with a purposeful stride, as if going to a familiar destination. I joined the throng of people heading to Ensenada's main drag, keeping Val firmly in sight. If he were involved in this theft ring, maybe he'd meet up with his contact. I almost lost him once on a busy street lined with busy shops made busier by their brightly colored signs advertising mariscos, cerveza, and Viagra. I caught sight of him again, partly obscured by a knot of tourists. He looked over his shoulder, then ducked down a small side street. I sped up and peeked around the corner in time to see him enter a small cantina. I pulled my hat down to hide my face and slowed, walking nonchalantly past the open door, facing straight ahead but looking sideways behind my sunglasses. Val approached a big man facing the bar and tapped him on the shoulder. The man spun around, a scowl on his pale face until he caught sight of Val. Then he broke into a grin, pulling Val into a bear hug.

Huh. Not the way I'd greet my criminal contacts.

"There's no business like show busine—" Shit, I forgot to turn off the ringer on my cell. And it was on the loudest setting. Nice detecting style, Ivy. The two men turned toward the sound. I ducked away, scrambling in my bag to turn off my phone.

When I was a couple blocks away, I stepped into a souvenir shop. After a few minutes browsing huarache sandals and scorpions encased in plastic, I determined that I hadn't been followed. I took out my phone, turned the ringer off, and redialed the number that had interrupted my spying.

"Ivy, where are you?" my friend Candy asked in her unmistakable Louisiana drawl. "Don't tell me you forgot your best friend drove four and a half hours into another country just to see you."

"Of course not." Actually, I didn't think Candy really meant it when she offered to meet me in Mexico. Sure, she'd mentioned it last week on the phone, but she said it kind of offhandedly, the way people do when they think something is a nice idea but they don't really believe it will happen. Plus, Ensenada wasn't that much closer than Phoenix and she hadn't visited there once since moving to L.A. four months ago.

"Well, I'm here," she said. "I'm at Hussong's and there's a nice icy margarita on its way, just for you."

"Good. I could use it. And I could use you too. Want to help solve a murder?"

"Girlfriend," Candy said, "what are friends for?"

CHAPTER 17

Old Companions and Associations

There was no mistaking Candy, even from the back. Her curly brown hair had the same optimistic energy as the rest of her. When she jumped up from the table at Hussong's and ran toward me, all the men in the area turned in her direction. She had that effect. I don't know if it was the brilliant smile spread across her face or the fact that she looked like she might bounce right out of her sundress. Probably both. Candy radiated a sunny sexuality.

"Ivy girl!" Candy hugged me so hard my hat fell off. Then, "Omigod—your hair."

"Audrey Hepburn, right?"

"The spittin' image."

We chatted as we walked to our table, catching up on our lives. I felt so good with Candy. Like I was on solid ground again.

Oh.

I was.

I'd thought I was doing pretty well with my water phobia, but I suspected it had been seeping into my mind all this time, wearing away my sense of wellbeing. I didn't notice my chronic unease until it was gone.

Nothing I could do about it at this point. I had to get back on the ship in a few hours. I mentally packed my fear away in watertight luggage, pushed it far back into the attic of my mind, and focused on the time I had now, with Candy, on dry land.

After all, there were margaritas to be drunk.

We sat at a table already outfitted with a paper boat of crispy tortilla chips, a cup of chunky salsa fresca, and two margaritas—a frozen one for Candy, one on the rocks for me. "So," Candy said, "what's this about a murder?"

I filled her in, swearing her to secrecy. After she was caught up, I said, "So I need to find out a few things that could help. I want to look up some information on your phone."

"Why not yours? You forget to charge it?"

I shook my head. "Do you know how easy it is for someone to hack into your phone? Get your texts, your browser history, even your voice commands?" I did. Working at Uncle Bob's PI firm had given me quite the education. "Since we're undercover, we're trying to keep any cybertrails to a minimum. Even my texts have to sound innocent."

Candy hauled her chair next to mine, pulled out her phone, and went to her browser. "All right, let's do this. First thing?"

"Find out what Keppra is used for. It's a prescription drug."

A few taps later: "It's an anti-seizure medication."

"Any interactions with Amoxicillin?"

Candy and I scrolled through several sites looking for drug interactions. Didn't see any issues with Amoxicillin.

"Can we look up something more exciting now?" Candy signaled the waiter for another round of margaritas. "Like how to kill your agent who promised you movies and can't even get you a commercial?"

"Oh no."

"Oh yes. She's only managed to get me a handful of auditions since I got to L.A. Keeps sending me on cattle calls I don't even need an agent for. And the only role I actually got was in an indie film where I played 'sex tent female.' Don't even ask." Candy rolled her eyes. "I actually dated 'sex tent male' for a couple weeks, but that went about as well as the rest of my Hollywood life. I almost miss Phoenix."

"Almost? Do you miss Matt?" They had dated for more than

half a year after I'd introduced them. Candy broke off the relationship when she moved to California to pursue a film career.

"I don't know." Candy stirred the slush in her margarita with a little straw. "Let's investigate your murder some more. It's less depressing."

"Really?"

"Really."

"Okay. Let's find out everything we can about Theo Pushwright."

"Ooh, is he onboard?" She tapped on her phone. "I love him."

"You and about a million others." I stared at Candy's tiny screen. "Wow, he's sold a lot of books. But that's not what I really want to know." Candy and I searched for something about Theo's personal life for over ten minutes. Nothing that didn't appear scripted by his PR firm. "Huh." I knocked a bit of the salt off the rim of my glass and sipped my margarita. "No mention of wives or kids or girlfriends at all."

"Maybe he's gay?"

"Jonas said Theo was his stepfather, so he had to be married."

"Doesn't mean he's not gay."

"I'm pretty sure he's not." I remembered Theo sneering at Timothy. "Moral weakness," he'd said. "Let's move on," I said to Candy. "See what we can find on Harley Locklow." I'd seen Harley's last name on her *Get Lit!* contract.

Candy Googled her. "Looks like she's on a bunch of social media sites, but...kinda funny. She only posts about twice a month, but then she writes a ton."

"That makes sense if she's been working on ships for a while. Probably only gets online in between cruises. Hey, does she mention being onboard any other ships?"

Candy studied her phone. "Yeah. *The S.S. Jack London* and *A Cruiseship Named Desire*. Ooh, maybe I should audition for that one. After all, I have spent my life depending on the kindness of strangers."

"Did you say *Jack London*?"

"Yep. She's even got some photos." Candy slid her phone toward me. There was Harley, smiling into a cup of coffee; then with a group of people; then in a swimsuit on a beautiful white sand beach.

"You sure that's *Jack London*? It doesn't look like Alaska."

Candy looked closer. "Oops, that's the *S.S. David Copperfield*. I can go back to *Jack*—"

"No, wait." I grabbed her phone and looked at the group photo. I recognized some of the people: Timothy and David and Val. The whole group had linked arms, but Harley stood especially close to Val, looking up at him with obvious affection. "Look up Valery..." How had he introduced himself? "Boyko," I finished.

Candy tapped. And tapped. And tapped some more. "Valery Boyko? You sure you got that right?"

"I think so. Why?"

"Nothin' on him. Not a mention anywhere. As far as the internet is concerned, the boy doesn't exist."

CHAPTER 18

The Damp Breath of an Unwholesome Wind

Two hours later, I stood on the bow of the *S.S. David Copperfield*, watching the coastline recede. My unease had returned, a slippery shifting feeling, as if I was floating unmoored on a too-small boat, a current pulling me farther and farther out to the edge of the watery world where monsters waited in the endless mist. I closed my eyes. If I was going to be on the ship for another week, I better get ahold of this fear.

I made myself look over the railing. The sparkling sea was nothing like the Spokane pond of my childhood. The dark deceptive waters of that pond froze the winter I was eleven—solid enough to skate on, we thought. Again, I heard the crack of the ice. I felt its roughness under my skates as I raced to the jagged hole where I last saw my brother. Again, I watched Cody's yellow hair float above him as he sank to the bottom of the pond.

I blinked to clear the vision from my head. This blue water was not that pond. And Cody was okay. He might have a brain injury, but he lived a good life. He loved his job at Safeway and his friends at the group home. He even had a girlfriend, Sarah. Everything was okay now.

Suddenly I wanted to talk to my brother more than anything. I pulled out my phone.

"Ivy," said a voice behind me. "I've been trying to reach you. I was afraid you were crab hors d'oeuvres at the bottom of the bay."

"Sorry." I patted Timothy's hand. "Everything's fine. I had a great lunch with Candy. And I learned that margaritas really help with the whole my-arms-are-going-to-fall-off-'cause-I'm-out-of-shape thing." I leaned in. "But I didn't get anything on Val, except that he eschews the internet." That was a little strange, but maybe not so much for a Russian guy who spent most of his time onboard ships with little (or very expensive) access to the internet. It was also really frustrating, since it brought up more questions than answers.

"You saw Candy? While I ate all by myself, just in case you needed me?" Timothy rolled his eyes dramatically. "You should have had your phone on. Especially while investigating."

"That's actually why I turned it off. *Anyway—*" My phone cheeped, alerting me to missed calls. "It's on now. I want to call Cody before we get out of range."

My phone kept making noises. "Arggh. I must have missed about a billion calls. Wait..." I scrolled through the numbers of missed calls. Most of them were from the same two numbers: Matt's cell phone and Cody's group home. Ice water dripped into my gut. "Shit." I punched in the group home number and paced while the phone rang.

"Hello?" One of Cody's housemates must have picked up.

"Hi," I said, "this is Cody's sister. Is he there?"

"No."

I looked at the time on my phone. Cody was usually home by now.

"Is he at work?"

"No."

"Do you know where he is?"

"Gone."

"Is Matt there?"

"Yes."

Thank God. I waited for Matt to come on the line and tell me everything was okay. I waited some more. No Matt, just breathing. Oops. Sometimes I forgot to be really concrete with the guys.

"Could you please ask Matt to come talk to me on the phone?" I asked.

"Sure. Matt!"

"Everything okay?" asked Timothy. I'd forgotten he was there. I crossed my fingers and nodded.

"Hi, this is Matt."

"It's Ivy. Have you or Cody been calling me? Because your phone numbers—"

"Ivy." A frantic edge in Matt's voice made me stop breathing. "Cody's gone."

CHAPTER 19

A Real Alarm

"What do you mean, Cody's gone?" My voice shook.

Timothy moved close to me, a solid presence.

"He left last night and hasn't come back," said Matt. "I've been calling you, but was afraid if I left a message you'd panic."

"You were right." I tried to catch my breath. "Where...what...shit." I couldn't think. "Do you know why he left?" I asked.

"He went after Stu. We're looking for him too."

"Shit. Cody left a voicemail asking me to talk to Stu, but then he said never mind, so I didn't think...Oh God." I slumped against Timothy, who put his arms around me.

"Ivy." Matt's voice was strong now. "The guys said Cody left the house right after calling you. You wouldn't have reached him."

"Okay, okay." I took a deep breath. "What do we do?"

"We're pretty sure he's following Stu, but I want to check any places Cody might go."

"You checked Safeway?"

"Yeah. He's not scheduled to work and hasn't dropped by. What about Bob's?"

I shook my head even though Matt couldn't see it. "Cody knows he's onboard the ship with me. Did you ask Sarah?"

"She hasn't seen him. She's really worried. Anywhere else you can think of?"

"Maybe Encanto Park, but I think he knows better than to hang out in a park after dark. Omigod." I couldn't breathe again. "He's been gone since last night? Where would he sleep? He doesn't have cash for a motel and..."

Cody was not streetwise. If he slept in a park, who knows what might have happened.

"Ivy?"

"Yeah, sorry." C'mon, Ivy. Concentrate. Think like a detective. "Why did Stu leave?"

"There's a new housemate, Geoff. They don't get along. Stu got fed up and took off."

"And Cody followed him?"

"Yeah." The doorbell rang in the background. "I have to go. The police are here. And the media."

"The media?"

"We want to get the word out." Matt's voice got tight. "We can't do an Amber Alert because Stu is an adult and we can't do a Silver Alert because he's under sixty-five."

"I'm not sure a media blitz is a great idea." Though alerts made sense when it came to kids and senior citizens, people weren't always kind to guys like Stu and Cody.

"We really need to find Stu right away. In fact, that's why Cody..." Matt swallowed. "Cody went after him because he knows Stu shouldn't be without his medication. He has epilepsy. Gotta go." He hung up.

I hung up too. Timothy's arms tightened around me. "I have to get off the ship," I said.

"I wish you could," Timothy said. "But they can't turn around."

"But this is an emergency."

"They can't do it." He hugged me against his chest. "And your brother will be okay. I know it." He released me. "Better call your uncle."

I speed-dialed Uncle Bob. It went straight to voicemail. "Call me STAT," I texted him.

"I'm going to go look for him," I told Timothy.

"I'll look too," he said. "You take the decks, I'll check the restaurants."

I took the elevator to the London Lido Deck and jogged around the swimming pools. Not there. I ran up a flight of stairs to the Drood Deck next. No Bob. Wait. There he was. I'd nearly missed him. I was looking for his usual Hawaiian shirt, but he was dressed in Bob Stalwart's western shirt and jeans. And he was with Bette. Shit.

I texted him again. He checked his phone and put it back in his pocket. Dammit. "Cigar bar in ten," I texted again.

I went to the bar and staked out the most isolated table, which wasn't hard because I was the only one in the bar. Everyone else wanted to be outside in the Mexican sunshine. Not me.

The dark windowless space suited my mood. I still felt the afternoon's margaritas, so I ordered a Diet Coke for me and a beer for my uncle.

Fifteen minutes later, he still hadn't appeared.

With his big laugh and jolly Santa Claus face, Uncle Bob appeared to be a laid-back guy, but I knew he was really a type A guy in a type B body. He was always on top of things, a step ahead of everyone else and never, never late. What was going on?

A few minutes later, he sauntered into the bar.

"Where have you been?"

"Hey, hey, keep your pants on." Uncle Bob slid into the booth opposite me. "I was having a great time with Bette and it's not like any of us are going anywhere."

I stared at the man opposite me, speechless. Who was this guy and what had he done with my uncle?

"Besides, it looks like Harley probably did die of natural causes. I slipped a few bucks to the local coroner," he said. "Maybe someone panicked and stuffed her in the closet. Hey, remember my idea for a coffin closet? There's a guy in Maine who's doing that, building furniture that turns into a coffin when you need it. Cool, huh? Bette told me." His sunburnt face crinkled into a smile.

I found my tongue. "Cody's disappeared."

The smile slipped from his face. "What? Shit. Olive, I'm sorry, I thought—what happened?"

I started to tell him the story, but he held up a hand. "Wait a sec." He pulled his cell phone out of a pocket. "Gonna call Pink." Detective Pinkstaff of the Phoenix PD was one of my uncle's best friends. I waited as Uncle Bob made the call.

"He's already on it," he said after hanging up. "In fact, if I'd checked my messages..." He trailed off.

This was *so* not like my uncle, and *so* not the time to scold him about it, so instead I told him the whole Cody and Stu story. "What can we do?" I asked. "Should we go home?"

"No." He shook his head slowly. "It'd be really tough to get off the ship at this point. They won't airlift folks unless it's a real emergency." I started to protest, but Uncle Bob put a hand on my shoulder. "Between the police and the media and the group home people—you said Matt's looking too, right?"

I nodded.

"We wouldn't be able to do anything they're not already doing. Besides," he cleared his throat, "Pink says your mom and dad are down there. Helping."

"Helping" meant standing around and blaming people. That was what my parents did, especially where Cody was concerned. Every so often they blamed Matt for things like letting Cody go on a date ("Inappropriate," they sniffed), or Uncle Bob for giving him a beer (on Cody's twenty-first birthday), but it was me who had burning coals of blame heaped onto my head on a regular basis. I was the one who didn't watch over Cody when we were skating, who let the accident happen, who later insisted that he move out of my parents' home and into the group home. Where he just disappeared from.

"Right," I tried to say, but couldn't. The thought of Cody sleeping on the streets...I took a sip of Diet Coke, hoping to loosen the knot in my throat.

My uncle reached a big hand over the table and covered mine. "It'll be okay, Olive."

"Bob?" a feminine voice drawled at my shoulder.

"Bette!" My uncle grabbed his hand back, his face red.

"I wondered where you got to." She eyed me, sizing up the competition. "You two know each other?"

"He knows my uncle," I said. "I was just asking for some advice. Cody, my...boyfriend, is...running around." I might have been a good actor, but I was lousy at improv.

"Honey, you should know better than to ask a man advice about another man."

Did Bette really think my uncle and I could be an item? He was thirty years older than me.

"Like I said, I think he'll come back." Uncle Bob slid out of the booth and looked seriously at me. "Try not to worry."

CHAPTER 20

New Fortitude and Firmness

As soon as Uncle Bob stood up, Bette clamped onto his arm like a mollusk. I watched them leave the bar arm in arm, then took a long drink of Diet Coke and checked my phone for messages. Nothing new, but shit, was that the time? I scrambled out of the booth, left a few bucks on the table for a tip, and hightailed it out of there.

I skidded into the theater just in time. The entire cast of *Oliver! At Sea!* was onstage ready to rehearse. I jumped up on the stage and joined them. Timothy slid next to me and touched me on the arm. "You okay?"

"I'm okay. Ready to go."

"Okay how?" said David. "Is something wrong?"

"Everything okey-dokey?" asked Val.

I motioned them away. "Later. I just want to be Nancy for a while." A minute later, I slipped into a Cockney accent and into Victorian London. Theater had been my place of refuge ever since Cody's accident. It was the one place I could forget everything around me and still feel safe.

Some people don't understand the "safe" part. They think it must be terrifying to be onstage in front of an audience. For me, it's more like reading a good book. I become another person, transported to another place and time. But it's even better than reading, because my chosen family is there onstage with me, reading the same book at the same time.

So by the time we took a break, I was feeling better. Still, I didn't want to talk about Cody, so I searched my brain for something else.

Oh! How in the world had I forgotten that I'd found Harley's knitting in Val's room?

"Hey," I said to Timothy, who stood next to Val and David onstage. "Do you know if they've recast Madame Defarge? Candy could use a job." I let my face fall. "Oh, would she have to knit? I don't think she's crafty." But I was, so to speak.

"She'd definitely have to knit," replied Timothy. "I swear the audition consists of knit one, purl two."

"Makes sense." In *A Tale of Two Cities*, Madame D. knits the names of the condemned into a scarf. I snuck a look at Valery. He was watching us, but his face was relaxed. Interested, but not nervous.

"What did she do with all the stuff she knit?" Still no change on Val's face.

"Half the time she'd just unravel it and start again," Timothy said.

"But sometimes she gave presents," Val said. "Like to me. I have nice scarf. It says Val."

"She knitted you a scarf?"

"Sure. We were buddy-buddy."

"Everyone!" shouted Jonas from the front row, his eyes on his cell phone. "A little change in schedule. I want to run 'Gruel, Glorious Gruel.' We're not going to have time to run the other numbers. Val, Timothy, you can go." The guys exited through the wings. Jonas walked to the edge of the stage and held out a hand to help me off the stage. "Ivy, could we talk a minute?"

I took the hand he offered. It was warm and strong and comforting.

"Timothy told me about your brother going missing. You doing all right?" He kept my hand in his.

"Yeah," I said, as much to convince myself as anything. "There are a lot of people in Phoenix working to find Cody, and there's nothing I can do right now anyway. It's good to have something else to think about."

"You sure?" I nodded and he smiled at me, one side of his mouth tipped up like a mischievous boy. "Well then, I could give you something else to think about."

Was Jonas flirting with me? First he said I had a delicious ass, and now...

"How about dinner tonight? At the captain's table?"

He *was* flirting with me. Hmm. Jonas was handsome and he seemed nice enough, but I didn't think I was into him. And there was another thing. "Don't we have silk rehearsal for the magic show?"

"Dinner is at the early seating. We'd be done in plenty of time."

"I didn't think crew members could eat at Delmonico's."

"We can eat in the dining room when we have family onboard. And you get to sit at the captain's table when your family is Theo Pushwright."

That decided for me. I didn't have anything solid on the theft ring or Harley's death yet, but I could find out more about Theo and Harley at dinner. Besides, I really wanted to dine at the captain's table. "Sure," I said. Visions of a fancy dinner danced in my head, with silent waiters and crystal goblets and men in tails and women in...Oh. "Um, I hate to sound like a girly girl, but I don't have anything to wear. Aren't we supposed to dress for dinner in the dining room?"

"More than you know. We dress in period clothing when we're at the captain's table. But don't worry. There are several onboard costume shops. Go to the one on the Upper Pickwick Promenade and tell them I sent you."

CHAPTER 21

All the Treasures of the World

I popped into Mrs. Chickenstalker's Sundries Shoppe on my way to the costume shop. I'd run out of Tums and needed more before dinner. My stomach hadn't felt exactly right for days, and Cody and Stu's disappearance sat heavy and queasy in my gut like slightly off Mexican food.

Or maybe it *was* slightly off Mexican food.

Like everywhere else, the store was done up Dickens-style, the walls lined with floor-to-ceiling dark wooden shelves.

Signs with fancy lettering announced the goods for sale, though if you looked carefully, you'd see iPod accessories among the aspirin and deodorant.

I took my purchase up to the counter and handed it to the shopkeeper. "We have better stuff than that for seasickness, you know." The shopkeeper wore a white shirt and brown vest, a sort of string tie around his neck, and a long white apron over the whole outfit. "Would you like to try some Dramamine?"

"Sure." I slid my packet of chewable Tums toward him too, just for good measure.

He turned and picked up a packet of Dramamine from a mirrored shelf behind him, which in a very un-Dickensian manner was filled with vaping supplies and cold and allergy meds.

"Why do you keep the Dramamine back there?" I asked. "Seems like it'd be pretty popular."

"Kids." The clerk sniffed. "They can abuse anything if they put their minds to it. I guess it has some hallucinogenic properties." He rang up my purchase.

I thought about asking him if Dramamine might also help with that dizzy feeling you got when you were twirling on a flimsy piece of fabric forty feet in the air, but figured I could find that out on my own.

I walked the few feet from Mrs. Chickenstalker's Sundries to the costume shop next door. Each *Get Lit!* cruise featured a fancy costume ball, so every ship had several shops full of outfits that fit its literary theme. A bell jingled as I opened the door to Madame Mantalini's Temple of Fashion.

Oh my. I'd reached heaven. Actors' heaven, at least. I reverently entered a room that shimmered with light reflected off silken ball gowns. Beaded bodices sparkled and velvet capes whispered of walks through manicured gardens. Neatly pressed men's suits in black and gray and brown looked proud and pompous, even on the rack. A few brightly colored waistcoats winked from among them. Bowlers and boaters and top hats perched on a shelf above the men's clothes, while a half dozen free-standing hat racks held confections for women made of feathers and lace and ribbons. Nearly hidden among all this finery were worn-looking cotton and wool costumes like the one I wore, and behind the shop's counter was a rack filled entirely with what looked like black robes. As I peeked over the counter to get a better look, a short elegant man emerged from a back room. "How may I help you?"

Once I told him what I needed, he brought out several gowns. I tried on a scarlet velvet dress (a little too low-cut for dinner), a gold silk-looking one (did nothing for my complexion), and a brocade gown in a soft sage green that set off my eyes. Perfect. Its off-the-shoulder neckline dripped with tea-dyed lace and its full skirt (hoop skirt included) emphasized my small waist. Or so I thought.

I came out of the dressing room to look at myself in the larger mirror in the shop.

"Hmm," said the costumer shop manager. "Do you want to try a corset?"

"Uh...Sure."

He sized me up with his eyes and handed me a front-lacing corset from a drawer behind the counter. I went back into the dressing room with the contraption. Once I was laced up tight, I slipped the gown back over my head and checked my reflection. Oh, *that's* why he suggested it. My waist looked tiny, which made the skirt look fuller. Plus I stood up straighter, probably because I couldn't bend in the middle.

"What do you think?" he asked from outside the door.

"I'll take it," I said, somewhat breathlessly. "Maybe it'll help me to eat less at dinner."

As the manager helped me pick out a blonde wig (neither my one-and-a half-inch orange hair nor my Nancy wig were going to fly), I gazed at the beautiful clothes in the shop. "Are all these costumes historically accurate?"

"They're of the time period," he said. "Though maybe not very Dickensian." He handed me a wig, an elaborate style with swept-up blonde hair and a few long curls spilling down the back. "Most customers want to dress like the upper classes, even though most of Dickens's major characters were low or middle class." He settled the wig on my head. "And our most popular costume doesn't fit into any of those categories."

"What do you mean?" I said, admiring the way the short curls on the wig framed my face.

He gestured at the rack of black robes behind the counter. "Our biggest seller, so to speak." I must have looked confused, because he said, "Bestseller is a bit of a misnomer. Costumes are free to all guests for the duration of the costume ball. Or when they're invited to sit at the captain's table."

"But what *is* that costume?"

"The Ghost of Christmas Future."

"The scary faceless ghost who points at Scrooge's grave? That's your most popular costume? Why would anyone want to wear a black robe when they had all this to choose from?" I waved at the finery that surrounded us.

"I know." The manager put my wig in a hatbox and handed it across the counter. "I think some people wear it because it hides absolutely everything. Allows the shy ones to still dress up, you see."

"You said some people wear it because they're shy. What about the others?"

"I think the others are just plain creepy," he said. "Do you want to see my absolute creepiest costume?"

"Of course."

He turned to the rack behind him and pulled out an innocent green velvet robe from among the black ones. "A Ghost of Christmas Present costume," he said. "But a special one given to us by a theater company." He opened the robe. From the white satin interior scowled two horrifying faces, gaunt children staring out of dark eye sockets, the flesh tight around their skulls.

"Ignorance and Want," I said, "the two monster-children who clung to the ghost of Christmas Present."

"'No change, no degradation, no perversion of humanity, in any grade, through all the mysteries of wonderful creation, has monsters half so horrible and dread,'" the clerk quoted.

"The costume almost looks new." The green velvet was plush and no stains or rips marred the white lining.

"It is." The clerk nodded. "Hardly anyone wears it. Who wants to be reminded of ignorance and want?"

CHAPTER 22

A Strong Appetite for Contradiction

I would have been on time to dinner, but I had to pee.

"Easier said than done," I mumbled to myself as I stared at the restroom stall, which was a good foot and a half skinnier than my hoop skirt. I squished the sides of my skirt down and walked into the stall. Doable. Wall-to-wall hoop skirt, but doable. I turned my hiney toward the toilet seat and felt a tug on my skirt. I let go of my hoop skirt so I could see what caught me, and *whoomph!* I felt like one of those exploding Poppin' Fresh crescent roll thingies, fully expanded to fill the space. I pawed through miles of green brocade, but couldn't see what had grabbed my skirt. "Dammit."

"Are you okay?" A small girl peered in the open stall door.

"Kind of," I said. I tried to push my skirt down at the sides, but now whatever I was caught on had grabbed my skirt but good. I let go of my skirt again so I didn't tear the fabric. *Whoomph!*

The little girl giggled.

"Can you see what my skirt is stuck on?" I pointed to the side of the stall where I thought my skirt was caught.

She stuck her head inside the stall and shook her head.

"Maybe if you come closer?"

She stepped into the stall with me and looked down at my skirt. "Oh, it's stuck on that thing."

"The toilet handle?"

"No."

"Toilet paper roll?"

"No."

"Toilet cover dispenser?"

"It's a box. Where my mom puts her mouse."

"Her mouse?"

"You know. It's a white mouse with a tail."

Hmm, white with a tail. "Her tampon."

"Yeah."

I am a detective, you know. So I was stuck on the tampon receptacle. "Could you unhook it for me?"

"It's stuck underneath."

"Maybe if I lift up my skirt, you could reach it."

"Okay."

I raised my skirt and she crept under it.

The door to the restroom opened. "Eloise? Have you fallen in? Whatever is taking you so...Oh." Eloise's mom skidded to a halt in front of my stall. "Is that my daughter under your skirt?"

It took several minutes to calm down Eloise's mom, a few more to get me unhooked from the tampon receptacle, and then several more to figure out how I was going to use the toilet (I really had to pee by then), so I ended up ten minutes late for dinner.

"My apologies, everyone," I said as I approached the captain's table. I decided not to go into the whole bathroom/tampon/hoop skirt story.

"No worries. I ordered for you." Jonas stood and pulled out a delicately carved wooden chair for me. He wore a well-cut black tailcoat. "You look beautiful."

"Thank you." Though the skirt and corset were pains in the ass, the glimpse I'd seen of myself in the bathroom mirror was small-waisted and full-skirted and pink-cheeked (probably from lack of air). I felt beautiful.

Until I sat down. Then my devil hoop skirt flipped up and hit me in the face, exposing my bright pink Victoria's Secret underwear, which I suspected weren't historically accurate despite the name.

"Oh dear." A woman jumped up from the table and helped me wrangle my skirt into place. "It happens to most of us the first time we wear a hoop," she said. "The trick is to sit on the edge of your chair. If you lean back, whoops, up goes the skirt."

I thanked the woman, who was dressed in a high-necked gown of deep blue. "I'm Rose," she said, sitting down next to a man dressed in a double-breasted navy blue suit with epaulets on his shoulders. "I'm married to Captain Steerwell here."

"How do you do, everyone." I nodded slightly at the five couples seated at the table. "I'm Ivy Meadows."

"Where are your manners, Jonas?" Theo sat next to Jonas and wore a similar tailcoat.

"My apologies. I was just about to introduce—"

Theo stood. "You probably know of me, Miss Meadows, but allow me to introduce myself. I'm Theo Pushwright, and this is my literary assistant, Madalina Botchick." Madalina was dressed in a gown of dove gray silk trimmed in black, her ash blonde hair pulled into a bun wound about by a braid of her own hair. My lacy dress and wig felt costume-ish by comparison.

"Nice to meet you, Mr. Pushwright," I said. "I understand you're Jonas's stepfather." A waiter silently deposited bowls of soup before each of us.

"Yes." As Theo studied Jonas's face, his eyes narrowed in disappointment and his lips puckered in disgust. "If I'd been his real father, perhaps things would have turned out differently."

"Excuse me?" I said.

"I'm the black sheep of the family." Jonas sank in his seat.

"Has to be old news," I said. "A directing gig for *Get Lit!* is quite a coup."

Jonas shook his head.

"Of course it is. Most theater directors have to go from job to job, or wind up doing theater administration too, which, let's face it, is not what most creative people want to—"

"I think our onboard theater is marvelous." The captain's wife broke in, obviously noting the tension I had ignored in favor of defending Jonas. "Both the entertainment and The Royal Victoria Theatre itself. I saw that you filled the space for your lecture, Mr. Pushwright. You must have many fans onboard."

At the mention of fans, Theo's face took on the charismatic glow I'd seen at his book signing. "Why, yes, I'm honored to have so many people who believe in the power of positivity."

"My former roommate Harley must have believed," I said.

Jonas gave me a sharp look. No one else seemed to notice that I used the past tense, though the captain's wife set down her water glass with a thump.

"She must have really been looking forward to your visit," I continued. "She already had a signed book and everything. You said she was positively perfect."

"Probably came to one of my Positively Perfect seminars." Theo sipped his wine. "They're weekend retreats designed especially for women, to help them realize the power and beauty of their femininity."

So the signature on Harley's book didn't imply anything— unless Theo helped Harley realize her feminine power and beauty in a one-on-one, up-close-and-personal situation. I watched him carefully, but his face showed nothing. No. The signed book was a dead end.

"Maybe you'd like to attend one of my weekends?" said Theo. "When you're in port, of course." He smiled at me, a bit too warmly it seemed. "I could arrange a discount."

Jonas shifted in his seat next to me. This was getting weird. Theo was now studying my face with an expression of interested delight, as if he'd just discovered a new Rembrandt. It was especially strange since the incredibly beautiful Madalina sat right next to him. I had the distinct impression he was using me to goad Jonas.

"Ah." Theo turned his charm on me full tilt. "I remember you. I wasn't sure because you wore a different wig and costume, but I recognize you now. You wanted to quit smoking."

"That was me, but—"

"You *can* quit, Ivy." Theo spoke my name like it was the name of his favorite cognac. Madalina leaned back in her seat in an amused "here he goes again" attitude. "People have conquered everything using the power of positivity," he said. "They've stopped smoking, overcome addiction, cured long-standing diseases. If everyone around the world thought positively, there'd be no more poverty of mind, body, or spirit. I mean, look at me. I was born a poor nobody, and now I'm one of the Forbes 400."

"But you're not saying that positive thinking can solve all the world's problems, right?" I said. "I mean, sure, I believe it can help somebody break a bad habit or become a better person or even get a better job, but it's not going to help some poor lower-caste woman in India get a four-bedroom house and a car."

"It could, if she truly believed."

I looked around the table. Everyone seemed very interested in their food. I knew I should let the subject go, but Theo's patronizing prattle had my dander up. "And what about my brother, who has a permanent brain injury? If he thought positively, could he become an Ivy League scholar?"

"The brain has been known to repair itself."

"You've got to be—"

"And your brother might be stunted by a lack of positive energy from his family members."

"Excuse me." Silverware clattered as I jumped up from my seat. "I'm going to have a smoke."

CHAPTER 23

This Train of Reflection

I shouldn't have brought up Cody. The storm that threatened to capsize me earlier circled back and the first teardrops gathered. I strode onto the deck outside the dining room, trying to shake off the tempest brewing in my heart. A salty wind lashed my face, whipped at my skirt, and tugged at my wig, but still my mind was full of Cody. It was night, and he was out there somewhere. Where? On a park bench? Huddled on a doorstep?

Through the big window I saw the brightly lit dining room. A few heads from the captain's table were turned my way. I faced the sea and pantomimed smoking/vaping a cigarette, one hand on top of my head to keep my wig from blowing away.

A few moments later, Madalina joined me at the railing. "It is nice night for a smoke. Too bad we do not have one." She stood beside me, looking out to sea. Her dress rippled in the wind, a beautiful silver wave.

"Thanks," I said to Madalina. "For coming out here."

"I like you. You talk back to Theo."

"I couldn't help it. How can he believe that my brother...that people are in bad places because they're not thinking positively enough? It's like saying they're to blame for their situation. It's, it's..."

"Arrogant. He is arrogant man, but not bad one. His message helps many people."

"You're his assistant, right? His literary assistant?"

"I write for him. I am spook."

She didn't look like CIA to me. Ah, she meant ghost. A ghostwriter. A gorgeous ghostwriter who didn't speak English well. Huh.

"He likes you, you know," she said. "You have fire."

I shook my head.

She looked over her shoulder. "See? Is true."

I followed her glance. Oh, she must have been talking about Jonas, who had just come out on deck and was walking toward us.

"I see you later," Madalina said to me. She nodded at Jonas as she passed him on her way back into the dining room. I turned back to the ocean. The wind had calmed. My worries about Cody too, though I didn't know why. I hoped we had some sort of psychic connection and he was telling me he was all right.

"Ivy." Jonas placed a hand on my back. "I'm sorry I didn't come out sooner. I wanted to make sure...well, to keep the family peace."

"At what cost? Does Theo always talk to you like that?"

"Not always, but...often." He shook his head. "Theo's like a lot of very successful men. He's convinced he's right about everything. His success is the proof. And my lack of success—at least as far as he sees it—is proof that I'm in the wrong."

"And he never is?"

Jonas shook his head. "That's another attribute of men like him. Regular rules don't apply to them."

"Like those politicians who get caught with their hands in the candy jars but insist it was part of a grand plan for humanity?"

"Yeah. But in some ways Theo can be worse, because he feels like his positive thinking validates everything he does. If he believes what he does is good, it is. He's not an easy man." Jonas scooted closer to me so that our shoulders touched. "But he likes you."

I was really confused. When Madalina said, "he likes you," did she mean Theo? If so, why did she say "is true" when she saw Jonas? And why did everyone care what Theo thought anyway?

"I appreciate you standing up for me," Jonas said. "More than you know."

When I turned to look at him, our faces were just inches apart. Maybe that's why he kissed me. It felt like a misplaced peck on the cheek. At first. Then he glanced toward the dining room, pulled me closer, and kissed me again.

Nope. Nothing there for me. I was just about to pull away when...

"A kiss for the boofer lady!" Oliver and a gang of orphans appeared at the same time as a gust of wind tore off my wig. We all watched as the blonde curls sailed out to sea.

"What are you, a black wizard or something?" I said to Oliver, who was doubled over laughing. "And boofer lady? What the heck is—"

"It's Dickens!" Oliver shouted as he turned and led his pack of boys back down the deck.

"From *Our Mutual Friend*," said Jonas. "That kid is too smart by half. Which reminds me, there's something I wanted to ask you."

CHAPTER 24

Good Training Is Always Invaluable

"No, really?" I didn't mean to whine, but there it was.

"Only when you're in costume," Jonas said. "It's just that your character is the most likely one to watch over Oliver."

The actress who formerly played Nancy was Oliver's de facto keeper. Now I was. Great. Not only did I find the little bugger *really* annoying, I was crap at watching over people. The Cody storm rumbled on the far edge of my mind, but I concentrated on the calm feeling I'd had just a few minutes earlier. Cody was okay. He was.

"Okay." What else could I say?

"We'd better get back."

Back inside the dining room, Theo was holding forth, the faces at the table turned toward him like plants toward a grow light—a fake sun that came with a price. I decided to act the part of a genteel Victorian lady and so kept my mouth shut and ate daintily (the corset did help). The rest of the meal was uneventful.

After dinner, I went quickly back to my room. As I got out of the gown and its accouterments, I wondered briefly if a hoop skirt might soften a fall onto a hard stage floor. I knew there was no way to perform in it, but I did like the image of me floating down to earth like Glinda the Good Witch. I got into leggings and a tank top instead and tried to stuff my dinner costume in the closet. No way. I gave up and tried to contain it on my twin bunk. It fit well enough. I threw my phone and some Gatorade and lip balm into my duffle, then swung the bag to work the soreness out of my arms as I made my way to the theater.

Jonas wasn't at rehearsal. Val was. "Are we still rehearsing the magic show?" I asked Timothy as I dumped my duffle bag in the seat between him and Val.

"Jonas sent a message." Timothy watched Ada drag a mat under a silk onstage. "He's with his stepfather, and thought we could do this without him since we're just working the silk choreography."

"Money before art." Ada kicked the mat and it unrolled with a *whoomph*.

"What's she mean?" I asked Timothy quietly. But not quietly enough.

"You think Jonas asked Theo on this cruise because he likes him?" Ada gave a mean laugh. "Ivy, check your rigging."

"Jonas is Theo's only family," Timothy said. "So it pays for Jonas to be nice to him. Literally. Jonas could inherit millions if he plays his cards right."

"So we are all nice to Jonas." Val watched me scoot up the ladder to the catwalk, obviously admiring the view.

"Why are you here tonight?" I said to Val as I stepped onto the metal walkway. "They haven't added you to the magic show, have they?" I checked the carabiners that held my silk. All locked.

"I am here because you want me."

"I do?" I headed back down the ladder.

"Sure. You leave note. On my bed. Last night I sleep with it under my pajamas."

"You mean under your pillow."

"No, I don't." He grinned at me as I stepped onto the stage.

"Let's go," Ada said. "Ivy, tie into your silk."

I did. Ada tied herself into hers too. "We're going to practice with the techs raising us with the pulleys. Watch me as much as you can without throwing yourself off balance. To start off, your outside arm starts in preparatory position." Like most choreographers, Ada used ballet terminology. I curved my arm in front of me. "The arm slowly rises into second position, as if it's helping to lift you," she continued. "It ends up over your head in third position by the time the pulley stops, when you reach the top of the proscenium. Ready to try it?" I nodded. "Okay, go!" she yelled to an unseen techie.

The fabric tightened in my hands as the silk started rising. I concentrated on timing the movement of my incredibly sore arms with the rise of the silk and so didn't really feel the height until my ascent stopped. Then I noticed Val and Timothy sitting in the audience. They looked much too small.

"Now we're going to do the moves you learned last rehearsal. Start with the Ship's Lady."

We went through a sequence of poses that had names like the Crucifix and the Wing Surfer and the Upside Down Splits. Yeah, I did say *Upside Down* Splits. And I was actually having fun. Though my heart beat fast and my arms burned and I couldn't look directly at the stage floor far below me, I was beginning to understand the lure of aerial work. I was even getting the hang of it (pun intended). I'd just tipped myself into a Half Buddha position—like the lotus position but with your head pointed toward the floor—when my cell pinged loudly from its spot in my bag in the theater. "Grab it," I yelled.

"She's in the middle of a family emergency," Timothy explained to Ada. He looked at my phone's screen. "It's a text from a guy named Matt. Says, 'Still looking. Try not to worry. O O.'"

"O O?" Val said. "What is that?"

Timothy looked at my phone. "I think it's hugs. Or is it kisses?"

"Should I be jealous?" said Val.

I was still upside down, Cody was still missing, and the blood was rushing to my head. "Let's just go on." I threw myself into the rest of rehearsal, hoping that by concentrating on the incredibly difficult task in front of me, I could stop worrying about where Cody was sleeping.

But I couldn't.

CHAPTER 25

No Very Great Consolation

Val followed me out of the theater. "Ivy, baby, I could not read your writing. On the note."

"I was wondering if you could help me out with my Cockney accent." I did have horrendous handwriting.

"Sure. We go to my cabin?"

"I don't think—"

"Maybe the bar?"

We walked toward the stairs. "It's sweet of you to offer, but not tonight. It's been a long day."

"I could rub your neck."

"I bet you could." My cell buzzed. I said a quick silent prayer before looking at it, but it was just a text from Uncle Bob responding to an earlier message.

"Try not to be sad, okey-dokey?" Val somehow made "okey-dokey" sound compassionate. I stared at him for a moment. Could he really be a thief, a murderer? "You change your mind?" he asked.

Maybe I was changing it. About some things. "No. I'll see you tomorrow." I made an attempt at a smile. "Okey-dokey?"

Val kissed me on the cheek and headed into the stairwell. I made my way to the library.

After a few texts back and forth, Uncle Bob and I had decided that the cigar bar might not be the best place to meet anymore, since Bette had seen us there.

The library welcomed me with the musty but wonderful smell of books.

My uncle sat reading in one of the leather chairs facing the fireplace, another book on his lap. I sank into the other one gratefully, thankful also for the bottle and two glasses on the small table between the chairs.

Uncle Bob put down his book when he saw me. "Thought you might need a drink." He poured golden liquor into a small-stemmed glass and handed it to me.

"Boy, do I," I said, taking a big swig. "It's been the day from—aaah!" I nearly dropped my glass. "What *is* this?"

"Harvey's Bristol Cream. It's sherry."

"*Sherry?*" My uncle was a beer man. Tequila if he was feeling rowdy.

"Yeah." He looked a little hurt. "I thought you might like it. It's kinda Dickens-ish." He sipped from his glass, which looked tiny in his big hand. "They have some rule about buying bottles of liquor onboard, but you can get wine for some reason. Sherry's a fortified wine. They add brandy to give it a higher alcohol content."

"I'll drink to that." I poured a bit more into my glass and sipped it carefully this time. Sweet, and heavier on the tongue than the beer or margaritas I usually drank.

"Bette introduced me to it."

Bette again. I'd get around to her later, but first: "Any word about Cody?"

"That media alert helped."

"They found him?"

He shook his head. "He's not back home yet, but he's okay. A few people called in to say they'd seen him. The last person who saw him said Cody was showing a picture of Stu around a bar."

"A bar?"

"I know. You got me. And just in case, I asked Pink to check the hospitals and..." Uncle Bob trailed off. He wouldn't look at me.

"And the morgues." I knew what he almost said.

"But he's not there," he said firmly.

We both stared at the fire for a moment. It perfumed the air with a spicy, slightly masculine scent...No, it was a gas fire. There shouldn't be a smell. I inhaled, trying to identify the aroma.

"What were you checking out this morning?" asked Uncle Bob.

"Oh." I couldn't believe I hadn't told him about Val. Then again, it had been an awfully full day. I filled him in: Timothy seeing Valery pick the man's pocket, Val's meeting with the big guy in the cantina, finding Harley's knitting in Val's room. "But I didn't actually see him do anything," I said. "And I just can't see him as a murderer. I've got pretty good intuition about people."

Uncle Bob nearly choked on his sherry. "You what?"

"I think I'm pretty good at—"

"Remember the guy who nearly killed you, oh, just a few months ago? The guy you thought was your mentor?"

"So I was wrong once."

"And then there was that boyfriend of yours who turned out to be gay."

"Bi. He was bisexual."

"And that actress in your show who poisoned me."

"Okay, okay. Uncle," I surrendered. "You find anything?"

"Not really. Didn't realize how tough this job would be. Never worked undercover around the clock like this. Any other time, I had at least a few hours I could go home or back to the office and look stuff up. Maybe in the dead of night, but still, it was an option. This time, even doing a simple background check is a pain in the ass. It's gonna have to be faxed to the ship instead of emailed, and it's gonna have to be encoded, in case any crew member takes a gander. I got my work cut out for me tomorrow. Got to look over hundreds of names."

"Hundreds?"

"The whole crew."

"Doesn't the cruise line do background checks?"

Uncle Bob tilted his hand back and forth: the universal "maybe so, maybe not" gesture. "Anyway, now they do. As part of our expenses. The encoding we're using is something pretty simple I've used before. I make it look like I'm checking a shipment of produce. The individual names get buried in the lists of farms, distributors, even varieties of produce. I also get dates, locations, everything. And the guy doing it for me flags anything big." He grinned. "I just gotta look for the bad apples." His smiled faded. "Speaking of something rotten, that coroner in Ensenada didn't find anything. The toxicology report will take a while yet, but no sign of anything." Uncle Bob grimaced, the way he did when something didn't seem right. "Weird." He stared at the fire again.

I sniffed the air. Maybe the spicy smell was coming from the books? I glanced at the ones facedown in Uncle Bob's lap. "What are you reading?"

"Oh." He grinned. "This is great." He showed me the cover of one of the books: *Hunted Down: The Detective Stories of Charles Dickens.* "Did you know Dickens was the first to write about a police detective? He made up some guy named Inspector Bucket in *Bleak House.* I haven't read that one yet. Thought I'd start with this one. Shorter."

"And the other book?"

Uncle Bob reddened. "*The Lost Art of Towel Origami.*"

"Really? Can I see?" I mostly wanted to figure out why Uncle Bob was blushing. Maybe they were dirty towels.

He handed me the book. Inside were instructions on how to make elephants, palm trees, and monkeys out of towels. No erotic towel-ry. But nothing to do with Dickens either. "You found this in the library?"

"No. Um...Bette bought it for me."

"Did she buy you the aftershave too?" Uncle Bob had never smelled of anything except Mexican food and beer, which is why it took me so long to finger him as the source of the scent.

"No. They were doing some Victorian Life talk at the Leather Bottle Bar today, and one of the bartenders made this for us to try. It's bay rum." Uncle Bob lost his shy embarrassed look and grinned at me. "Did you know you could actually drink it too? It's basically rum infused with bay leaves, spices, a little orange peel, and vodka."

"It does smell tasty. Does Bette like it?" This was my way in, but I had to tread carefully.

"Uh, yeah." Uncle Bob flushed pink again.

I swallowed a big gulp of sherry for the liquid courage. "So tell me about her."

"She's a nice gal."

Oh no. It was worse than I suspected. This was what Uncle Bob said about all his girlfriends.

"She's from Golden, Colorado, outside of Denver. Her husband died about a year ago. He was in oil, I guess."

"She a big Dickens fan?"

"Not really. *Get Lit!* Cruises just sounded fun to her. She could travel and learn something at the same time."

And meet her next rich husband. "I thought maybe she was onboard to see Theo." I remembered Bette asking a question at Theo's book signing. Timothy had thought Theo recognized her.

"No. She doesn't believe in that New Age crap."

Another bad sign. Uncle Bob's last girlfriend, Echo, had been a big New Ager and it sat just fine with him. Now he was okay with whatever Bette believed.

"Hey." Uncle Bob looked at me over his glass of sherry. "Why so interested?"

I wanted to say, "Because I wonder why she's after a fifty-ish overweight rancher if it's not about his fake money," but that would be insulting. After all, I thought Uncle Bob was quite a catch. It's just that it usually took people a while to see beyond his not-so-suave exterior. The bigger reason, though, was that I knew Bette's type. They were the ones who showed up at theater galas in too much makeup and too many jewels and treated the actors like waiters. Who snapped at the servers. And who played footsie under the table with their friends' husbands. But I couldn't say any of that, because I loved my uncle. So instead I said, "Just keeping an eye on you."

And Bette. I was definitely keeping an eye on her too.

CHAPTER 26

A Conversation of Some Importance

I grappled with Bette and tore the key from her hand. I raced to her car and unlocked the trunk, where she'd kept Cody this whole time. Could he breathe? I opened the trunk. An alarm went off.

My cell phone buzzed beside my pillow where I put it last night.

A Phoenix area code number I didn't recognize. Please, not the police, not the hospital, I prayed. I picked up.

"I need your help."

"Cody?"

"I still can't find Stu."

It *was* Cody. He must have found a pay phone. Thank you, thank you, thank you God. "Where are you?"

"Downtown."

"Thank God you're all right."

"Keep it down." Ada's voice was groggy. "Some of us are trying to sleep."

"Hang on, Cody." I hopped the few steps to the bathroom and shut the door. "Okay. I need you to go back to the group home—"

"No. I've got to find Stu. He needs his medicine."

"Can't you conduct your search from the house?"

"No. They'll be mad at me for leaving."

Yeah, they would. "Maybe you could go to the police."

"NO. Are you going to help me or not?"

Once Cody got an idea in his head, he didn't let it go until he was ready to be done with it. It may have been part of his brain injury, or just a family trait.

"Okay, okay. How can I help?"

"I don't know where to look."

"Did I hear you've been looking in bars?"

"Yeah. Stu likes beer. But he's not supposed to have it." Cody rattled pills in a bottle. "Do not combine with alcohol," he read slowly. "That means he's not supposed to have beer when he's on Keppra."

Keppra. That again. "You have Stu's medicine with you?"

"Duh. He needs it so he doesn't have a seizure. That's why I'm looking for him." Cody sighed exaggeratedly. "You're no help. I'm gonna go."

"No, wait, wait. Um..." Where would I look for Stu? "Think about where Stu might want to sleep. Look for him there at night." Did I just tell Cody to stay out on the streets after dark again? I nearly slapped myself in the forehead. "No, wait, that's not a good idea—"

"Yes, it is." Cody's voice brightened. "Thanks, Olive-y." He hung up. I called the number right back but it rang and rang.

Damn. I couldn't believe I'd done that. My phone said 6:02 a.m. I usually wasn't up for another hour (or two), but there was no way I could go back to sleep. I snuck quietly back into our cabin, grabbed a t-shirt and jeans out of my drawers, and dressed quietly in the bathroom. I slipped outside and checked my cell phone. It still had one bar. I speed-dialed Matt.

He picked up immediately. "Ivy?"

"Cody called me. He's okay."

"Oh, Ivy, thank—"

Dead air. And no bars. I redialed, just in case. I really really wanted to talk to Matt. No, the signal was gone. At least Cody had been able to reach me. And now Matt could rest a little easier.

I ran up to the Pickwick Promenade and used one of the deck-to-cabin phones to call my uncle's room. "Hey, it's me."

"You're up?"

"I know, I know, but I talked to Cody. He's okay."

Uncle Bob sighed with relief.

"But...I think I encouraged him to stay out another night." I told him what I'd done.

"Hon," said Uncle Bob, "you know your brother. Do you really think you could have talked him into going home?"

"No."

"Cody must be staying somewhere safe. He's a careful kind of guy." It was true. Cody liked order. "And it sounds like he's got a plan. I really think he'll be fine."

I did too. Even though my mind was trying to latch on to worry, my heart felt comforted, like it did last night after dinner. I hoped it was our psychic sister-brother connection and not just wishful thinking. "Okay. See you at the library tonight?"

"I'm going to that costume ball thing, but afterward."

After we hung up, I went to Boz's Buffet where I celebrated with a full English breakfast. I sat down at a table facing the ocean (take that, water phobia) and devoured my entire fry-up: eggs, fried bread, a fried half of a tomato, sausages, and black pudding. I was just mopping up the last bit of egg with a slice of fried pudding when Timothy sat down across from me, a cup of coffee in his hairy hand. "I can't believe you're eating blood pudding," he said.

"Please don't call it blood pudding this early in the morning. I was just starting to feel good." I told him about Cody's call.

"Thank God," he said, scooting his chair back from the table. "And good thing you ate a big breakfast. Today is the day from hell, you know. Think I'll go see if I can scrounge up something not fried." He wandered off in the direction of the buffet line.

The day from hell? It wasn't going to be that bad. We were off until lunch, at which time all ambient characters would encourage the passengers to attend Mr. Fezziwig's Ball tonight (and to get their costumes before three p.m.). Then we had a half-hour lunch before attending *Oliver! At Sea!* rehearsal, then a two-hour break for dinner, then the costume ball where we'd dance with the guests, then our last rehearsal for *Fagin's Magic Handkerchief*, which premiered tomorrow night. Plus I was supposed to keep an eye on Oliver, the little brat. I guess it was the day from hell.

But what the heck. I was off until lunch. I planned to let my breakfast settle a bit, soak out the soreness in my arms and shoulders in one of the hot tubs, then head to the onboard art auction at eleven o'clock. Seemed like a good opportunity for a thief to learn which travelers were potential marks.

At 10:59, I was in position behind a potted palm where I could scan the auction audience members without being seen. Most of them wandered around, gazing at the artwork on the wall and peering into glass cases, mimosas in their hands. Waiters circulated, balancing trays of crystal flutes filled with the sunny orange drinks.

The squeal of a microphone announced the beginning of the auction. "Welcome to Cruikshank and Cattermole's Art Auction," said a too-amplified voice. "Today's auction items include Dali prints, Russian nesting dolls by master artist Lonuchenkova, and a rare copy of *David Copperfield* from 1914, written entirely in Chinese." Pretty impressive, some of this stuff. Definitely worth stealing.

But I didn't see anything suspicious as I peered through the palm fronds or hear anything that piqued my interest. For about ten minutes. Then I heard semi-familiar voices. Familiar, because I'd heard them both before: Theo and Bette. Semi, because I'd never heard either of them spitting mad.

"Are you following me?" Theo's voice was low and full of menace.

"Why would I do that?" Bette's Western accent was gone. "Oh, because you ruined my life?"

"You did that to yourself."

"That's right. We're all the masters of our own destinies, right?"

"You can be, if you decide to—"

"Stuff it, Theo. We both know what—"

"What do you want?"

"I want to give you one more chance to—"

"Why are you hiding behind a tree?" Arghh. Oliver's timing couldn't have been worse, and from his grin I think he knew it. He quickly rearranged his face into an innocent look and pointed at my hiding place, just in case Bette and Theo hadn't noticed me.

"Just...lost...an earring back," I said as they glared at me. "Thought it might have flown back here. Here it is." I bent down to pick up the invisible back and pretended to attach it to my earring. "See ya," I said to all involved. I scooted down the hall to a bar that hadn't opened yet and found a quiet place to sit. I wanted to think about Theo and Bette. To think about Bette's lack of accent during their argument. And to think about what I would tell Uncle Bob.

CHAPTER 27

The Devil's in It

Lunchtime didn't start off too badly, except for the complaints from the cooks who were overloaded with orders for gruel. Seems Oliver had convinced all the orphans to order it for lunch.

After lunch, I stood outside on deck talking to a gaggle of senior citizens: "Ladies and gents, you'll want to outfit yourselves for the fancy dress ball tonight, and Madame Mantalini's Temple of Fashion has all the flounces, feathers, frills, and furbelows you'll want, so—oof!" My feet went out underneath me, and I sat down hard in something slick and wet and lumpy. Oh no.

"Oh dear." One of the ladies pointed at the mess I'd slipped in. "I'm afraid someone's been seasick."

I picked myself up carefully, my stomach churning with the thought of having to clean myself off when I heard a smothered giggle. Oliver and a few orphans watched from a distance. Hmm. I swiped at the yuck covering the back of my skirt and lifted a finger to my nose. A few of the seniors looked horrified, others entertained. I gave the stuff an experimental sniff. Yep. Gruel. I shook a sticky finger at Oliver, who ran off laughing.

On my way back to my room to change into my other (now clean) Nancy costume, I ran into a traffic jam. I pushed my way through the crowd, in a respectful sort of way.

"Did you decide who you'll be for the ball tonight?" a woman asked the man next to her.

Ah, the bottleneck was right outside the costume shop.

"I'm not going to the party. I wish to be left alone."

"You're kidding," she said in a crestfallen voice. "You were so excited about it earlier."

"Bah humbug," said her husband. Then he laughed, a big hearty laugh. "Get it?" he said. "I'm practicing to be Scrooge already."

"You!" His wife smiled and swatted him.

Excited travelers swarmed the costume shop and dozens more spilled out in a long line that filled the hallway. I had nearly made my way past the crowd when I saw Jonas's blonde head. He had sent me a text last night after rehearsal: "Amazing night. All because of you." Ack. Jonas was nice and handsome and...not for me, romantically at least. But I still thought there was something fishy about Theo, and Jonas was my best way in. Mata Hari would have led him on. But that just seemed mean, especially since I liked Jonas. I decided to be friendly but not flirty, and hope he didn't get the wrong idea.

I started to wave to him when he looked over his shoulder, furtively it seemed, then ducked into Mrs. Chickenstalker's Sundries Shoppe.

Being a natural snoop, I crept to the door of the shop, keeping myself well hidden in the throngs of people. Jonas pointed to something behind the shop's counter. The clerk grabbed it from off the shelf, but I couldn't see what it was. Jonas left the store, a small paper bag under his arm.

I changed clothes and went to rehearsal, arriving a few minutes early for once. I spent the time working on my Cockney accent with Val. And trying to find out more about him and Harley.

"Have you worked on any other *Get Lit!* ships?" I asked. "I always wanted to see Alaska, and 'arley said she really liked the *Jack London*." A big fib: Harley never said anything to me except "no," but maybe I could find out where she and Val met.

"This is only ship for me. And Alaska is cold. Try last line again with more Cockney."

"'Arley said she really loiked the *Jack London*," I said. "And Oi fought Russians loiked the cold."

"Put words in the front of your mouth," Val said.

"You are Russian, roight? I didn' see anyfing abou' cha onloine, but—"

"You Google me?" Val grinned. "You like me. Yes, I am Russian. Try another sentence."

"Doncha eveh go onloine?"

"No. Too much money." Val scooted closer. "You have to know me in person, not by computer. Much better that way."

"Oi see."

"Better. You almost have it. Push your lips forward." I did and Val leaned into me.

"Are you trying to kiss me?" I said in my regular voice.

"Can you blame me?"

Right then Jonas walked in. But maybe he didn't notice Val trying to kiss me, or maybe he wasn't the jealous type, or maybe I was all wrong about him liking me, because he just clapped his hands and said, "Everyone! We're going to run the show from the top, but let's go over Nancy's ballad and her death scene first."

Go over? It was more like "let's do them for the first time." All of our rehearsal time had been spent on blocking orphans and running their musical numbers. Oh, I knew it made sense, them being volunteer amateurs and me a paid professional, but still.

I headed backstage. As soon as I was in place in the wings, the click track (the recorded accompaniment) began, playing the first few bars of the tune of "Where is Love?" from the original musical. I stepped onstage, gazed wistfully into the distance, and sang, "Whe-eh-eh-eh-ere...is food?" Not exactly the poignant song Oliver sang in the movie. "Are the pork chops any good?" I sang. "Should I drink my tea, or maybe see...if coffee's freshly brewed?" I guess *Oliver! At Sea!*'s lyricists had decided that food was the one thing the story and the ship had in common. "Whe-eh-eh-eh-ere...is pie? Should I order ham on rye? Or fish and chips, or Spotted Dick, or a pasty with fungi?"

"Really?" I stopped. I couldn't stand it anymore. "I'm afraid the audience will throw things at me."

"Don't worry," Jonas said. "They eat it up." He grinned.

I knew I was sunk, so I started in again. "As long as he feeds me..." This half of the song used "As Long As He Needs Me," a lovely ballad of heartache, and they'd turned it into a song that featured Bangers and Mash. I finished the stinker and exited stage right.

"Great. Let's move on," Jonas said from his place in the audience.

I opened my mouth to protest the fact that I'd practiced my big ballad exactly once with no feedback or anything, when I realized that if I did complain, I'd have to sing the song again. I shut my mouth.

Val and I got into places for Nancy's death scene. *Get Lit!*'s playwrights had played this part of the story seriously. In both *Oliver! At Sea!* and the original *Oliver Twist*, Nancy tries to help Oliver, but Bill Sikes erroneously believes she's given Fagin and him up to the authorities.

The click track began again: this scene was choreographed to music and played behind a scrim, so the audience saw only our shadows. I entered, took a few steps, and tentatively looked back. Holding my shawl tightly around my shoulders, I walked a few more paces.

Strong hands clenched my shoulders and whirled me around. Fingers dug into my neck and I looked up into a face crazed with pure hatred.

Val was gone. Bill Sikes threw me to the ground, raised his walking stick over his shoulder, and swung with uncontrolled rage. I screamed as the stick arced toward me, its heavy metal head hitting the pillow next to me with a sickening thud. I whimpered as the stick came down again and again, until finally it stopped. Bill's ragged breathing rang in my ears. The lights faded to black.

"Great. Thanks," called Jonas. "Places for top of the show, everyone."

A hand reached down to me. I raised my eyes. Val smiled at me. "We are still friends, yes?"

I couldn't speak so I nodded, and he pulled me to my feet.

CHAPTER 28

A True Tale of Grief and Trial

After rehearsal, I wanted some air, so I took a detour outside before heading to Food, Glorious Food for a quick supper. My cell buzzed in my skirt pocket. This whole in-cell-range/out-of-cell-range thing was mystifying.

Timothy said it had something to do with my carrier and satellites and vectors. Whatever.

The number on my phone was one I didn't recognize, and not an Arizona number. Normally I wouldn't pick up, but who knew who might be calling about Cody?

"Hello?" said a tentative female voice. "Is this Ivy Meadows?"

Not about Cody then. Anyone calling about Cody Ziegwart would have known me as his sister, Olive. "Yes," I replied, "but I'm at work right now, and—"

"On the *S.S. David Copperfield*?"

"Yes..." How would a stranger know that?

"*Get Lit!* gave me your number. Oh, I'm sorry, this is Sue Locklow."

Locklow, Locklow...Oh. "You're related to Harley?" I held my breath, really hoping she'd been notified of Harley's death.

"I'm her mother...was her mother."

So she had been notified. I let go of my breath in a whoosh, then immediately felt guilty for feeling relieved. "I'm so sorry about Harley, Mrs. Locklow."

"That's why I'm calling. I just wanted to talk to someone about her. You were her roommate, right?"

I'd spent just minutes with Harley when she was alive. "Yes, but—"

"And you found her?"

Oh boy. "Could you hang on a second?" I made my way to a single wheelchair accessible bathroom, the nearest private space I could think of. I stepped inside and locked the door. "Yes, Ms. Locklow, I found her."

"Was she...harmed?"

"It didn't look like it." I left out the "stuffed in a closet" bit. Didn't seem necessary or kind.

"Do you think it was drugs? Did my daughter do drugs? You can tell me."

"I don't think so." No one had ever mentioned drugs when talking about Harley. Ada did say she thought Harley was selling her wares, so to speak, but again, I didn't think that information would be pertinent, and I didn't want to cause Harley's mom any more grief. "They said it was natural causes."

"But she was twenty-nine. She was just twenty..." Sue gulped a breath and didn't say any more. Like she couldn't.

"Um, did Harley have epilepsy?"

"What?"

She sounded shocked, so I rephrased the question. "Did Harley have any medical conditions?"

"I think she had some sort of sleep disorder, but...I don't know. I don't know anything about her anymore!" An anguished wail spilled from her, followed by deep wracking sobs.

Then it all came out. How Harley had left home at sixteen after a fight about a boyfriend. And had never come home again. Never called. Never written. "I'm sure she was just trying to find herself." I didn't know what else to say.

"I kept trying to find her too. That's how I knew she was onboard the *David Copperfield*. A private detective told me. I wrote to her, but..."

"She got your letter," I said, glad I had a scrap of comfort to offer. "She kept it in her desk drawer."

"Do you think she knew I loved her?"

"I'm sure." I knew it was the right thing to say.

"Thank you," Harley's mom whispered. "And Ivy?"

"Yeah?"

"I'm glad she had a friend."

CHAPTER 29

A Strange Sort of Young Gentleman

"Please, sir, I want some—"

A passel of orphans swept into the Leather Bottle Bar before I could place my order.

"Gin!" cried Oliver. "Gin for everyone."

"Out!" I shouted, waving my arms at the lot of them and startling one old fellow off his barstool. The great thing about playing Nancy was that I could say or do pretty much anything I wanted. Even better if I did it loudly.

"Shut up and drink your gin," said Oliver.

"That's not Dickens," I said.

"It's from the movie."

I grabbed the little hellion by his collar. "It's also out of character."

"The kids drink gin in *Oliver Twist*."

I beat down the urge to make his little snub nose even stubbier and instead said, "Get out of here, or I'll sic my Bill on you."

"Talk about breaking character," said Oliver. "You're supposed to be my protector. C'mon, boys," he yelled to his troop. "Let's go pick some pockets."

The noisy wave of kids swept out as quickly as they'd swept in.

Except for one. "I'll have a pint of stout," said the Dodger, sidling up to the bar, top hat in hand.

"When I said out, I meant everyone."

"I'm twenty-two."

"Right."

"It is right," said the bartender. "I checked his ID when he first started working onboard. David Hu, age twenty-two. Hey, that rhymes."

"Sorry about that," I said to David.

"It's okay. I wouldn't be playing Dodger if I didn't look twelve."

"You don't look twelve." He looked fourteen. "Can I buy that beer for you?" I said.

"Sure." He sat down at the bar, placing his hat on the stool to his right.

I pulled out the barstool to his left. Perfect. I'd wanted to talk to David for days, as he seemed to be the only one really upset by Harley's death. "Could I please have a Diet Coke and whatever will fill me up the most?" I asked the bartender. "I have the feeling this will be dinner." He nodded at me as he slid a pint of dark beer toward David.

As I sat down, I noticed Bette and Madalina by themselves at a nearby table. Huh. I hadn't seen them together before, and the only connection I knew they had was Theo. And though they had to know I was in the bar, they leaned in toward each other, so engrossed in their conversation they didn't even look up when a waiter deposited drinks on their table. Interesting. But now I had a dilemma: spy on them or question David? I decided to go with the orphan-in-the-hand and try to eavesdrop on the other two birds at the same time. I turned my head to keep one ear in their direction.

My phone buzzed in my pocket. A text from Matt: "Good news. Cody spotted again."

"Thank heavens," I texted back. "Keep me in the loop." I texted my uncle with the news and put my phone back in my pocket. I'd felt like my brother was okay, and he was. It may have been denial, or the fact that I was miles out to sea and couldn't do anything, but I decided to trust my feelings and my brother.

The barman set down my Diet Coke and a small wooden board topped with bread, ham, a slab of cheese, and a small dish of brown stuff that looked like mincemeat. "A Ploughman's Lunch," said the bartender. "Should hold you." I poked at the brown jam or whatever it was. "Branston pickle," he said before walking away.

"Sort of like chutney. It's good." David took a sip of his beer, its creamy head leaving a little beer-foam mustache on his smooth upper lip. "Thanks for the beer. And in case you're wondering, I'm off-duty 'til the ball."

"Don't worry, I'm not everyone's keeper. Just Oliver's." I strained to hear what Bette and Madalina were saying but couldn't catch a word.

"He needs one," said David. "That kid is a menace. I can hardly wait until his voice drops and we can get rid of him."

"You've worked with him before?"

"This is his third summer." David took a long drink. "Thank God he's underage or we'd have to put up with him all year." The *S.S. David Copperfield* did five shows in rotation: *Oliver! At Sea!* in the summer; *A Tale of Two Cities* in the fall; *A Christmas Carol*, of course, during the holiday season; *David Copperfield* for the rest of the winter; and *Great Expectations* in the spring. All adult major characters from all the novels were onboard all year, so that guests could drink with *David Copperfield*'s Mr. Micawber, eat wedding cake with *Great Expectations'* Miss Havisham, or join *Two Cities's* Madame Defarge's knitting circle.

Madame Defarge. That's who I really wanted to talk about. "I'm so sorry about Harley," I said. "I just talked to her mom."

"Her mom?" David's forehead wrinkled. He must have known they were estranged.

"Yeah. She was glad Harley had a friend." Sure, I knew she meant me, but I also knew she would have been glad David had been a friend to Harley, so it wasn't a fib. "How long did you know her?"

"She came onboard the *Copperfield* about a year ago."

Not an actual answer. "And you met her then? Or maybe on another ship?"

"This is the only *Get Lit!* ship I've worked on."

Another non-answer. I switched directions. "You know, I was surprised more people weren't upset when she died. She must have had friends."

"Just a few. Harley kept to herself."

"Kinda hard to do in a place like this, isn't it? Oh, but the private room must have helped."

"Yeah."

"She was pretty upset when she found out I was going to room with her. Said she'd been promised no roommates ever."

"Yeah."

Arghh. I'd get more answers out of a clam. I took a leap. "Ada said Harley had a private room because *Get Lit!* was pimping her out."

David carefully set his glass on the counter and turned to me. "That is *not* true." His voice was low and his black eyes burned with barely restrained rage. "Harley had a private room because of a medical condition."

Now we were getting somewhere. "Do you know what it was?"

"Something to do with her sleep."

Harley's mom had said something about that too. And Ada said that Harley made freaky sounds. Still, a private room?

Crash! A glass shattered behind us. I turned to see Madalina's wine goblet in shards, red wine sluicing off the table into Bette's lap. Darn.

Madalina jumped to her feet. "Children? No!"

"I wouldn't make it up." Bette dabbed at her lap with a napkin.

"You know this for sure?" Madalina's eyes could have set the place on fire.

Bette nodded. "But why are you...?" The question died on her lips as Madalina dashed from the room, nearly running over Scrooge and Marley as they walked in.

The two actors approached the bar. David took his top hat off the stool to make room for Marley and settled it on his head. His *top hat.*

"Hey," I said. "Were you following me the other morning?"

"Why do you ask?"

"Just a feeling I had."

"I do watch people," he said. "I find it useful."

"For acting?"

"Sure," he said. "For acting."

CHAPTER 30

Unite Business With Amusement

I planned to take David's tack at the costume ball: watch instead of dance. After all, this event seemed like a good opportunity for pickpockets. I wanted to keep my eyes peeled for any suspicious behavior, especially from Val or Oliver. Plus I wanted to save my energy for the silk rehearsal after the dance. But all was lost as soon as I stepped through the door of the ballroom. A full orchestra played and men bowed and ball gowns glittered—oh, it was glorious.

"Isn't it great?" I said to Timothy, who'd accompanied me.

"Fancier than my underwear," he replied, then sidled toward a long table that held crystal punch bowls and glasses.

The floor was crowded with Dickens characters. As the costume shop manager said, most people were clothed in upper-class period dress, so it was hard to tell what characters they were. I did recognize a couple of sailors, several Miss Havishams in tattered wedding dresses, and a couple shady-looking characters from Dickens' criminal underworld. Then, of course, there were the ghosts from *A Christmas Carol*. A black-hooded Ghost of Christmas Future stood talking with Madalina, who made a beautiful Ghost of Christmas Past with a shimmery blue gown and jeweled stars in her hair.

A black hat blinked in my peripheral vision. David must be around. I tried to spot him but couldn't. I did see Oliver and his gang weaving through the dancers. They tripped a few people and lifted up a few skirts, but didn't steal anything as far as I could see. Val staked out a spot near the punch bowl. He greeted a few people, slapping them on the back in a buddy-buddy sort of way, but mostly he drank punch, spiking it with something from a little flask he took from his inside coat pocket. He didn't seem to care if anyone saw him. I guess it would have been in character for Bill Sikes, and Val didn't have to rehearse tonight like we magic show actors did.

"And Mr. Boyko drinks a little." Jonas had come up behind me and followed my line of vision. I really needed to work on snooping more subtly.

I turned and smiled brightly, hoping to distract Jonas from my investigative gaze. The orchestra was playing a lively tune with lots of fiddle. "Shall we finish out this song?" I said.

Jonas's eyes flitted toward Madalina, who practically shone in her silver and blue costume. He seemed satisfied with whatever he saw. "You bet." He led me onto the dance floor. "I heard that you talked to Cody. So he's okay?"

"Yeah. He's okay." I needed to believe that.

"Good. Let's dance." Jonas spun me round and round in some sort of energetic polka. It was invigorating, but really difficult to do anything besides keep up with the music. I finally caught my breath and said, "So you and Theo..."

"Things are good," Jonas said. "We made up."

"Made up? Were you fighting?"

"Not anymore. It's all past history." The orchestra played a final chord. "And so is our dance." Jonas kissed me on the cheek. "Enjoy the rest of the party. I'll see you at rehearsal later." He walked away from me and out of the ballroom.

Off-again/on-again Jonas was beginning to freak me out. Not because I wanted him to be on-again, but because I was beginning to doubt my instincts. And because on-again Jonas was more likely to tell me about Theo.

I started to follow him, but was intercepted by Valery.

"Now I dance with you." He smiled a snaggledy grin.

I craned my neck, trying to see where Jonas was going. "I'm not sure I feel like dancing."

"You feel like something bigger and better?" Val waggled his bushy eyebrows at me.

"What's the news, my dears?" Timothy said as he approached us. He had a bit of beef from dinner stuck in his fake beard. It looked kinda Fagin-ish so I didn't tell him.

"Jonas just said he made up with Theo." Val and Timothy exchanged a knowing look. "What were they fighting about?"

"Probably his 'moral weakness,'" said Timothy.

"What?"

"Ivy does not know she is Jonas's mustache," said Val.

"His beard," said Timothy.

"He isn't gay," I said. "He took me on a date last night." I looked around, but couldn't see Jonas anywhere. So much for following him.

"Did he kiss you good night?" asked Timothy.

"He did, as a matter of fact."

"Not like I would kiss you," said Val.

"That's probably true," I said. Val did everything with abandon.

"You'd be better off with Bill Sikes here," Timothy said.

"I promise not to kill you." Val downed another cup of punch and winked his bi-colored eye.

I stared at it, fascinated by its yin-yang quality. "You have the coolest eyes," I said to Val. "I've never seen anything—"

"Come, and know me better, woman." A large fake-bearded man in a crown of holly and a fur-trimmed green robe glided up and held out his hands to me.

"Perfect." I curtseyed to Uncle Bob. "You are the epitome of Christmas Present."

"A big guy who likes to eat?"

I took my uncle's hands. "A big *jolly* guy who likes to eat. And you look good with a beard." He did. He looked even more like

Santa Claus, which was pretty nice in my books. "Hey," I said as he led me into a waltz, "I didn't know you could dance."

"Took a few lessons onboard. This cruise stuff is pretty great." Uncle Bob's robe billowed around him as we danced and I slid a look at the lining. Phew, no Ignorance and Want.

"So what had you never seen before?" he asked.

"What? Oh." My uncle was a notorious eavesdropper. "Val's eyes. One is blue and the other is half-blue, half-brown."

"That's called heterochromia. It's pretty rare," said Uncle Bob. "It can be genetic if it's different colored eyes, but if one eye is bicolored, it's usually due to something that happened in the womb."

"Sheesh, do you know everything?"

He sighed. "I still don't know much about this case we got. I did get some info from one of the guests. Seems she was one of the folks who was robbed on another ship."

"The *Jack London*?

"No. The *Virginia Woolf*."

"I'm not sure I'd name a seagoing vessel after a writer who drowned herself."

"It's *Get Lit!*'s singles ship. Something about a room of your own? Anyway, this lady said a bunch of the theft victims traded info among themselves—I think they're looking to sue the cruise line—and she said they're nearly certain it's a gang of Eastern Europeans working all the boats. They have operatives on each ship—"

"Operatives. I love spy language."

My uncle wisely ignored me. "Who steal small stuff off people—mostly phones and jewelry—and also break into cabin safes where they—"

"Did you see that YouTube video 'How to Break into a Hotel Safe in Sixty Seconds'?"

"Would ya let me finish?"

"Wait, are you the Ghost of Christmas Cranky?"

Uncle Bob rolled his eyes. "Where they take whatever's in the safe, usually more jewelry, plus wallets, artwork, and passports, and hide them onboard until they get off in port, where they meet with their higher-ups."

I remembered Val's meeting in Ensenada. But surely his crime boss wouldn't hug him.

I looked back at him, and he waved at me as he tossed back a big glass of punch.

Uncle Bob continued, "The guys—or gals, we shouldn't make any assumptions—they have fences for the goods in all the ports. And they have people who pay them for the information."

"What information?"

"Are you asking the Ghost of Christmas Cranky?"

I stuck my tongue out at him, in a good-natured way.

"The information they get from the phones, wallets, and passports. They're not just stealing money and jewelry. They're stealing identities."

"That's big stuff, but...do you think you can trust what this woman's telling you? Maybe she's part of the criminal ring and she's trying to throw you off the scent."

"I'm gonna have her checked out, but I think she's legit. She's an old friend of Bette's."

"Lord, my ears are burnin'." Bette gave her loud attention-grabbing laugh. She must've been stalking Uncle Bob. "Why are you dancing with this wench when you could be dancing with me?" She was dressed just like me, but in green. Weird. Did she really think Uncle Bob had a thing for me?

I held up my hand and stepped away. "I ain't goin' to fight you for him," I said in Nancy's voice, "seein' as how I got my Bill. This fella's all yours, Miss...Nancy, is it?"

"Nah." She took Uncle Bob's arm. "It's Bet."

Of course. Bet was Nancy's fellow tart in *Oliver Twist*, a character so minor she was cut from *Oliver! At Sea!* and called Whore Number Two in *Fagin's Magic Handkerchief*.

And I thought Bette didn't know anything about Dickens.

"Just a second, hon."

Oh no. Uncle Bob called her hon.

"I was just telling Nancy here a joke. Can't leave without giving her the punch line." Bette took the hint and gave us a bit of space, stepping away with a forced smile on her face. Uncle Bob leaned into me. "Watch that director of yours."

"Jonas?"

He nodded. "Been decoding that background check all day. He's one of the rotten apples."

CHAPTER 31

A Very Bad Boy Indeed

I needed to think. I found a corner of the ballroom that wasn't crowded with people and let my eyes wash over the crowd while my mind ran over what Uncle Bob said. Jonas was a criminal. The new information didn't just throw a wrench into my investigation, it put a stick in the spokes of my self-esteem. Was I really that bad at judging people? And if so, what kind of private investigator would I make?

I stayed in my corner for several minutes, turning things over in my mind, and yes, trying not to worry about Cody, who was out there in the night. Though I made sure to look as if I was watching the dancers, my focus was internal, so I jumped when I felt a tug on my skirt.

"Miss Nancy?" said the littlest of the orphan actors. "I lost my marble. Can you help me find it?"

A marble? Maybe the kids were supposed to play Dickens-era games. No matter the reason, a marble underfoot at a dance spelled trouble.

"Sure." I bent down next to him and looked in the direction he pointed. "What color is it?"

"Gu...green." Something in his voice made me look up at him. At him and Oliver and several other orphans who stood next to him, looking down my top.

"Buzzums!" said Oliver, then, "It's Dickens."

I'd had enough for one night. I stomped out of the ballroom and down the stairs to the employee deck. I unlocked the door to my cabin, wrenched it open, and stopped dead.

"Hello, baby!" Val was in my room—in my bed—buck-ass naked. His you-know-what stood up like the mast of a ship amongst a sea of sheets. He waggled it proudly. "I make you forget all about gay Jonas."

I slammed the door shut.

"Baby?" he said, muffled by the closed door. "Come back. It's okey-dokey."

I cracked open the door. Still naked. I shut it again. I couldn't slam it, but I did try to make as much outraged noise as I could.

"Ivy? Please. I put clothes on." Not only did Val use my name and sound appropriately regretful, but several employees had come out of their cabins to watch the show. I went back in my cabin, closed the door behind me, and snuck a look at my bed.

"Val," I said, squeezing my eyes shut. "You said you put clothes on."

"I did," he said. "Socks!"

I left, trying again to slam the door. No luck. Maybe I'd go to the crew bar. Nah. Ada wasn't at the dance, so I was pretty sure she was holding court from her regular barstool there. I headed back toward the ballroom. What the heck. Maybe I could get Uncle Bob away from Bette, just for a dance. I missed hanging out with the old fart.

Though the ball was only supposed to last another half hour, the party was still in full swing when I stepped through the door. I watched the dancers, looking for Uncle Bob, when a Ghost of Christmas Future stumbled toward me. Oh no, really? Maybe I could sneak out of the room...Nope. The costumed ball-goer was definitely headed my direction. He even pointed a robed arm at me, like the Ghost showing Scrooge his grave.

Great. I was going to have to dance with a drunk ghost. Might as well make the best of it. "Well, sir," I said in a hearty Nancy voice, "I'll give you a spin if you fancy one, but as you seem a wee bit in your cups, maybe you'd rather a nice sit-down. What do you say, sir?"

He didn't say anything.

He just fell on top of me.

CHAPTER 32

The Mighty Fallen

Two hundred pounds of dead weight is near impossible to move, especially when you're stuck underneath those pounds and tangled up in yards of sweaty black fabric. Even worse was the smell of vomit that came from underneath the Ghost of Christmas Future's black mask. I held my breath, trying not to barf myself, and squeaked, "Help."

I was pretty sure no one heard me, but someone must've seen what happened because two crew members pulled the man off me.

"Get his mask off," I managed to say. "I think he's vomited. We don't want him to aspirate."

The crew members grappled with the costume's mask, which was a long hood sewn to stretchy fabric that fit over his face, sort of like a ski mask. They couldn't seem to get it off, maybe because the unconscious man was lying on the bottom half of the hood.

A ring of anxious women surrounded us.

"Sidney?" said one.

"Harold?" said another.

"Edwin?" said yet another.

"Who is it?" The women's fear for "their" Ghosts of Christmas Future produced a miasma as thick as the strangely sweet stench that came from beneath the man's costume.

A familiar figure pushed his way through the circle. "It'll be okay," I said to the women. As Uncle Bob knelt down beside the man, the women's faces relaxed—his calm confidence often had that effect on people. He grasped the Ghost of Christmas Future's hood and gave it a mighty pull. The mask and attached hood came off. He tossed them aside, then held his ear close to the man's vomit-covered face.

"I'm sure whoever it is will be able to sleep it off," I said.

"I'm afraid not." My uncle placed two fingers on the man's neck, then shook his head. "He's dead."

"It's Theo Pushwright!" said an onlooker.

It was Theo, and he was definitely dead, his slightly sunburned face frozen in a grimace.

"Oh my God!" Jonas skidded to a stop near me, staring openmouthed at his stepfather.

"Help!" a man yelled from another part of the ballroom. "I've been robbed!"

An hour later, Timothy and I finally made it out of the ballroom. "But no rehearsal?" I said. "We just have this one last rehearsal before the magic show tomorrow. I've never even rehearsed in costume."

"You're kidding, right?" Timothy said. "After all this?"

"All this" had been a nightmare. The scene at the ballroom had nearly turned into a riot after people discovered their jewels and phones had been stolen. Then ball-goers began getting sick to their stomachs. Rather than blaming the storm that had blown in during the dance, they were all sure they were sick with something serious and were going to die like Theo. A man was dead, the onboard hospital was full, dozens of people had been robbed, and I was worried about rehearsal. Pretty petty, Ivy.

"You're right," I told Timothy. "I mean, my costume is a leotard and wig. No big deal."

"Speaking of costumes…" Timothy looked pointedly at mine, wrinkling his nose.

"Yeah. I'll go change into something less barfy."

"You know, a man just fell down dead on top of you. You're taking this awfully well."

"I am, aren't I? I guess it's because I've dealt with a few murders in the last year or two." Murders of *nice* people, I didn't add. "A natural death like this is somehow easier."

"Natural?"

I shrugged. "Guys Theo's age die of heart attacks all the time."

CHAPTER 33

Reluctant Admissions

So I made an assumption. It was not an uneducated one. I knew that the number one cause of death in America was heart disease. I knew that men over fifty-five were especially at risk. I knew that vomiting during a heart attack was common.

And yeah, though I still suspected Harley's death wasn't due to natural causes despite the coroner's report, I didn't think Theo's death could be connected to hers.

"Besides," I told my uncle later that night in the library, "Theo was an ass, but not a bad enough guy for someone to murder him." I sipped my glass of sherry. The stuff was growing on me.

"How was he an ass?"

I told Uncle Bob what Theo told Timothy about "moral weakness," how he treated us all at the captain's dinner, and how he believed that everyone's problems were their own fault because they didn't think positively enough. "He even said that about Cody." The mention of my brother stopped me. "Have you heard anything else?"

"I talked to Pink. Someone called the police station today, thought they saw him."

"God, I wish we could get off this boat."

"Me too." Uncle Bob reached across the little table between us and patted my hand. "But you know, there's really nothing more we could do."

"I know." I sat back in my chair. "I wish we could do more here too. We're halfway through the cruise and don't have anything concrete." That ten-thousand-dollar bonus hummed in the back of my mind like a rebuilt car engine. "Or maybe we do. You said you found out something about Jonas?"

Uncle Bob blew out a breath. "Nothing we can take to the bank, but I did get some stuff from that background check."

Turned out the *S.S. David Copperfield* had eleven crew members with some sort of criminal record. None of them were murderers, thank heavens. There was an embezzler, a drunk driver, a bunch of people with drug possession, and several thieves. Including Jonas.

"What did he steal?"

"Not sure. My guy just turned up a juvie record. Gives only the bare bones of the case."

"Aren't juvenile records sealed?"

"That's the thing. You have to apply to have them sealed. So either Jonas didn't apply or he didn't qualify. There are a bunch of reasons somebody might not qualify—like further criminal behavior."

"Wouldn't that show up on the background check?"

"Probably. I'm having my guy dig a little deeper on all the rotten apples we uncovered. Still, we know he was a thief at least once. Just keep your eye on him."

Jonas. I just didn't get a criminal vibe off him. A hot-cold vibe, sure, but nothing more suspicious than that. Was I being naive? I sat and looked at the fire for a moment, its gas flames pretty but not quite real. Kind of like a certain blonde. Talk about someone being naive. "So was Bette upset about Theo?"

"Sure. Everyone was."

"I thought maybe she'd be more upset since she knew him and all."

My uncle's eyebrows drew together. "Bette didn't know Theo."

I knew she did. I also knew I needed to tread carefully. "I thought since she asked that question at his signing..."

"She read his book. Thought it was a load of horse manure."

"But—"

"Olive, what is with you?"

"I..." I didn't think I should come right out and tell him about eavesdropping on her and Theo. Not yet, anyway. I needed more information first. "I...don't trust her."

"What? Why?"

"She's..." What could I say that wouldn't sound like I thought she was a lying opportunist? Mention her fake Western accent? No, then I'd have to go into the whole Theo thing. I remembered her big laugh. "She's too jolly."

"Too jolly? You're kidding, right? You don't like someone because they're happy?"

"No one's that happy. Especially after being recently widowed." Hey, maybe I was on to something. Score one for the old subconscious.

"You never like anyone's girlfriend."

"Not true."

He looked at me, eyebrows raised.

"I like Cody's girlfriend now." I admit it had taken me a while.

"And my girlfriends? Like Echo?"

"She was *so* woo-woo. I mean, vortexes?"

"And Debbie?

"Did you really want a surgically enhanced social climber?"

"And Mary?"

"Way too short for you."

"Olive."

"Yes." I poured myself another glass of sherry. "I see your point."

"And I see your problem," he said. "Olive, I am not your folks."

"Thank God for that."

"I'm being serious."

"So am I." After Cody's accident, my parents were basically non-parents. They did speak to me, usually to remind me who was to blame for what happened, or to tell me how Cody's life ("such as it is," they always said, which made me want to slug them) was so much worse since he moved into the group home, or sometimes to belittle my choice of career, just for a change of pace.

"Just because I have a girlfriend—"

Oh no. He called Bette his girlfriend.

"—does not mean I'll abandon you."

I stopped my internal whining and looked at my uncle. "That's what Matt said when I was getting used to the idea of Cody and Sarah. He said that Cody wasn't leaving me."

"He's a wise man. And I'm an old tired one, so I'm going to bed. Tomorrow we both need to see what we can find out about the thefts at the ball. We've got nothing to show our clients so far." Uncle Bob heaved himself out of his leather chair. "I'll see you tomorrow. Same bat time."

"Same bat channel," we said together.

CHAPTER 34

Talk of Books

When I went back to my room, I caught sight of the books on my shelf and my face grew hot. After all, my parents did do a few things right. Like teaching me not to steal—especially from libraries. And there they were, *Little Dorrit* and *A Tale of Two Cities*, sitting on my shelf like I owned them. I felt especially bad since Uncle Bob and I were using the library as our private meeting room. I decided to go back and check the books out right then. Maybe the librarian hadn't noticed them missing yet.

I walked through the nighttime-quiet corridors of the ship to the library. I opened the heavy wooden doors, stepped inside, and stopped. Something rustled behind one of the standalone bookcases. A mouse? No. Too big. Someone was in the library. At one o'clock in the morning. Maybe other people had figured out the library was a good place for assignations. It would have been smart to come back later, but my natural nosiness got the better of me. I tiptoed around the stack. Bill Sikes's back was to me. What was Val doing here and why was he still in costume?

I must have made a noise because Val turned. When he saw it was me, his face lit up. "Ivy baby." He seemed remarkably sober, considering how often he'd tipped his flask at the ball. "You followed me here? Maybe you want me now?"

"Just checking out some books that I kind of forgot to check out the first time."

"You are a bad girl. Maybe I punish you?"

"Maybe not."

"I like 'maybe.' Is good word." He followed my eyes to the bookshelf in front of him and pulled out a book. "I get book too. To make me sleep." He slid out a copy of *Our Mutual Friend* from the shelf.

"Dickens makes you sleep?"

He shrugged. "Not enough action."

"*Great Expectations* has an escaped prisoner, *Oliver Twist* has a murder, and *A Christmas Carol* has ghosts. What more do you want?"

"Not enough action with women."

"Okay. True enough."

We walked into the library's main room with our books. Val stopped in front of the still-blazing fireplace. "Did you like what you see tonight?" He grinned at me. "You know, my big—"

"Tattoo," I finished. "It was very nice." I had briefly glimpsed the tattoo on his chest. "Is it a plant or something?"

"You want to see?" Before I could say no, Val unbuttoned his shirt. A tree spread across the top left side of his chest. "It grows over my heart," he said. Though the tattoo had the green-blue color of amateur ink, it was beautifully wrought, from the roots that curled down to his stomach to the branches that arced over his left side. There were only two leaves on the tree, both inscribed with Russian characters

"Why aren't there more leaves?" I asked.

"Is family tree. I add you when we marry, to make three leaves."

"But..."

Val pointed to one leaf. "Nikolay is my cousin." He fingered the gold chain he wore around his neck. "This is gift. From him."

I looked at the tree with its many spreading branches. Empty branches. "Where's the rest of your family?"

"I do not know them. I am orphan."

"So this is?" I pointed to the other name.

"Tuzik. My only other family. He is dead." Val looked sad for the first time ever. "My dog."

CHAPTER 35

Trembling in the Balance

I don't know exactly what I dreamt about—I think it involved my mother and maybe a dog—but I woke up early with family on my mind. I wasn't one of those people who put a lot of stock in where I came from. I had never been really interested in my ancestry, didn't know most of my extended family, and did not look forward to the annual Christmas get-together with my parents. In fact, before yesterday, if someone had asked me if family was the most important thing in my life, I probably would have said no. After all, I was single, no kids, and my parents and I barely spoke. But I had somehow missed the fact that the two most important people to me in the world were my uncle and my brother. And now, I suddenly was slapped upside the head with the fact that I might lose them. Oh, I knew I was being dramatic. Cody would probably be home by nightfall and Uncle Bob wasn't going anywhere, even if it felt like it. That's it. I *felt* it, that potential for loss. My conversation with Val last night really drove it home. How would it feel to be completely alone in the world?

My cell rang.

"Omigod, doesn't anyone call you during normal hours?" Ada said from the bottom bunk in a groggy, pissed-off voice.

I grabbed my ringing cell from near my pillow, looked at the number, and clambered out of the top bunk. "Matt?" I whispered as I padded to the bathroom.

"I can still hear you," Ada said. I shut the bathroom door.

"God, I'm glad I caught you, I've been trying for hours."

I sat down hard on the toilet lid. "Tell me."

"They found Cody."

"And?" I held my breath.

"Oh, shit, I'm so sorry. I haven't been sleeping. I'm not thinking straight."

"Matt."

"Sorry. Cody's okay. So is Stu. I left a bunch of messages, but I hadn't heard from you." I suspected all those messages were queued up on my phone now that we were in range again. I really needed to get a better cell plan when I got back to Phoenix. "I wanted to make sure you knew, and to thank you."

"To thank me?"

"Cody said you helped him find Stu."

"I did? Where was he?"

"Costco."

I smothered a laugh. "Of course." Stu loved Costco. The guys from the group home took regular trips there for cheap lunches made up of food samples and hotdogs.

"Cody said you told him to think about where Stu would feel safe at night. He figured it out right away. Your parents convinced the manager to let Cody in after hours."

My parents?

"And he found Stu hidden between stacks of cookies and the wall. He'd made a little nest there for himself with a bunch of pillows and lots of chocolate." Stu's sweet tooth was famous. "Costco isn't pressing charges, given the situation, but Stu's going to have to pay them back for everything he ate."

I laughed out loud, mostly out of relief, but also at the image of Stu happily eating his way through Costco's candy section.

"*Ivy*," Ada said from the other room.

"And Stu's okay?" I whispered.

"Looks like it. He didn't have any seizures while he was gone. They checked him out at the ER to be safe. Everything looks fine."

"And Cody?"

"You should see him, Ivy. He found his friend in time to keep him safe. He's so proud. And so are your parents."

"They're not pissed?"

Matt laughed. "Yeah, well, a little. But they also got to see what Cody's capable of. It's like they're looking at him with new eyes. I wish you were here to see it." He paused. "Actually, I just wish you were here."

"Me too." I let out the breath I'd been holding for days. "Thank you, Matt. Thank you, thank you, thank you." I pressed the phone against my cheek, as if I could embrace Matt through the phone line.

"It's all right." Matt's voice sounded husky. "Everything's all right. But still, come home soon, okay? Come home soon."

CHAPTER 36

More Than a Trifle in Liquor

After I texted Uncle Bob, I showered away the soreness in my muscles, got dressed in my Nancy costume (I was on ambient character duty at nine), and ran up to the London Lido deck. I wanted to share my news with someone other than Ada, who had chewed me out for talking so loudly at the ungodly hour of eight a.m. I wandered among the crowd on the outdoor deck, enjoying the fine sunny morning and the salty-smelling breeze.

Hey, was that David?

I blinked and the Dodger's battered top hat was gone, swallowed by the sea of passengers. But bobbing among their faces was a familiar square-jawed profile. "Jonas," I said. "They found Cody. He's all right."

"Great, Ivy." Jonas sounded like he needed coffee and looked like he'd been made up for some plague movie, his face yellowish, purple shadows under his eyes. "Good for you."

Good for me? Was that sincerity or snark?

"Have you seen Valery?" he asked.

"What? No."

Jonas's eyes scanned the crowd on deck. "Maybe he's around the corner." He turned away.

Okay, this was more off-again than usual. Way more. What was up with—

"Omigod, I am such an idiot," I said to Jonas's back. "Here I am talking about finding my family when you've just lost yours. I'm so sorry about your stepdad."

He faced me with a half-smile that I couldn't read. "It was pretty quick, so he didn't suffer. And we weren't exactly close." He leaned into me, presenting me with the sour smell of booze on un-brushed teeth. "Because I didn't want to be. Theo was a horrible, horrible man."

"I thought you two made up."

"Oh, there's Valery." Jonas lit out for Val, who puffed on an e-cigarette while talking to a couple of young women. I followed, just to keep an eye on Jonas. I wondered if he'd slept. I wondered how much he'd had to drink last night. I wondered if he was still nipping at the bottle this morning.

"Valery!" Jonas said, too loudly. He slung an arm around Val's skinny shoulders. "We have things to discuss."

Val puffed out another stream of vapor before putting the e-cig in his pocket. The smell it left behind was sweet, like a Jolly Rancher, but it also made me feel slightly sick. Couldn't say why.

"Ivy, sweet pea." Jonas turned to me. "I'm not mad at you. How could I be, with all you've done for me?"

"All I've done?"

"But if you would excuse us." Jonas steered Val away from me. "We're going to get a drink."

"Maybe he wants a Bloody Mary," I said to Timothy when I found him at the breakfast buffet. "That's good for a hangover, right? Hair of the dog and all that?"

Timothy made a little "pfft" noise like a cynical Frenchman.

I trotted next to him as he filled his tray with breakfast meats (but no blood pudding). "I'm sure that remark about Theo being horrible was just the booze talking."

"Pfft." Timothy reached for a very un-Dickensian onion bagel. I took the opportunity to steal a piece of bacon from his plate.

"I mean, he wouldn't have gotten so drunk if he didn't care."

"Pff—"

"If you keep doing that your face is going to freeze that way."

Timothy stretched his lips just to show his face wasn't going to freeze any time soon. "You're not lusting after Jonas, are you? Because if you are, you're going to be very disappointed."

"I am only interested in Jonas as a friend." And as an investigative lead/maybe suspect. "But he's not gay. He hasn't had a boyfriend since you've been onboard, right?"

"Closeted doesn't mean straight."

"Pfft," I said to him.

"Well, whatever bus he rides, the competition will be stiff now."

"What? Why?" I said, eating my stolen piece of bacon.

"Didn't you hear? I mean, it was you who said Jonas and Theo made up."

"Yeah, so?"

"Theo changed his will. Jonas is now worth millions."

CHAPTER 37
A Real and Thorough Bad One

I went outside on deck. I needed time by myself to think, but there was really no place to be alone on the ship. The deck was the next best thing.

The wind had picked up and the air was salty enough I could taste it. Just a few people ambled up and down, chatting or looking for dolphins. I turned my back to the ship and all the people and distractions and faced the sea. The water was gray and foamy white, but no icy hand clenched my gut and the ship deck felt stable underneath me. Cody was fine and water was not my enemy.

I tried to organize my thoughts. It may have been just my relief over Cody's safety, but everything seemed to revolve around family: Jonas's stepdad, Harley's mom, Val's...no one. And those connections tangled with my investigation questions. Was Jonas still a thief? Was Harley murdered? Was Val a pickpocket? I'd been on the ship nearly five days and I had more questions than when I'd begun. That ten-thousand-dollar bonus seemed further away than ever.

Focus, Ivy. Jonas first. It seems he was a thief, at least a juvenile one. Could he still be a criminal? I thought back over all of our interactions, every time I'd seen Jonas. Nothing seemed suspicious.

And Harley. How did she die? Death by natural causes was awfully weird for a twenty-nine-year-old. If that were the case, why would someone shove her in a closet? Was she connected to the thefts somehow?

Then there was Val. That was who I really needed to think about. It did seem as though he'd picked that guy's pocket at breakfast the other day. But Val was naked in my bed when the thefts occurred during the ball. That didn't mean he couldn't have stolen things throughout the evening. People didn't often notice things missing until later. And Val confused me. In the middle of all that goofiness there was a core sweetness, like a nutty candy bar with caramel at its center. But I'd also seen his Bill Sikes. Acting or Val's dark side?

As I pondered the Val question I saw Oliver out of the corner of my eye. He was without his clutch of sea urchins for a change. And he was picking a man's pocket.

"Oliver!" I shouted, advancing on him. "Give that back."

He started, as did the elderly man whose wallet he had just lifted. A gray-haired woman next to them shook her head. "George," she said to her husband. "For heaven's sake. I *told* you to leave your wallet in the room safe."

"Begging your pardon, sir," said Oliver, handing the man back his wallet. "But I was hungry." He scampered off.

I caught him by the collar of his jacket. "Hungry, are you? And with all these free buffets."

"Works every time," he said in a whisper. "Don't say anything and I'll cut you in on the next deal."

Could the answer to the theft ring really be this simple? "How about I turn you into ship security instead?" Oliver squirmed, but I had a good hold on him. "Or maybe you could tell me everything you know about the thefts onboard."

"Mom!" he yelled. "Nancy's hurting me."

A plump woman in a nautical-themed top steamed toward us. "Again?"

"Again?" I said.

"The last Nancy manhandled my boy too. That's why she was dismissed."

Dismissed my ass. I bet she practically ran off the ship.

"What is it with you actresses?" The stripes on Oliver's mom's t-shirt quivered with indignation.

"What is it with your son? I just saw him steal that man's wallet."

"Oh, that." She smiled as if Oliver had done something cute. "He's just playing at being Oliver Twist. He always gives them back. Don't you, Ollie?"

Oliver's face screwed up upon hearing his nickname. I filed away that useful fact away for later.

"And you, miss," said his mother. "If you don't stay away from my son, there will be yet another Nancy onboard. You can take that to the bank." Her face blanched as the ship rolled, but she swallowed hard and managed to stalk away, head held high. Oliver trailed behind, sticking out this tongue at me when she wasn't looking.

The sweet scent of e-cig vapor floated on the air. "That boy," said Madalina's heavily accented voice behind me. "He should be fed to the wolves. And that woman should not wear stripes."

Both were true. Regarding Oliver, well, that was self-explanatory. And Oliver's mom may have been going for the French sailor thing, but she looked more like a buoy. Madalina, on the other hand, was like a pearl in a short off-white linen shift with just a touch of sheen. A dress like that had to take a big chunk out of a ghostwriter's salary. If Madalina was a writer. I mean, why would Theo hire someone with such a limited grasp of—yikes, Ivy, remember your manners. "I'm sorry about Theo," I said.

Madalina lifted one shoulder in a languid shrug. "I was employee, not friend."

"Are you still an employee? I mean, are you going to finish his memoirs?"

"Probably not." She turned to face the sea.

"So you're out of a job?"

"I was paid in advance, and I am never out of a job for long." Her voice sounded jaded and weary.

"Did Theo put you in his new will?" Arghh. A little obvious, Ivy. I really needed to be craftier about this stuff.

"Of course not. Like I said, I am employee. Ah, you want to know about the new will." Yep, really needed to work on subtlety. "I was there as witness." Madalina didn't seem to mind my question. Maybe she appreciated directness. "Jonas is now very, very rich. You helped."

"I did?

"Theo liked you."

"I don't know why everyone cared so much."

"That is one reason I like you. Too many suck up Theo." She tilted her head. "Or is it 'suck up to?'"

"The second." Good thing Madalina liked me. Maybe she wouldn't mind another fairly direct question. "Who was the other witness?" You could legally write a will without a lawyer, but there did need to be two witnesses.

"The captain. His wife was there also." Madalina's voice was low and throaty, her accent similar to Val's. Which was Eastern European.

"You have a beautiful accent," I said. "Are you Russian?"

"Rumanian." She blew out a final stream of vapor and put her e-cigarette into a small crossbody bag. "Though I think my father was Russian."

"You think?"

"I did not know him. Or my mother. I am orphan."

"Really?"

"Really." She turned to me, her eyes hard. "You think I joke?"

"No, sorry, sorry. It's just that Val—he plays Bill Sikes—he's from Russia. He's an orphan too."

"There are more of us than you think. Especially from our part of the world."

My mind pulled up grainy photos of children in long rows of rickety cribs.

Big heads on malnourished bodies, babies tied to beds, enormous pleading eyes. "Sorry again. Really," I said. "And I am sorry about Theo. Even though you weren't friends, I know you must be upset."

"I do not get upset."

Except for outbursts at the bar. Hey. Since Madalina obviously knew Bette, maybe she could help me figure out the connection to Theo. "Do you know anything about Theo ruining someone's life?"

"Hah." Madalina gave an elegant snort. "Theo ruined many people's lives."

CHAPTER 38

A Strange Interview

I hoped Jonas was still drunk. Probably not the nicest thing to wish on a friend at ten o'clock in the morning, but something was up. I wasn't sure what, but I did know I was interested in Val and Harley and Madalina, and Jonas was the only person I could think of who knew all three. I was especially intrigued by Theo's ghostwriter. The night of the captain's table dinner, Madalina said Theo wasn't a bad man. Now she thought he'd ruined lots of people's lives. I might be able to find out more if Jonas had a few drinks under his belt, and hey, he started down that road himself.

By the time I found Jonas five minutes later hanging out near the outdoor pool, I had completely rationalized my intent to ply him with alcohol. "Can I buy you a beer?" I said, steering Jonas toward the George and Vulture Pub.

"No."

Dang.

"I'll buy *you* a beer. I'll have a cocktail." He was already tipsy enough that he said "coch-tail," like some German sailor on shore leave.

I guided him to a back corner booth where no one would hear what we said. "I'll have a Mai Tai," said Jonas. "And she'll have..."

"A Diet Coke."

"No, you won't. I'm not drinking alone."

"But I'm on the job." I nodded at the Nancy outfit I wore.

I was supposed to be encouraging guests to get their photos snapped in our ship's brig, which looked like a nineteenth-century jail. This morning, cruisers could get their picture taken in the Marshalsea Prison with some of Dickens's criminals, like Fagin and Bill Sikes and Magwitch from *Great Expectations*.

"I'm your boss and I say you can have a drink."

"A Guinness," I said to the waiter. It was the healthiest alcoholic drink I could think of. They used to drink it in Irish hospitals, you know.

"So..." I said, not knowing exactly where to start.

"Did you hear I'm rich?" said Jonas. "Filthy rich?"

Okay, we could start there. "Because of Theo's death?"

"Because of you! I could kiss you. I think I will." Jonas leaned over and planted a sloppy kiss in the vicinity of my mouth.

"Because of me?"

"Because Theo and I made up."

"What does that have to do with me?"

"The son of a bitch liked you. Oops," he said, putting a finger to his lips. "Shouldn't speak ill of the dead."

"I'm still confused about how I helped—"

"Ivy, sweet pea, I'm rich." Jonas closed his eyes and smiled like a happy cat. A happy drunk cat.

Time to get him back on track. "So Theo put you in his will."

"Correct. You win another beer. Waiter!"

"I haven't got my first one yet."

"Pah. Another beer for the lady," he said to the waiter he'd flagged down.

"Why did you and Theo need to make up?"

"He disowned me. I used to be bad." He hung his head in mock sorrow. "I was a juvenile delinquent."

"Jonas," I whispered. "I don't think you should be saying—"

"Doesn't matter. I don't need this job anymore. I'm a millionaire. Or maybe a billionaire. Not sure."

"Were you really a juvenile delinquent? What did you do?"

"Stole a motorcycle."

"You stole a motorcycle?"

"Just for a joy ride." He showed his white teeth to the waiter who dropped off a Mai Tai and two pints of Guinness. "Prob'ly good the cops caught me instead of the owner of the bike. Was a Harley," he slurred.

Okay, Jonas was not gay. Gay men did not ride Harleys. And Jonas had just given me an opening for my next line of questioning.

"Do you think Harley was named after the bike?" I didn't say it was a smooth opening.

He wrinkled his forehead in thought. "Harley?"

"You know, my roommate? The one who died?"

"Nope."

"She wasn't named after a motorcycle?"

"It's not coming back to me. Harley..."

"She played Madame Defarge."

"The knitter!"

"Right." You might be able to get more information out of drunks, but boy, it took patience I wasn't sure I had. "Do you know much about her?"

"Knitted. Kept to herself. Not many friends, except for David and Val."

Another opening. Maybe patience was a virtue. "I knew she and David were friends, but Val?"

"Like this." Jonas tried unsuccessfully to twine two fingers around each other. He gave up and wrapped his cherry stem around the little umbrella that accompanied his Mai Tai. "Inseparable."

Huh. How had Val described it? Buddy-buddy? "Val didn't seem too broken up when she died."

"He was probably on to some other girl by then. He doesn't stay long with any of 'em." Jonas swirled his drink, then looked up at me. "You're not interested in him, are you? 'Cause he's no good that way. Besides being unemployable, he's got the whole orphan thing going on. Fear of abandonment and all that. Dump them before they dump you."

"Let's go back to the orphan thing." I was not about to pass up the golden egg that had been laid in my lap. "Did you know Madalina was an orphan too?"

"Nope. I did know—do know—that she's a prostitute."

"Really? I didn't believe the memoir story, but..."

"Thought he was her sugar daddy, didn' cha?"

I hadn't actually given it much thought but nodded to keep the conversation going.

"Being a sugar daddy requires commitment. Madalina is bought and paid for so he can return her when he's done. When he *was* done," Jonas corrected himself. "He only kept each girl for a month or two."

"And ruined their lives?"

"What? No, I don't think so. It's not like they haven't been in the business for a while."

"Wow. If that ever got out, Mr. Anti-Moral-Weakness hiring hookers..."

"It won't. Lots of rich guys use this particular outfit. The girls are paid *very* well to keep quiet." Jonas over-enunciated the words with drunken carefulness. "Waiter! Could I have another Mai Tai?"

I persevered. "There's a woman onboard named Bette. Do you think she could have had something going with your stepfather once upon a time?"

"Not unless she's a pro. I am the closest thing Theo ever had to a real relationship. Which is why I am rich." Jonas began to sing: "Oh, yes, I am a rich man..."

Could Bette be a pro?

"...bubba deedle diedle, yowsa frowsa..."

Could Harley have been working for the "particular outfit" Theo patronized?

"...beetle biedel dum." Jonas stopped mangling the lyrics to "If I Were a Rich Man" and said, "Hey, do you think the *Fiddler* writers did that because they couldn't think of rhyming words?" he said. "The deedle deedle bit?"

"Yes."

I was pretty sure the answer was no, but I never disagreed with a drunk. "One more thing," I said. Might as well ask everything while Jonas was so willing to answer, and before he started singing again. "What happened to the last Nancy? I heard there was an Oliver incident."

"An Oliver incident!" Jonas laughed so hard his Mai Tai lost its umbrella. "You could say that. The little bugger led her into the swimming pool during a game of Blind Man's Bluff. The deep end. While she was in costume." He frowned. "It actually could have been serious. That wet costume probably weighed a ton."

"Yeah, it could have been bad." I'd had a close encounter with a nun costume and a swimming pool not so long ago. "So she quit?"

"Yeah, but not after tying the little imp to the Charles Dickens statue in the lobby." He grinned. "In just his tighty-whities."

The waiter glided over with a fresh Mai Tai just as Big Ben bonged the half hour. Must be ten thirty. I took a last sip of my barely touched Guinness and then a sip of the other untouched one so it wasn't completely wasted. I pushed my chair from the table. "I've got to go encourage people to go to jail...Oops." Dang, would I ever learn to think before I spoke?

"No worries. This former criminal is not offended." Jonas lifted his glass. "But before you go, let's toast my good fortune and our bright future." We clinked glasses and I left Jonas admiring the lovely sunset colors of his new drink.

I was halfway to the brig when a thought stopped me in mid-stride. *Our* bright future?

CHAPTER 39

Under Trying Circumstances

After convincing a number of people to get their photos taken behind bars, I had a few hours free. Time to get back to detective work. I checked my phone. No bars.

I was in a pickle. My investigative tools (the internet, the phone, Uncle Bob) were severely limited. I couldn't ask for records or interview people or snoop like a normal PI. But though I couldn't act like an investigator, I could behave like a silly girl.

No matter what anyone thought, I was not a silly girl. I was always a rough-and-tumble type of kid. Creative, sure, but more interested in playing pirate than house. As a grown-up, I scoffed at the type of women who pretended they couldn't do anything for themselves in case they'd break a nail or soil their white pants (though I did understand the white pants bit, which is why I did not wear them). So no, I was not a silly girly girl. But I was an actress.

"I'm afraid for my safety," I said breathlessly to the buzz-cut guy who opened the door to the security office. "After what happened at the ball last night."

"There's no need, miss," he said, sticking out his chest. "We've got it all under control."

"I just really need to talk to someone." My lip quivered and I looked up at him with moist eyes.

"Aww." Had him. "Why don't you come in for a minute? You can tell me all about whatever's bothering you."

I stepped into the small security office which, like most of the crew section of the *S.S. David Copperfield*, looked less like a floating hotel and more like a ship. The guy, who was built like a brick bungalow (he was on the short side), took a stack of papers off a chair and motioned me to sit.

"So, miss, tell me what's bothering you."

I had to be careful.

Not only did I need to maintain my cover, I needed to remember that these guys might be in on whatever was happening onboard.

Talk about having your hands tied. But I did have another body part I could use.

I still wore my low-cut Nancy costume, so I leaned forward. Might as well give him both barrels, so to speak. "This morning when I ate breakfast at the crew mess, everyone said thousands of dollars were stolen at the ball last night—if you count all the money and jewels and stuff missing from the safes, I mean." The entire story was made up, but it sounded plausible to me.

"Did you have anything stolen?" he asked.

I was about to give him a story about my grandmother's pearl necklace when he said, "Weren't you working?"

Oops, almost hoisted by my own petard. Of course he would know I was working, which meant I'd be in my Nancy costume, which meant no expensive jewelry. "I was, but..." I stalled for time so my brain could come up with some plausible reason for being afraid. I smoothed my skirt and felt my phone hidden in my pocket. That would work. "I can't find my phone." I remembered what Uncle Bob said about identity theft. "And it has a lot of personal information on it." I leaned a little farther forward.

"Now that is serious." Evidently my boobs were also serious, since that's where the guy's attention stayed. "When did you last have it?"

The security office door opened.

I recognized the smirking face—the security guard who'd come to my room after Harley's death.

"If it ain't Miss Rubber Gloves," he said.

The guy across from me raised his eyebrows in a lewd question mark. I wanted to melt into my seat, but instead had to act like everything was better than blueberries. Good thing I was an actress. I smiled at the newcomer. "So nice to see you again."

The buzz-cut bungalow said to the other guy, "Miss...uh..."

"Meadows," I said.

"Miss Meadows just told me she was worried that her phone may have been stolen."

"I think someone might have taken it during the ball, when they took all that other stuff," I said. Sheesh, I hadn't gotten an ounce of information out of these guys.

"When did you see it last?" said Smirky.

"Hey, I'm questioning her," said the first guy. "When did you see it last?"

"I don't know. I didn't know it was lost until I went to look for it."

"Do you remember where you saw it last?"

"Not sure. In my room?"

"Did you ask your roommate?"

"Yeah. She didn't know anything." I really really hoped they wouldn't question Ada. Wow, this conversation had gotten away from me. I took back the reins. "And this ball thing really freaked me out."

"You and about a thousand other passengers." Smirky smirked.

"Do you think the thieves planned the heist—"

"Heist?" His smile dimmed.

Oh, not ditzy enough. "Isn't that what they call it in all those movies with handsome jewel thieves?" I asked Brick Bungalow. He was my best shot, given that he seemed a little slow on the uptake. Plus he was enamored of my chest. "Anyway, do you think they planned it or just took advantage of Mr. Pushwright's death?"

"I'll tell you something on one condition." Brick winked at the other guy, who said, "Look at that, time for a smoke break." He left.

"Okay..." I began to get nervous. I was in a small office far away from everyone and flirting with a guy who might be in league with criminals. "The condition?"

"Have a drink with me later."

Phew. "Oh, dang. I would but I've got a show tonight."

"Before dinner then."

"Okay." I got up to leave.

"Wait, don't you want to hear what I was going to tell you?"

He was going to tell me now? Before I fulfilled my one condition?

If this guy was in league with a gang of criminals, he sure wasn't the mastermind. I sat back down.

"This'll all come out tomorrow, so you have to keep it close to your chest 'til then." I thought it was "close to the vest," but didn't want to correct him. "Not only did someone take advantage of Mr. Pushwright's death..." Brick paused for best effect. "Someone caused it."

"Someone gave him a heart attack?" I could see Oliver doing that.

"A heart attack? Where'd you hear that?"

"I was there when it happened. That's just what I thought." Hey, a bit of truth amongst all my fibs.

"Did you see the body?"

I was about to tell him that I saw, felt, and smelt it, but didn't really want to go there, mostly for my benefit. Instead I nodded.

"Notice anything unusual about the guy's face?"

"Not really." I willed my mind back to the scene. Theo's face had been frozen in a grimace, and..."I guess he was a little sunburnt."

"Wasn't the sun that did that." The guy sat back in his chair to deliver the punch line. "That was poison."

"Theo left Agatha-style," I texted my uncle as soon as I had a bar on my cell phone. "Agatha-style" was our code for "poisoned," since

Christie, who once worked as an apothecary's assistant, often used poison in her novels.

"You sure?" he texted back.

"Pretty sure."

"Do you think we should be worried about the butler?"

"Butler" stood for "killer," as in "the butler did it." Should we be worried? If the poison was caustic, that meant it was applied topically, so Theo was most likely the target. Probably not a serial killer.

"I think we're OK," I texted him. "Are you with Bette?"

"Yes."

"Be careful." Theo's murderer might not be a serial killer, but it didn't mean he or she wasn't dangerous.

"Give it up, Olive."

CHAPTER 40

A Man-Trap!

But I couldn't give it up. Bette was up to no good. I just knew. Yeah, okay, I also knew I might have a teensy problem with my uncle having a girlfriend, but more importantly, I was sure Bette wasn't being straight with him. I wanted to protect the old fart, but I had to know what I was protecting him from before I could do anything.

I was on ambient character duty, so I used the time to pace up and down the deck in costume while I figured out what to do. Made it look like Nancy was a thinker.

Here's what bugged me: No matter what she told Uncle Bob, Bette *was* connected to Theo. Their whispered conversation had made that clear. In fact, Theo had "ruined her life." There was also that conversation with Madalina in the bar, the one that ended up with a drink in Bette's lap.

"What are you smiling at?" asked Timothy/Fagin as he caught up with me.

"Just a fond memory." What had Madalina said as she upended the drink? Something about children? Maybe Bette had children with Theo?

"Earth to Ivy."

"Hang on. I'm thinking, and I can't think and talk at once."

"No comment."

I ignored Timothy. What was the other thing that bothered me? Right. Bette had dropped her accent when talking to Theo. I didn't know who she was, but I was pretty sure she wasn't the recent widow of an oilman from Colorado.

"Ivy?"

"Not done thinking." The biggest question of all: why was she after Uncle Bob? It could be his supposed money, but—"Omigod."

"What? Did you hurt yourself thinking?"

Bette had to know Uncle Bob was a PI. She was working so hard to distract him because she was involved in something she didn't want him to find out about. Like theft. Or murder.

"I've got to go." I headed to the stairs.

"Wait." Timothy hurried after me, his long green coat flapping. "I'm your sidekick. Remember?"

I didn't know when Timothy decided he was my sidekick, but I needed one right then. "Okay," I said as we hurried down the stairs. "I'm going to break into someone's room and you're going to help me."

Timothy's shaggy Fagin eyebrows shot skyward.

"Right, sidekick?"

He hesitated, then nodded. "Whose room?"

"Bette, my uncle's new girlfriend." She could have been on to him from the start. From the plane ride, even.

"How do you know which room is hers?" he asked as we emerged from the stairwell onto the Queen Street Deck.

"I followed her once before." After Bette's conversation with Theo, I had tailed her to her cabin. "Just watching out for Uncle Bob, you know."

"Ivy, do you think—"

"You know who the best sidekick was?" I asked. "Tonto."

"Because he always had the Lone Ranger's back?"

"Because he hardly ever said anything."

"Whoa, Miss Bossypan—"

I turned on Timothy. "You want to be a sidekick, Tonto?"

"Yeah, I—" He shut his mouth and nodded.

"Great. Help me figure out how to get into Bette's room." I stopped in front of a cabin. "It's this one." I looked at the door, which unlocked with a keycard. Dang. I really wished I could talk to Uncle Bob. I bet he knew how to unlock a door like this.

Suddenly Timothy came to life. "Greetings, ladies and gents," he said to a family coming out of their cabin a few doors down from Bette's. "May I hold the door for you?" He looked sideways at me, and I sprinted a few steps to stand behind him. "Are you planning to attend my magic show tonight?" he said to the somewhat flummoxed family. "Let me give you a preview." I stood innocently by the door to the family's cabin, keeping it just a tad ajar with my foot. Timothy untied the long red scarf he wore around his neck. "I don't mean to keep you," he said to the little group. "We can walk and talk and do magic." He led them a few feet down the hall and then retied his red scarf, pulling it tight around his neck. "Watch carefully." He pulled on the two ends of his scarf. Instead of strangling him, the scarf slipped off his neck in one piece. "Ta-da!"

"Lame," said one of the kids.

"Balconies," Timothy mouthed to me over his shoulder as he ushered the family down the hall. "Lame, you say? Maybe you'd be more impressed by this." He presented the kid's phone to him with a flourish.

"How'd you do that?" the now-impressed kid asked as they rounded the corner toward the elevators.

"I learned to pick a pocket or two," said Timothy.

I waited until the elevator bell dinged, then slipped into the family's cabin. I crossed the room and let myself out the sliding glass door onto the balcony. Whoa, shit, we were a long way up. A fog was beginning to roll in, but it didn't completely hide the ocean beneath us. I had no idea how high I was, but the water looked like a solid blue floor from this high up. And it was *water*.

My heart rate sped up, but I took a few deep breaths. "For Uncle Bob," I chanted to myself. "For Uncle Bob."

I peeked around the edge of the balcony. The other room's balcony wasn't far.

All I had to do was climb up on the rail, hold on to the partition, and reach my right leg to the rail of the next balcony. I could do this: I was a dancer—I was an *aerial* dancer. This was just another dance move.

I wasn't convinced.

Holding on to the partition, I climbed up onto the rail, making sure to not look down. I snaked my leg over and felt the other railing. Good. Or not. I was straddled between the two balconies. The wind tugged at my skirt. Damn costume. Should have tucked it up in my waistband. Too late now. Now I needed to shift my weight past the partition over to the new rail. Good thing I'd been doing those core exercises.

I slipped my left foot over to join my right on the new rail. Then, still holding onto the partition, I swung out and pushed myself onto the new balcony. Now I just had to let go of the partition and jump onto my new perch. Ignoring the thought of falling hundreds of feet into an icy ocean miles from nowhere, I focused on the sliding glass doors on the next balcony and jumped.

Bravo. I patted myself on the back once I'd made contact with the balcony. Only four more to go. The fog was beginning to close in. Couldn't waste any time. I tucked my skirt and petticoats into my waistband and readied myself. Stretch...and...leap!

Piece of cake.

The next stretch and leap went fine too. I reached my left foot around the next partition—and someone grabbed it.

"Hey!" A man's voice. "What the hell do you think you're doing?"

"I'm...Nancy," I said. "I'm an aerial dancer in *Fagin's Magic Handkerchief.* I'm doing a preview." I silently thanked Timothy for the inspiration.

"What?" The man's grizzled head peered around the corner at me. The fog was now so thick I couldn't see his shoulders.

"Hey, folks." I waved at an imaginary audience below. "Tonight only, *Fagin's Magic Handkerchief*!"

The man released his grip on my ankle and I swung myself onto his balcony. "Luverly to meet you, sir. Please forgive me intruding like this." I climbed up onto his rail, prepping to climb onto the balcony next door. "Aerial dancers," I said to my invisible audience. I swung my leg onto the next balcony. "Thrills and chills, but no spills!" I leapt quickly before the fog cleared and the guy realized there was no audience below me, unless he counted fish.

CHAPTER 41

Worse Luck!

Bette's balcony. Finally.

I tried the sliding glass door to Bette's cabin. Unlocked. I hoped she'd been as lax about the rest of the place.

Her cabin was one of the nicer ones: a queen bed, small sitting area, and of course, the balcony. It was also very tidy, everything put away except for a few shopping bags from Bette's Ensenada excursion. I began the search with her closet. The clothes that hung there were expensive, but that just meant she had money, not that her money came from where she said it did. The first few drawers of her dresser yielded nothing. I searched the bottom drawer. Just a bunch of lacy underthings and nightclothes. I scrounged around to make sure nothing was hidden underneath, and pulled out a berry-colored silk robe.

Sheesh, she even had it monogrammed. I folded it up and put it back in the drawer.

Wait. I grabbed the robe again and shook it open. There on the left side in white embroidery was the monogram: B.W.

Not B.F. for Bette Foxberry, the name she'd given us.

I had that weird feeling you get when you're right about something you wish you weren't right about, like when you got the first rumblings in your belly after eating the shrimp that smelled fishy but you ate them anyway. Bette wasn't who she said she was. And she was after my uncle.

I put the robe back in its place, making sure to put the impostor's underthings back exactly how I'd found them.

Who was Bette really? Maybe B.W. had some prescriptions. I stepped into the bathroom, which was bigger than mine, but still tiny with a toilet, a small curtained shower, and a sink with a medicine cabinet above it. I opened the mirrored cabinet. Lots of potions, makeup, and hair products. Some Dramamine and Aleve. No prescriptions with names printed on them.

I shut the medicine cabinet. Boy, it made a lot of noise, almost like—Shit. It was the cabin door.

Bette was back.

Footsteps padded across the carpeted floor. Wait, were there more than one pair?

"It ain't the Ritz, but it'll do." Bette laughed her insincere laugh. Who was she talking to? "The toilet is right through there."

I jumped into the shower stall and pulled the curtain closed just as the bathroom door opened. Someone walked in. I held my breath. The room was so small that I was just a few feet away from the person who'd entered.

That person began to whistle. Oh no. It was my uncle, and I was hiding in the bathroom of his paramour after breaking and entering.

Then something worse happened.

"Thanks for letting me use your toilet," he called.

I heard him lift the lid and sit down heavily. On the toilet. About a foot away from me.

"Don't know if I would have made it to my room," he said. "That Bubble and Squeak is really living up to its name."

"Cabbage'll do that to you," said Bette.

Some might call my new personal hell "being trapped while hiding just a foot away from your uncle who's on the toilet in the throes of intestinal distress." Others might just say, "Crap." Either one would be unfortunately accurate.

After what felt like ten minutes, Uncle Bob finally flushed. I heard him stand up, zip his pants, and buckle his belt. He stood so near me that the shower curtain moved as he stepped toward the sink. I held my breath so he wouldn't hear me breathe, and because I really really needed to.

Finally, Uncle Bob left the bathroom. "How would you feel about a walk in the fresh air?"

Yes! I nearly shouted.

"Sure," said Bette. "Unless you'd care to help me with a little problem."

"What's that?" asked Uncle Bob.

"I think this mattress is a little soft. What do you think?"

No no no no no no no no no no.

"Aw, hon," said my uncle. "I'm still a little bubbly and squeaky. Best to wait 'til later. How about that walk?"

"You bet," said the fake Bette. "But I'm taking a rain check."

When I was sure they'd gone, I let my breath go in a rush. Thank the Lord. That was much too close. In more ways than one.

And my uncle was dangerously close to being taken in by this woman. What if he fell in love with her? What if she murdered him in his bed?

I needed to find out who Bette really was. I double-checked the medicine cabinet. Still nothing there. I went back into the sitting room and re-searched. Nothing. Tried the bedroom again. The drawers and closet held only clothes. I pulled back the covers on the bed, dislodging a towel in the shape of a palm tree. Just sheets and a blanket. I made the bed again, complete with towel tree. I really hoped it wasn't from Uncle Bob. I tried to look under the bed, but a wooden platform ran from the floor to the mattress. A too-soft mattress—what a lame line.

I straightened up, inadvertently kicking one of the three shopping bags lined up along the wall. Hmm. I went through them, one by one. I unfolded each piece of clothing and unwrapped each souvenir, including every piece of an onyx chess set from Mexico. I rewrapped the final piece—the black queen—in tissue paper, and turned over the chess board. Yes! A receipt was taped to the bottom of the board.

A credit card receipt for the American Express card of Bernadette Woodward.

CHAPTER 42

Blending Truth and Fiction Together

After I left Bette/Bernadette's room (by the door this time), I had just enough time to change into street clothes before meeting Mr. Brick Bungalow for a drink in the crew bar. I didn't really need to keep our date. After all, he already gave me the bit of information he knew. And I'd promised Ada I would stay away from the bar. Still, I showed up right on time, partly because I might be able to wheedle some more information out of him, partly because I was curious to see the place, but mostly because I hated being stood up and wouldn't do that to anyone.

But maybe not showing up wasn't such a bad idea if the guy you were meeting was dressed from head to toe in black leather, wore a studded dog collar around his neck, and greeted you with "Hello, Miss Rubber Gloves."

Needed to shoot down that misconception but quick. "I'm afraid your friend misunderstood," I said as I slid into the booth where he waited. "I'd been cleaning." I hoped his buddy hadn't told him that both Uncle Bob and I wore gloves. "I'm a teeny bit OCD."

"Clean is nice too," said BB. I briefly wondered if scrubbing the toilet could be a turn-on but decided I didn't want to know.

"So," I said, "I've never been here before. It's nice." The place was nice, in a bar sort of way. As with the rest of the crew areas, *Get Lit!* had dropped the literary theme. Instead, neon signs sang the praises of Bud Light, an old-fashioned jukebox sat in one corner, and all the surfaces were easy-wipe-clean. Definitely a no-nonsense drinking establishment. And everyone was here. Jonas was with the clerk from the sundries shop and a couple other men at a table a few feet away. David sat nearby at the bar by himself. Ada was laughing with a group of guys that included Val. Everyone was so engrossed in their own conversation (or their drinks) that no one noticed me. Or so I thought.

"Bet they sell a lot of vodka here." I nodded at a group of guys speaking some Slavic language. "Seem to be a lot of Eastern Europeans onboard."

"Yeah. Cruises are good money for them," said Brick. I really should ask his name, but it might make me appear too interested. "Most of them don't have a pot to piss in."

I giggled. "You're funny." He wasn't. "Do you think maybe they're the ones who are stealing stuff, since they're so poor and all?" A little on the nose, but I hoped my general air of ditziness would make me seem less investigator-ish.

"Could be. I have a theory about all that. You want to hear it?"

I should have known I didn't need to worry about sounding like a detective. People love to tell you stuff, especially if they think it'll make them look smart. "Yeah," I said breathlessly, just for effect.

"I think some of them are stealing IDs so they can pose as American citizens after they're done with their contracts onboard. You know, get off in Alaska and just disappear into the wilderness."

Maybe this guy was smarter than I thought.

"In fact," he leaned in so close the tag on his dog collar was dangerously close to his beer, "I've heard they have an underground compound outside of Anchorage where they're storing up weapons so they can stage a coup and take Alaska back for the Ruskies."

Nah, I was right about his intelligence to begin with. Still, it was kinda fun to play along. "Isn't the ground, like, really frozen up there?"

"Yeah."

"So how would they dig a big underground compound?"

"Oh. Well, first they'd probably steal some dynamite—"

"Hey, Ivy baby." Val stood next to our table, a puzzled look on his face. "Do you like dogs?" he asked the leather-clad BB.

"Uh, no." Brick fingered the collar around his neck. "I just—"

"I know S and M!" Val laughed and clapped him on the shoulder, then sat down in the booth next to me. "But I don't know what they stand for, the S and the M. Can you tell me?"

Brick's forehead furrowed. Either he wasn't sure if he was being put on, or he didn't know what S and M stood for.

"Ivy, if you want to eat before the show tonight, you'd better leave now." Ada stood beside our table, hands on her hips.

"Right." I pushed Val out of the booth so I could get up.

"I hear there's something special on the menu tonight." Ada narrowed her eyes at me. "Dead meat."

I got in line at Food, Glorious Food. While waiting, I checked my cell. Yay, one bar. I called the group home, crossing my fingers that Cody was there. He was. For about a minute.

"Olive-y!"

"Hey, I'm so glad you're back ho—"

"I found Stu. You were right. He was in a safe place."

"That's so cool, Cody. But we were worried about you too."

"You shouldn't have been. I was in a safe place too."

"But where did you—"

"Gotta go. Mom and Dad are taking me and Stu for pizza." Cody started to hang up.

"Wait, can I talk to Matt?" A clunk as Cody put down the phone. The group home still used a landline. Kept down expenses, especially since they'd canceled long distance after the guys decided they wanted to hear a real Australian accent.

"Hey, Ivy," Matt said.

I was startled by the change in his voice. "Wow, I just realized you sounded like crap these last few days."

"Thanks. I love you too."

"No, seriously."

"Me too."

"What?"

A pause. "Never mind. I finally got some sleep."

"You sound way better."

"We're all better. I got sleep, Cody got an enormous breakfast, and Stu got his meds."

At the mention of meds, a tiny lightbulb flickered in the back of my mind. "That was Keppra, right?"

"Yeah. Why?"

No one I'd asked seemed to know if Harley had epilepsy. "Is that medication just for seizures?"

"Not sure. Why?"

"Could you do me a favor? I can't really use the internet here. Could you find out a bit more about Keppra for me?"

"Sure."

"And one more thing. Could you find out if someone can die from epilepsy?"

CHAPTER 43

Who's Afraid?

A half hour and a quick dinner later, I skidded to a stop outside my cabin door. I was supposed to be at the theater for *Fagin's Magic Handkerchief* in five minutes. I fumbled in my skirt pocket for my keycard. Why, oh why was I always late? It was as if my internal clock ran ten minutes behind the rest of the world.

Since I was busy berating myself (which I soundly deserved), I nearly stepped on the small object someone had placed on the floor, tucked against my door. I pulled my foot back at the last minute, and bent and picked up a wooden doll, painted to look like a Russian peasant woman in a blue dress and scarf. I looked up and down the hallway. No one. Huh.

Maybe someone had left me an opening night present? I took my treasure into the cabin and examined it. Yes, it was a little Russian nesting doll. I unscrewed the outside doll to find a smaller version inside, this one with a yellow headscarf. I took that one apart to find a green painted figure. Was this the final doll? No. A hairline fissure circled its middle. I pried the green doll open with a fingernail. Her insides held a tiny red doll cloaked in a scrap of paper. I unrolled the paper carefully. In minuscule print someone had written, "You're on the right track."

I stared at the note. What right track? What had I learned today? I knew Bette was Bernadette and I knew Theo had been murdered. What else did I know? And more importantly, who thought I knew something? Shit, I was supposed to be undercover and at least one person knew I was up to something. And sure, that person might be cheering me along "the right track," but why? And why didn't he or she just come out and say something instead of hiding a note inside a Russian...

Duh. Inside a Russian doll. When had I mentioned Russians? Once with Madalina, and then again in the bar. Both times there were scads of people around.

No time to think. I was supposed to be at the theater right this minute. I slipped the doll into my pocket, grabbed my costume for *Fagin's Magic Handkerchief* off its hanger, and ran.

"We've got places in five," Ada announced as I ran through the dressing room door. "And you still have to get dressed, put your makeup on, and check your rigging." She turned right before she left the dressing room. "Good luck."

Nice. She basically just cursed me. There's a reason actors say "break a leg" instead of "good luck." Actually, I don't know what it is. I just know that saying "good luck" pretty much ensures the opposite. I set my opening night present, sans note, on the counter. Maybe someone at the theater would recognize the doll, maybe even let slip who gave it to me.

I scrambled into my costume (a red leotard cut and trimmed to look like a Victorian bustier), slapped on some makeup, and checked my rigging, all in record time.

I was in place when a blackout and music announced the beginning of the show.

I watched the first act from the stage left wing. Timothy pulled a string of handkerchiefs out of his pocket, did his "scarf through the neck" trick, and made a hankie dance while he danced a jig. Then he said to the audience, "Gents, I need a volunteer for my next feat." About a dozen arms shot up into the air. "But," Timothy said, "I need a bloke who's carrying a pocketbook." All the arms went down. "That's a wallet in twenty-first century parlance." Only a few men raised their arms again. Most people left their valuables in their room safes.

Timothy pointed at a nattily dressed man wearing a bow tie. "Would you please join me on the stage?" The man trotted up next to Timothy, who said, "Kind sir, do you think I could pick your pocket without you feeling it?"

"Perhaps," replied the guy in a British accent. "But I've a particularly sensitive bum." The audience laughed appreciatively.

"Could you please show the audience your wallet, so they can take a good look at it?"

"Of course." The man reached toward his back pocket. "It's..." He patted his rear. "It's gone."

"But not too far." Timothy wiggled his fingers in pick-pockety delight. "Dodger!" David ran on, bowed, and presented the man with a wallet. "Is this yours, sir?" asked Timothy.

"It is, indeed," stuttered the man. "How did you ever?"

"Ah, ah, ah, there's a code of silence among thieves," said Timothy.

"Isn't that code of honor?" asked the man.

"It's both," Timothy said, a bit gruffly.

Must have fluffed his line. Didn't matter. The audience roared.

Then the lights dimmed. My cue. Time to fly. I think I can I think I can I think I can. I'd be the little Ivy that could.

Very un-Dickensian pulsing electronic music played. Timothy stood in the middle of the stage and opened his arms wide in a grand gesture. The two silks dropped on either side of him, and Ada and I ran out and took our respective places. No mats underneath the silks this time. I grasped mine, tied onto the silk with my foot, and struck a pose, one arm swinging out and around as my free leg hooked around the front of the fabric. I held my breath as the pulley engaged and lifted me slowly skyward. When I could nearly touch the curtain that ran along the top of the proscenium, the pulley stopped. I smiled and moved into my first pose—and fell.

What the hell! The ground rushed up at me. My foot tangled in the fabric and my hand still clutched the fabric, so I hadn't slipped. What—Ow! Shit! The silk yanked tight around my instep as the free fall stopped. My foot felt nearly broken by the force and my arms ached from the death grip I had on the fabric. I looked up. The silk was still attached to the hardware. I looked down. Just ten more feet and I would have smashed into the stage.

The audience, which had been holding its collective breath, erupted into applause. Ever the performer, I smiled and waved. Someone maneuvered the pulley so that it floated me gently down to the stage, where I took a bow. Then I walked offstage and collapsed. Literally. My rubber legs wouldn't go any farther than a few steps into the wings. I sat there on the hard wooden floor and burst into tears.

A blackout, and Timothy rushed over to me.

"Did I pee my pants?" I asked him. "Please tell me I didn't pee my pants in front of everyone."

"You're okay," he said.

Jonas appeared next to me, Ada behind him. "God bless us." Jonas sat next to me and hugged me. He still smelled of booze.

A worried-looking techie shook his head. "Just like Har—"

"Why didn't you check your rigging?" Jonas said.

"I did. I checked it. All of my carabiners were locked."

"It was the knot. You didn't check the knot. It slipped because it wasn't tied right."

"Oh." Fear had sucked away all my brainpower, but several thoughts circled the fuzzy ball that was my mind.

I remembered being told to check the hardware, but did anyone ever tell me to check my knot?

The knot was just fine yesterday. Why had it been retied?

Most importantly, who retied it?

CHAPTER 44

We're All Afraid

"That slip, was that part of the show?" Uncle Bob's face looked a little pasty, even in the fire-lit library.

"No." I took a big gulp of sherry. Its warmth slid down my throat and helped me stop shivering. "The knot slipped. See, the silk is knotted around a piece of hardware called a rescue eight that's attached to the pulley, which is attached to—"

"Olive, did you forget to check your knot?"

Dang. I had hoped the extra information would distract him. I didn't want to tell him about some stuff yet—not about the note in the Russian doll and not about the knot, which I was pretty sure had been tampered with. Not until I saw how he'd respond to the news about Bette. So instead I appealed to his love of trivia. "Did you know that aerial silks have only been around since the eighties? I guess a Canadian gymnast with Cirque du Soleil came up with the idea. Before he did, aerialists only used trapezes and—"

"Olive. The knot."

"I...sort of forgot."

I let Uncle Bob lecture me for a minute, knowing his anger was out of love and fear, and knowing I had never been told to check that stupid knot. When he finally ran out of steam, I said, "You want to hear how Cody found Stu?"

He chuckled appreciatively as I related the Costco story. "Pretty smart, that brother of yours," he said. "So glad he's safe.

Now, back to work. This security guy, he said Theo was murdered?"

I told Uncle Bob what I knew, how the slight burns on Theo's face indicated poison. "Should we notify the police that there's been a murder?"

"Ship security should have already done that. Unless they didn't, if you know what I mean."

"Right. If they didn't provide the police with the information, there's a reason they're sitting on it. Do you think Theo's death could be connected to the theft ring?"

"Probably. I'm surprised this security guy told you anything."

"He's a few peas short of a casserole."

"Were you wearing that booby dress?"

"If you are referring to my Nancy costume, then yes."

"Got it." Uncle Bob set down his sherry glass and stared at the fire. "I don't think we should say anything yet. I checked with the medical staff. All the passengers at the ball who thought they were sick are okay—no signs of poison. We're too far at sea for the police to bring anyone on board and it would probably put the kibosh on our investigation. It's a tough call, but I don't think anyone is in danger."

Oh boy, here it came. "I think someone may be in danger."

"Who?"

"You." I sped ahead, not looking at my uncle. "I think Bette's on to you."

"Olive—"

"I know you like her, but she knew Theo. She hated Theo. She's not who she says she is, and I think she's...she's playing you."

Uncle Bob banged his sherry glass on the table so hard its stem shattered. "Goddammit, Olive, this has got to stop."

"But—"

"Yeah, Bette did know Theo. She told me today. Used to work for the son of a bitch, until he fired her."

"What did she do for him?"

"I don't know, public relations or something."

"You sure she wasn't..." I stopped. Not the time to pursue this.

"Wasn't what? Come on, you started this. Spit it out."

"You sure she wasn't a...call girl?"

"Oh, for God's sake, Olive." Uncle Bob stood up and stomped to the library door. "You've got a problem."

CHAPTER 45

Shrouds with Blood upon Them

If things are okay when you go to bed at night you expect them to be the same when you get up in the morning. So I ignored the slight sense of unease I had upon waking. Probably just a lack of coffee.

Ada wasn't there. Must have risen early. I ignored that clue too (Ada usually slept even later than I did), performed my morning ablutions, and opened my closet.

"Aaaah! Shit! Oliver!" The little urchin was stuffed in my closet, eyes shut in a grimace, trails of blood dripping from his mouth and ears. "Shit!"

I raced the whole twelve inches to my desk, picked up my phone, and started to dial. I couldn't stand the kid, but I didn't wish him dead either. Maybe they could do CPR, or...

Wait. I stopped dialing and sniffed the air. It smelled different than normal, sweet and fruity like...candy? I put down the phone, walked back to the closet, and gave Oliver's body a sniff. Suddenly Theo's death flashed back into my mind. The same sickly sweet smell, albeit mixed with vomit.

I grabbed my rubber gloves from my drawer, put them on, and went back to the body. The odor came from the face area. I put a gloved finger on his lips. Maybe someone had placed something inside his mouth...

"Aaaah!" I screamed again as the little miscreant opened his eyes and grinned at me.

"Got you." Oliver stepped out of the closet and licked the stage blood from his lips. "What were you going to do to my mouth?"

"You smell funny, like...apples or something." I was too startled to be pissed.

"Jolly Rancher." He sucked noisily on the candy in his mouth. "Want one?" He produced another one from a pocket.

"I just want you to go away." The kid made me very, very tired.

"That's what everyone says. Ha. You screamed like a girl."

"I am a girl. Now get." I shooed him away. "No, wait." Of course Oliver opened the door to leave. I grabbed him by the shoulders before he slipped away. "Did you ever give Theo a Jolly Rancher?"

"Who's Theo?"

I searched his face. He looked sincere, but he was an actor. A good one too, the little bugger. "Did you mess with the knot on my silk last night?"

"I was with my parents all night. You can ask my mother."

Something knocked on the door of my coffee-less brain. Silk...knot...mother...Harley. Last night, didn't one of the techies say something about..."Hey, did Harley—she was Madame Defarge—"

"The dead one?"

"Yes, the dead one. Did she ever do the silks?"

"Yeah. Nancy was supposed to, but she hurt her hand. I have no idea how." Oliver gave me the "cherubim have nothing on me" look.

"Did Harley fall once? From the silk?"

"Yeah. Sprained her wrist. Ada had to do the magic show by herself for a whole week." Oliver squirmed under my grip. "Can I go now?"

"One last question: How did you get into my cabin so you could hide in the closet?"

"Ada let me in."

Of course.

* * *

I didn't know why the smell of Jolly Ranchers stayed on my mind, but I just couldn't let it go. After a quick breakfast, I trotted down to the ship's infirmary.

"Hello?" I knocked on the door. A stout woman in a white doctor's coat opened it wide and I caught a whiff of disinfectant.

"Yes?" she said in a friendly tone. "How can I help you?"

"Is it possible to pay my respects to one of the deceased?"

"Welcome to sick bay." A short African-American man in blue scrubs held up a hand in a split-fingered Vulcan salute. "Live long and prosper."

"He can't decide if he's Bones or Spock," said the woman, swatting him on the shoulder.

"I want to be Captain Kirk." He winked at me. "But she's in charge."

She shook her head at him, then said to me, "Please come in."

The infirmary was a model of organization. Every bit of space was used. Locked cupboards full of medications and medical equipment surrounded a bed, while backboards and stretchers were affixed to the wall. It looked like a cross between a hospital room and an ambulance.

"Would you like a cup of tea?" asked the doctor.

"You do the Dickens thing here too?"

"Oh, no. I just like tea. And we rarely get visitors. Well ones, anyway." She bustled around getting cups and teabags from a small cubby that also held an electric teapot. "We also don't get that sort of request too often. Are you family?"

"No, but the man died on top of me."

"Oh my." She shot a "don't you dare say anything" look at the guy in scrubs.

"Not that way," I said. "He just fell on me. At the ball."

"You must be talking about Mr. Pushwright. I'm sorry, but since you're not family we can't take you down to the morgue."

"You have a morgue onboard?"

"A lot of older travelers like to cruise, and it's not uncommon to have a death at sea. The morgue isn't anything fancy, basically just a set of refrigerated drawers."

"But I can't see it?"

The doctor shook her head.

"We'd have to move the prime rib," the guy said.

"Jamie! Not funny." Then the doctor smiled. "Space *is* at a premium onboard, you know. So we do keep flowers in the drawers when they're not in use. It's the perfect temperature." The kettle must have been one of those super-duper ones, because she was already pouring hot water into our cups. "Why did you want to see Mr. Pushwright?" she asked.

"Just to satisfy my curiosity. There was a smell about him."

"Was there ever," said Scrubs.

"Do you know what it was?" I asked.

"Vomit," he said. "They're going to have a tough time cleaning *that* costume."

"Cleaning it? Wouldn't they just throw it away or burn it or something?"

"Just between you and me, dear, those costumes are quite expensive," said the doctor. "They do everything they can to clean them up, no matter what dirties them—vomit, blood, urine." She smiled at me. "Do you take anything in your tea?"

CHAPTER 46

Exhibiting Decided Marks of Genius

After a very nice cup of tea, I made my way to Madame Mantalini's Temple of Fashion. I suspected the robe and mask had been cleaned, but having worn my share of stinky costumes, I knew that smells often lingered.

As I turned the corner to the shop, I caught a glimpse of a familiar top hat. Like always, when I looked for David, he wasn't there.

The guy really did belong in a magic show.

I walked inside the costume shop and my spirits lifted. Sure, I was looking for a dead man's clothes, but what actress's heart doesn't swell at the sight of all that silk and lace?

"Hi again," I said to the manager. He looked at me blankly. "You outfitted me for dinner at the captain's table the other night? A green brocade dress—you convinced me to wear a corset?"

"Sorry," he said. "I get literally hundreds of people through here. And most of them should wear corsets."

"No worries. I'm really here about Theo Pushwright's costume."

"That was disposed of, of course."

"But even if it wasn't—which I would never tell anyone about in a million years—someone had to handle it, right?"

The costume shop manager pursed his lips, appraising me. "You know, I suddenly have the urge for a cigarette and some chocolate. Would you go next door and get me a box of Godiva chocolates and some vaping liquid? I like Dead Man's Party."

"You do?" Visions of the black-robed costumes danced in my head.

"It's a vape juice flavor. Blueberry lemonade."

"Got it." I started out the door.

"And don't forget to bring me my change."

"But you didn't give me any mon—Oh. Right. Sure thing."

I went next door to Mrs. Chickenstalker's Sundries and got the chocolates and the vape stuff.

But now I had a problem. I dialed Timothy.

"Hey Tonto, do you have any cash on you?" Since everything was paid for by my onboard account, I didn't bring much actual money. I had only about thirty dollars in cash left, and it was back in my cabin.

"I've got about fifty dollars."

I hoped that was enough. I'd never bribed anyone to tell me about a barfed-on Ghost of Christmas Future costume before. "Great. Meet me in the costume shop as soon as you can."

"Perfect. I need to go there anyway. Need a new Fagin beard."

I went back next door and gave the goods to the manager. "Your change is on its way."

"Good." He took an e-cigarette out of his pocket and carefully filled it with the vaping fluid. Something niggled at the back of my mind. "How do you work those?" I pointed at the gadget.

"You just suck on it to activate it."

"I've heard that before," Timothy said behind me.

The manager smiled a slow smile at my sidekick. "Want to try it?" he said, offering the cigarette to Timothy.

"Aren't you supposed to use those outdoors?" I said.

"I'll try anything once, twice if I like it, three times to make sure," Timothy said in his best Mae West voice. He took a long sensual drag on the cigarette.

"Timothy," I said pointedly as he fluttered his eyelashes. "Don't you have something for the nice man?"

"Do I ever." He slid a hand into his front pants pocket while blowing out a stream of fruity-smelling vapor.

"Cut it out. I want to talk about dead people." I stopped. "Wait, do that again."

"This?" Timothy slid his hand slowly into his pants pocket, leering at the manager.

"*No.* Blow that vapor at me, would you?"

"Sure." Timothy complied and I finally realized what had been bugging me.

And what had killed Theo.

I ran back to the sundries shop. "Forget something?" the clerk asked me.

Even though I didn't see anyone close by, I lowered my voice, just in case. "Wasn't there a story in the news not too long ago about some kid accidentally getting killed with vaping liquid?"

"Yeah. Vape juice can be pretty dangerous. That's why we keep it behind the counter. I heard as little as a teaspoon can kill a kid."

"It smells like candy too, so it'd be easy to slip into someone's drink, I guess," I said, thinking out loud. "But that doesn't explain the burns."

"I don't know exactly what you're getting at," said the clerk. "But this stuff is toxic if you get it on your skin too. A couple of months ago a guy ended up in the infirmary. Had a seizure after spilling some liquid on him. Doesn't take much, I guess."

"Right." Things were falling into place. "Who has access to vaping liquid?"

The clerk shrugged. "Anyone over eighteen."

Damn, that let Oliver off the hook. I really wanted to nail him for something.

I wished I could talk to Uncle Bob, but he hadn't replied to the apologies I texted him earlier. I should probably let him cool off. And my idea wasn't well-formulated or urgent. Still, I wanted to talk it through while it was fresh in my mind.

Matt. I could call Matt. He'd listen, and he'd tell me the right thing to do. He always did.

I pulled out my phone. No bars. No Matt. I sighed, thanked the clerk, and walked next door, where Timothy was still flirting with the manager. "Come on, Tonto," I said. "We've got some thinking to do."

CHAPTER 47

A Fit of Professional Enthusiasm

"Looking forward to wearing your beard next to my skin," Timothy called to the manager as I dragged him out of Madame Mantalini's, a bag tucked under his arm.

"How do you make everything sound dirty?" I said.

"It's a gift."

I hauled him down the hallway. "Let's go back to your cabin."

"Oohh, baby."

I stopped. "Are you flirting with me?"

"Sorry," Timothy said. "Force of habit."

"Who's gay, who's straight—it's all very confusing right now."

"You don't seriously think that I could be strai—"

"Of course not," I said. "Hey, let's stop by the kitchen first. I need some butcher paper."

About ten minutes later, Timothy unlocked the door to his cabin. I stepped in, a nice clean roll of paper under my arm. "Let's get to work."

I was a visual thinker. I needed to see things in front of me. Investigations were especially tricky, what with all the clues and suspects and such. Back at Uncle Bob's office, I used a whiteboard. Here onboard the ship, I was going to have to make do with what was at hand.

I unrolled the piece of butcher paper and duck-taped the edge to the frame of the top bunk.

"The famous duck tape." Timothy pronounced the name carefully ever since I'd told him the story of the tape's real name (it was used to keep ammo dry in World War II, and worked "like water off a duck's back"). "I guess it does come in handy."

I always kept a roll in my purse. I used it to repair flip flops and car hoses, and..."Did you know I could tape someone's mouth shut with this?" Timothy zipped his lips as I taped the other edge of the paper to the frame underneath the bottom bunk. "Makes a nice temporary set of handcuffs too." I stopped back and admired my taped-up handiwork. "Ta-da. Instant whiteboard." I grabbed a Sharpie out of my purse.

"What can you do with those? Sharpies?" asked Timothy.

"Um, write?" I hadn't had much time to ponder Sharpie's possibilities. Yet. "You said there's no chance your roommate will walk in on us, right?" Timothy roomed with the actor who played Pip in *Great Expectations*.

"Nah, he's on character duty all day. I would be too, if it hadn't been for Oliver." He stepped toward me and stroked his cheek. "See how smooth?"

The left side of Timothy's face was hairless as a baby's bum. He turned the other side of his face toward me. It had what looked like a three-day growth of beard, Timothy's typical five o'clock shadow. "The little turd put Nair on one side of my fake beard. When I took it off last night, I also took off all the hair on that cheek. Brat ruined my only beard too." He shook his new beard out of the bag from the costume shop.

"You're just lucky he didn't put it—"

"Oh, he thought of that too," said Timothy. "He must have soaked my underwear with it or something. I am even smoother than normal down there. Like a cucumber. A cucumber with a rash."

"Oh, oh, oh!" I was so excited I dropped my Sharpie.

"I know, it really itches."

"You just helped me figure out how Theo was murdered." I grabbed the pen and stood back up.

"Theo was murdered?"

"Sorry. Let me back up." I wrote "Theo" on the paper as I explained about the burns on Theo's face. "But I couldn't figure out how anyone could have smuggled poison onboard the ship. Plus, when he died, he had an odd sweet smell I couldn't identify—until a few minutes ago at the costume shop."

"The e-cig vape."

"Right." I wrote "poisoned by vape juice" underneath Theo's name. "It's straight nicotine. Can kill you pretty easily."

"And it's available to anyone onboard."

"Anyone over eighteen," I said.

"Crap," he said. "I was really hoping we could pin something on Oliver."

"You and me both. I figured someone slipped some in Theo's drink at the ball, but I couldn't figure out the burns on his face. But your baby face—"

"Baby face," sang Timothy. "I've got the cutest little baby—"

"Hey, *Tonto*." I zipped my lips for emphasis.

"Sorry," said Timothy. "Sometimes a boy's just gotta sing."

"You want me to get out the duck tape?"

He shook his head.

"Okay, so now I think someone tampered with Theo's costume. His Ghost of Christmas Future mask was made of fabric that fit tightly over his face. Someone could have doused the fabric with the nicotine and—omigod, we have to make sure no one else wears that mask."

Timothy took out his phone and texted someone. "Done." He smiled. "I just happen to have the costume shop manager's phone number right here. What's next?"

"People who had a reason to kill Theo, I guess. Bette sure seemed to hate him." I wrote down her name. "I overheard her say he ruined her life. Oh, and Madalina too. She was his, um, paid companion."

I wrote her name next to Bette's.

"Is that a reason to kill someone?"

"No, but something happened between them to change her mind about him."

"Maybe he carried a roll of duck tape with him."

"*Timothy.*"

He grinned an innocent Oliver-type smile.

"I guess I need to add Jonas," I said, writing his name on the butcher paper.

"Right," said Timothy. "He just inherited a buttload of money. And don't forget—"

"Val. Yeah." I put his name down too. "If Theo's murder is connected somchow to the thefts, and if Val is a pickpocket, he could have..." I shut my eyes, the better to think. "Yeah, I guess he would have still had time. I was thinking he couldn't have done it, since he wouldn't have had time to get dressed. But of course, he could have poisoned Theo's drink and costume earlier."

"Did you just say get dressed?"

"Remember you said he likes to get naked when he's drunk? I came back that night to find him in my bed, in just what he was born with."

"Ooh...is it true?" said Timothy. "Does he have a big—"

"Tattoo? Why yes, he does." I went on before Timothy could ask another question about Val's physical attributes. "It's a family tree—a really sad one, actually. There are just two names on it, his cousin's and his dog's. He doesn't even know his parents' names so he can't put them on..." I stopped.

Val had been duped.

Or he was lying.

CHAPTER 48

A Creeping Sickness at His Heart

I wanted to talk to Val immediately, but first things first. "You sure this will be safe?" I folded the butcher paper "whiteboard" and handed it to Timothy.

"Yeah," he said, tucking it inside a magazine. "There's no way my roommate's going to flip through the pages of *Inches*."

"Great. I need to get going." We'd talked through the investigation for a few more minutes, but it was painfully obvious I didn't have much to go on. And it was painfully obvious where I needed to begin.

Val was the best lead we had. He was Eastern European, Timothy saw him steal T-shirt Dad's wallet, and he was the only one obviously connected to Harley. I couldn't see a connection to Theo, though. Maybe Theo had learned about the theft ring? Or he was involved in it? After all, Theo was rich before he started writing his positivity books. That money had to come from somewhere. Maybe Val knew?

After changing into my Nancy costume (ambient character duty again), I headed for the indoor swimming pool where Val often hung out.

Yep, there he was, dressed in costume, talking to two young women in bikinis standing near the edge of the unfortunately named Little Nell's Natatorium—I mean, c'mon, who names a swimming pool after a poor little dying girl?

"Bill Sikes!" I put my hands on my hips, Nancy-style. "I don't care for this, not one bit. What do you think you're playing at, with all these women? I thought I was your—"

"Stand off from me, or I'll split your head against the wall."

Whoa. I stepped back.

"That's right," Val continued in his Bill Sikes voice, "you be quiet now, or I'll quiet you for a good long time to come." He stared at me with the flat eyes of a killer, then turned back to the girls, all charm. "Now if you'll excuse me, ladies." He doffed his hat and took my arm roughly. "Pretty good, you think?" Val whispered to me in his own voice as he pulled me away from the group. "I do that for the play tonight. Now they come. Nice foreskin, yes?"

"Foreski—I think you mean foreshadowing. Oh. You knew that, didn't you?" Val grinned at me. No sign of Bill Sikes now. He pulled me closer. His aftershave was somehow familiar. "Is that bay rum?" I said, trying to get his murderous look out of my head.

"No. Something someone gave me. You are okay from last night? Your fall?"

"Yeah." The few bruises and fabric burns I had were piddly compared to what might have happened.

We strolled for a minute while I tried to figure out how to get him talking.

"You are quiet," he said. "Are you worried about your brother?"

"I can't believe I didn't tell you. They found him and Stu."

"He was eating stew?"

"What? No. My brother's friend—the one who he went after—is named Stuart, but Cody calls him Stu." Ah, here was a way into the conversation. "Did I tell you he calls me Olive-y?"

"Because you like martinis?"

"No. Because my real name is Olive."

"Olive?"

"Olive Ziegwart. My dad says it means 'victory nipple' in German."

Oops, mistake. Val's attention moved to my chest.

Though my breasts sometimes proved useful in interrogation (e.g. Mr. Brick Bungalow), I really wanted to see Val's eyes. When interviewing subjects, Uncle Bob had taught me to begin with a question people could answer truthfully. I would note where they looked when they told the truth. Then with further questions, I'd watch to see where their eyes moved. I stopped walking and tipped Val's chin back up so his eyes met mine. "Do you know what your name means?"

"Valery means brave." Val puffed out his chest and looked up and to the right.

I was pretty sure that was correct (think about the word "valor"), so right was Val's truthful place.

"Also a girlfriend told me it means 'a deep inner desire for a stable loving family or community.'" As he spoke the memorized words, his eyes stayed where they were. Good. True.

"Was the girlfriend Harley?"

"No." His eyes flitted back to me, then to the left. "She was not a girlfriend."

A lie. "So she never saw your tattoo?"

"That is only for special girlfriends. I show it to you again tonight."

"I was trying to remember the names on the tree's leaves. There was Tuzik, your dog, and..."

"Nikolay. My cousin." His eyes moved to the right.

So he hadn't been lying about his cousin. Huh. I needed to proceed carefully. I began walking again, his arm tucked under mine. "I think I've heard his name before. Oh, didn't someone tell me you were going to meet him in Ensenada?"

"Who told you that?" Val's voice had changed again. Not exactly Bill Sikes, but someone to be wary of.

"I don't remember." I shook my head and moved to safer ground. "He's your cousin?"

Val nodded.

"It's so cool that you found some of your family. It must have been hard to do."

"What do you mean?" Val stopped walking and looked at me.

"You don't know who your parents were, right?" The bare branches on Val's tattooed family tree haunted me. I really didn't want to do this to Val, but I forged ahead. "So how do you know that Nikolay is your cousin?"

"He found me. He knows we are cousins because of my eyes. He has two-colored eyes too. Is family trait."

Oh. Phew. Maybe I was wrong about this whole thing with Val's cousin. But didn't Uncle Bob say...Dang. I sighed before I could stop myself.

"What?" Val said. "What is wrong?"

"Um. What you have—the bicolored eye? That's really rare. And your type isn't usually genetic."

"But Nikolay has a brown eye and a blue eye. He must be family."

"So he doesn't have an eye like yours? His eyes are completely different colors?"

"Yes. That is rare too, no?"

"It is rare, but...Didn't you say he found you? Did he know you had a bicolored eye?"

"Everyone knows. What is 'but'?"

I didn't want to go ahead with this. I chewed my lip instead.

Val gripped me by the shoulders. "What is 'but'? You said, 'Is rare, but...'"

"But it's pretty easy to fake with a contact lens." I said it all in one breath, the verbal equivalent to ripping off a Band-Aid.

Saying it quickly didn't seem to make it hurt less. Val looked like someone had taken away the only Christmas present he'd ever been given. "Nikolay found me," he said slowly. "He knew I did not know my family. He knew about my eyes. He wanted me to think we are related. You are right. And I am stupid."

CHAPTER 49
A Weary Catalogue of Evils

Val strode away without looking back.

I felt like shit. And now I was going to mess with someone else's head. How did Uncle Bob do this every day? My family didn't talk. We didn't even have regular "how was your day" conversations. These "sacrifice a soul for some information" talks were way beyond anything I was used to.

Still I soldiered on. After all, two lives had been lost. It sucked that I liked the victims less than the people I was interrogating.

It was lunchtime, so I wandered through the Solitary Oyster, Boz's Buffet, and Food, Glorious Food looking for Target Number Two. Ah, there she was. I grabbed a tray, went through the buffet, and loaded my plate with the first things available. I walked quickly to Madalina's table.

"Mind if I join you?" I sat down before she could answer. I needed to talk to Madalina about her relationship with Theo. If he had been just a john, why would she change her opinion of him? Or had she just let her mask slip after his death? "Boy, I'm starving. I could eat a horse."

"You may be eating one." Madalina looked pointedly at my plate. "Along with rest of barn." Madalina had a shrimp salad. My plate was filled with meat pies, sausages, blood pudding, and lamb chops. Must have loaded my tray in the meat section.

"Have to stay in character, you know."

"What is your character?"

"I play Nancy, from *Oliver Twist*. She's a—" I caught myself before I said "whore."

"A...?"

"You know, it's interesting. Dickens never comes right out and says what her profession is," I babbled, "but it's implied that she's a...lady of the night."

Madalina arched a sculpted eyebrow. "You are afraid to offend me?"

"It's just that..." How do you ask someone if they're a sex worker?

"Maybe because you think I am whore?"

Guess I didn't have to ask. Or avoid the W word.

"Is true. So? Is my life." She picked a bit of shell off a piece of shrimp.

"It doesn't have to be." I leaned across the table to her. "I could introduce you to my agent. She reps models too. I'm sure you'd get lots of work."

Madalina pursed her perfect lips. "Acting and modeling. They are much like prostitution."

"Not really."

"Do you kiss men you don't like, for acting?"

"Yeah, but—"

"Would you take off your clothes?"

"I haven't."

"But would you, to be big star?"

"Madalina, I'm just trying to hel—"

"You judge me. I have enough of that." She pushed her salad away and scooted her chair back.

"Wait," I said. "I don't want to judge. I want to understand. And to help if I can."

Madalina stood up and began to walk away.

I took a deep breath and said, "I am chained to my old life. I loathe and hate it now, but I cannot leave it. I must have gone too far to turn back—and yet I don't know."

She stopped and looked at me.

"One of Nancy's lines," I explained.

Her eyes traveled my face. She must have seen something in me, because she sat back down. "You cannot help. There are other people involved. It is not so easy to walk away."

"Other people? Like Theo?"

"He was no one to me."

"But—"

"You want to understand or you want to ask questions?"

Actually, I wanted both, but decided to stay silent.

"I have worked for these people since I was twelve." Madalina did not look at me, but held her head high in defiant dignity. "They come to orphanage where I was raised. They say they were social workers who had training program for young girls. We think sewing, maybe even computer work. It was not that kind of work."

I imagined a twelve-year-old Madalina, a little blonde girl in threadbare clothes, excited at the prospect of a new life, then...I didn't want to imagine any further. "Couldn't you run away?"

"Some tried. When I saw what happened to them, I did not try. And now I am lucky one. I do not work the streets. I am not beaten. Many have it worse than I."

"But—" My throat closed up and I couldn't finish. Besides, I didn't know what to say.

"Is worst for those who feel. I do not. I am dead inside. Only once in my life did I feel something. Then, poof. Dead again. It is way with orphans, you know. If no one loves you, you do not learn to feel. Or even to want. You just hope to live."

CHAPTER 50

The Arts of Cunning and Dissimulation

The weight of Val and Madalina's lonely lives sat heavy on my chest, and my meat-filled lunch did the same for my gut. A walk would help.

I was on ambient character duty, so I swished my skirts and smiled at guests as I strode the decks, but I didn't talk to anyone. Besides confirming my suspicions, I hadn't learned much this morning, and so needed to continue the conversation I was having in my head. Why would someone kill Theo? The obvious answer was money. The next obvious answer was that whoever inherited his money would be the killer, but I really didn't believe Jonas was capable of murder. There had to be another angle. Thieves? Unlikely. Theo had lots of money, but I was pretty sure that a savvy businessman like himself wouldn't have brought cash onboard the cruise, so...Ah.

My serendipitous wanderings had brought me to The Crystal Palace (Fine Jewelry for Discriminating Tastes). I slipped inside the small high-end shop. The burgundy carpet was plush under my feet, beveled glass cases winked at me, and the air smelled faintly of roses. It had that hush that typifies very expensive shops, and it made me supremely uncomfortable. Sure, I was surrounded by beautiful things—Victorian pearl necklaces, butterfly brooches made of gemstones, cherubim earrings carved from coral—but I was also afraid I might do something wrong. Like say, "Fancier than my underpants" to the elegant man who approached me. Damn Timothy and his quotable ways.

The clerk didn't say anything in response, but smiled genteelly, like a butler dealing with an ignorant master. I curtseyed. "I'm Nancy," I said in my best Cockney accent. Maybe he'd take the underpants line for a character thing. "I'm just curious," I continued in my Nancy voice, "to know if you sell many of these trinkets to the swells onboard."

"We do well," the clerk replied.

"What's the most precious bit you sold?" I asked in a conspiratorial whisper.

"Why are you interested?" he whispered back, relaxing a bit.

"Humor me?" I said in my real voice.

He shrugged. "We sold a ten-thousand-dollar diamond and emerald necklace this time—a one-of-a-kind Victorian antique."

"Wow."

"It's not that unusual on these cruises," he said. "*Get Lit!* serves a high-end clientele, guests are often here for romantic reasons, and we stock Victorian-era jewelry that people won't find elsewhere."

"Wow," I said again, partly because I couldn't imagine anyone spending ten thousand dollars on a necklace, partly because the thieves had picked a great cruise line to burgle, and partly to convince the clerk that my next question was innocent. "Who bought the necklace?"

"I'm afraid I can't give out that information." His manner grew stiff and formal again. Guess the innocent act didn't work.

I'm not sure why I tried the same tactic at the art gallery, but it bombed again. After that failure, I ambled into the atrium and stared at the statue of Dickens, hoping for inspiration. A bell sounded, and there it was: my next idea.

That sounds pretty woo-woo. It wasn't. It was just the noise from a slot machine in the nearby casino. I made my way to the Golden Hall Gambling Establishment. Like most casinos, the room was windowless and filled with felt-topped tables for craps and cards. But in a nod to the ship's Victorian theme, there was no neon, no flashing lights, and no mechanized music from the slot machines. The slots themselves looked like antique reproductions, decorated with scrolled metalwork, spinning wheels, and dancing tin monkeys. Small chandeliers and lamps with fringed shades illuminated the playing areas. The whole effect was one of civilized entertainment, the sort of place where the upper crust might lose the deeds to their estates.

I spied a guy wearing a green eyeshade standing at the side of the room, probably a dealer waiting to go on shift. "How does this work?" I asked him. "Do guests use cash or sign-and-sail cards?"

"Either," he said. Did he have an accent? "But if they use cards there is small fee, so many prefer to use cash." Yep, another Eastern European. Was that suspicious?

"How about the payout? Do they—" I asked.

"Woo hoo!" A curly-haired woman jumped up and down as a shining waterfall of tokens spilled out of a slot machine.

"You are good luck. Maybe you stay and say 'pay out' more often?" The dealer smiled at me. "About your question, guests turn in tokens and chips for credit on their accounts or for cash now."

"Do big winners ever choose cash?"

"Sure. Up to certain amount, of course."

I sidled up close. Might as well try. After all, the dealer had smiled at me, and I was wearing my "booby dress." I leaned toward him. "Had any big winners this cruise?"

"Yes." Didn't look like he was taking the booby bait. "But of course I cannot talk about them."

Oh well. "Of course. Thanks. Hope someone else gets a *payout*." I said it loudly and scanned the room to see if anyone else had gotten lucky. I didn't see any winners, but I did see a familiar back of a head sitting at one of the card tables. Great, maybe I could apologize to Uncle Bob in person.

I headed toward my uncle, who looked like he was having a great time. "Did you know that a popular food item was invented so someone could go on gambling?" he said to his fellow card players.

"A nobleman ordered his servant to bring him sliced meat between two pieces of bread, so he wouldn't have to stop playing. He was the Fourth Earl of Sandwich."

The table laughed appreciatively. One laugh in particular stood out and I stopped where I stood. I hadn't recognized Bette because she wore a hat, a straw skimmer that looked jauntily Victorian and modern at the same time. I slipped behind a bank of slot machines and watched whoever-the-hell-she-was whisper in my uncle's ear.

I was going to have to stop this.

CHAPTER 51

An Opening Presents Itself

"Bernadette Woodward, a.k.a. Bette Foxberry, worked in the media relations department for Positivity Productions for ten years before being fired at age forty-eight." Timothy and I were both on duty as ambient characters, so we chatted like Fagin and Nancy as we strolled down to Scrooge's Haunted House. In reality, Timothy was updating me after doing research via his smartphone (he had a way better cell plan than me). He continued: "There was a scandal where it looked like she was embezzling, but nothing was ever proved."

I went to open the door of the haunted house where we could talk a bit more privately. As I did, the doorknocker changed into a ghostly face.

I decided it was fine to talk outside the house. "Pretty hard to get another job after that," I said. Was that how Theo ruined Bette's life? "Anything else?"

"That's it. She dropped off the radar. No social media accounts, not under Bernadette Woodward or Bette Foxberry. Nothing."

The clock bonged twice.

"Big Ben has spoken," said Timothy. "Time for me to go. I've got an afternoon date with Marley."

"Isn't he a little old for you?" The actor playing the ghost from *A Christmas Carol* looked at least sixty-five.

"Not him." Timothy looked like a kid about to meet Santa. "The costume shop manager has promised to dress as Marley. But with just the chains." He scooted off.

I ambled up to the Drood Deck, where I stood looking out to sea in the hope that no one would bother me. I needed to know more about Bette/Bernadette. It looked like the only way I'd get more information was to talk to her directly, but I didn't see how that was going to happen. I wasn't exactly her favorite person.

"What's the matter?" The familiar voice behind me projected well. Oliver.

I turned to see David next to him. They were both in costume. "Hush," said David. "Do you see that old cove at the book-stall?"

"The old gentleman over the way?" said Oliver, an adorably earnest expression on his face. "Yes, I see him." Ah. Oliver's fake sweet look gave it away. They were acting out a scene for the crowd on deck.

"He'll do," said David. He tripped Oliver, who fell against the "old gentleman."

"Cor blimey, sir," said David. "We didn't see you at all. Please accept our apologies." While Oliver steadied himself, David slid a stealthy hand into the oblivious man's back pocket. Then he presented the man's very recently stolen goods back to him. "Your keycard, my fine sir," David said with a bow. After a stunned moment, the man began clapping. Pretty soon the entire crowd was applauding. "Come see *Oliver! At Sea!* Tonight only," said David. The pickpocket team gave one last bow, David disappeared, and Oliver began to walk away.

But not fast enough. I collared the little creep. "Give it back," I whispered.

"What?"

"Whatever you took out of that woman's purse when everyone was applauding." I pointed at a woman in a pink polo shirt.

"It's just a phone," Oliver whined as he handed it to me.

I said in a loud Nancy voice, "And you thought the show was over." Not very Dickensian, but my best shot at improv. "Madame, your pocket has been picked!" I gave the phone back to the woman and began the applause myself.

Then I hauled the little bugger out of earshot of the crowd. "Just a phone. You're kidding, right? It's not as if people just use them for calls. They have half their lives typed into the things, and if they lose..."

Oh. Yes. I knew how I could get Bette to talk to me.

"Yeah, yeah. Let me go, Nancypants." Oliver tried to wriggle away, but I kept hold of him as I tried to catch a thought that was slipping away like a minnow. I stared at the kid. Oliver. Phone. Pickpocket. That was it. For a little kid, Oliver was awfully good at stealing. "Who taught you how to pick pockets?"

"Fagin did."

"Tell the truth, Ollie."

He shrugged off my grip. "Just because he's your friend doesn't mean he doesn't know how to steal."

CHAPTER 52

Getting to the Bottom of This Mystery

I knew it was a deal with the devil, but I didn't have any other options. "There she is." I pulled Oliver behind the statue of Charles Dickens in the grand lobby and pointed to Bette, whose arm was wrapped tightly around Uncle Bob's, like that seaweed that tangles up unlucky divers and drags them to a watery death.

"Finally," said Oliver, who'd been hauled around the ship for twenty minutes before I spotted Bette. Then he giggled.

"What?" Oliver laughing was a bad sign.

"Didn't you see it?"

"See what?" Admittedly, I was distracted. Though I didn't believe the little stinker, Oliver had planted seeds of doubt in my mind. After all, how well did I really know Timothy? We were just theater friends. I didn't know where his family lived or if he even had any family. I knew he was the one who suggested *Get Lit!* hire Uncle Bob and me, but that didn't mean he wasn't in on the whole theft ring.

"*That.*" Oliver nodded toward Bette and Bob, who were staring at the statue along with a dozen other people.

Keeping a firm grip on Oliver, I snuck around the back edge of the knot of people. Ah. The statue of Charles Dickens now sported a large stick-on handlebar mustache.

"And it's red." Oliver grinned gleefully. "Dickens hated red hair."

"How did you do that?" The statue's face was about fifteen feet from the ground.

"I'll never tell."

In a way, you had to admire the kid.

"So you want me to steal her phone?" Oliver said.

"Right. I'll wait for you around the corner. Bring it to me, and I won't tell your mom that you stole from that woman."

"Like that's a threat. I'd just say I was acting."

"Then I'll tell your little gang of orphans that Ollie wears girl's underpants. Pink ones with bunnies."

"But I don't wear—"

"They'll believe me. I'm an actress."

Oliver scowled at me, then put on his angel face as he worked his way toward Bette and Bob, who still had their backs to us. When he got in range, he nodded at me. I stepped around the corner, where I was mostly hidden but could still keep an eye on the action.

Oliver pinched the bum of a large woman next to Bette. She squealed. Bette turned, and Oliver slipped behind her and stuck his hand in and out of her blazer pocket in a flash. He trotted over to me, and I ushered him into the stairwell.

He handed over Bette's phone. I took it and tapped an email icon. Her email address, "woodfox," wasn't helpful, but the first message I checked was signed Bernadette Woodward.

"Jackpot," I said

"Jackpot? What are you, like eighty or something?" Oliver said.

"What would Dickens say?"

He thought a minute. "'In luck, then.' Or maybe he'd call me a clever dog."

"All right: we're in luck, then, you clever dog. Now scram. And remember, don't breathe a word of this or—"

"Girl's panties, right." He scooted away.

A lame threat, I knew. I hoped it would hold.

My cell buzzed in my skirt pocket. Matt. Yes.

I picked up. "I'm so glad it's you."

"And I'm glad it's you. Wait, I called, didn't I?"

Upon hearing Matt's voice, a great wave of relief crashed over me. "Really. I am. God, it's good to talk to someone I can trust." Tears pricked my eyes.

"What's wrong?"

"It's not so much what's wrong as what's not right."

"Matt waited for me to explain. He was good that way.

"You know that feeling you get when you're the new kid on the block, and you don't know which kids are going to be your friends, or which dogs might bite you? Or the way you feel when your best friend has found a new better friend? Put those two together and then add your brother going missing and..." I swallowed the lump in my throat. "But talking to you is like coming home and your dog is there and so happy to see you, and you hug him and everything is all right again."

"So I'm like your dog?" I heard the smile in Matt's voice and I smiled too.

"Best dog in the world," I said. "Thanks. I appreciate it more than you know. So, everything back to usual there?"

"Pretty much. I missed an exam, but they're letting me make it up." Matt was getting his Masters in Social Work at Arizona State. "In fact, I'm on my way to meet with my professor now." He was probably at ASU downtown already, crossing the street with his relaxed stride, maybe carrying a few books, smiling at the people he passed..."I wish I had more time to talk, but I'm nearly there, and I wanted to tell you what I found out."

"Right." Back to the task at hand.

"Okay, as far as I can tell, Keppra is only used to treat seizures."

So Harley didn't just have a sleep disorder. She had epilepsy. She must have been diagnosed after leaving her mom's house.

"And yes, people can die from epilepsy. It's called Sudden Unexpected Death in Epilepsy, or SUDEP. About one out of a thousand people die from it per year."

"Do they have any idea what causes it?"

"Not really. People with poorly controlled seizures are more at risk." It sounded like he was reading now. "As are those taking multiple anticonvulsant drugs and people who have long-standing chronic epilepsy."

"Hmm." That didn't really sound like Harley. "Any other risk factors?"

"Generalized tonic-clonic seizures—what they used to call grand mal seizures—and nocturnal seizures, and also—"

"Wait, night seizures?" That sounded like Harley.

"Right."

"Go on."

Matt continued reading: "Also, not taking medication as prescribed or stopping medication."

Harley's prescription bottle had been empty. "What does death from SUDEP look like?"

"Like natural causes. Even during an autopsy, they have to rule out every other cause of death. And of course, they have to know that the person had epilepsy."

"I think you may have just solved a mystery."

"Did someone die?"

"Two people did. But now it looks like just one was murdered." With this new information, I strongly suspected Harley died of SUDEP. Whoever was with her must have panicked and stuffed her in the closet.

"Murdered? I can't believe I have to hang up right after you tell me that. But—"

"But you need to take that exam. I understand. Break a leg, all right?"

"Yeah. And Ivy, be careful, okay?"

"I will."

CHAPTER 53

The Sneaking Way

"Consider yourself onboard," a voice sang. "Consider yourself one of the barnacles." David was giving another preview, singing the ensemble's song all by himself. Perfect. I'd grab him once he finished. I could find out if he knew about Harley's epilepsy *and* I could ask him to deliver a note to Bette. I'd planned to use Timothy as messenger, but considering what Oliver said, I thought it best to keep him out of the loop for a while.

David's preview would last a few more minutes. I found a little cubby next to the shore excursions desk and composed the note to Bette quickly, using paper and an envelope I'd snagged from the guest services desk.

"Dear Ms. Woodward," I wrote, "I found your phone. I thought about turning it into lost and found, but know there have been a number of thefts onboard and so decided it was best to return it to you personally. Please meet me in the back corner booth of the cigar bar at 4:30 p.m." I scrawled an illegible signature and added, "P.S. I apologize for sending this note via messenger, but am booked for a spa treatment. I've shown an employee a photo of you (from your phone) so that he'll deliver this note to the right hands."

Perfect. It sounded completely innocent on the surface, but hinted that the letter writer had been rummaging around on her phone. Bette would definitely show up. I sealed the envelope and tucked the note in my pocket just as David bowed to a smattering of applause. I joined the little group of people around him. "Nicely done, Dodge," I said. "Could you spare your Nance a minute or two?"

"Anything for you."

I smiled. "I'd Do Anything" was one of my favorite songs from the original *Oliver!*

"What is it, milady?" David said once his fans had left.

"Do you think you could deliver a message to someone for me?"

"Sure."

I handed him the envelope. "Her name's Bette Foxberry." I pulled her phone out of my skirt pocket and scrolled through the photos until I found a selfie. The photo showed a laughing Bette standing next to Uncle Bob, and the way he looked at her made my fillings hurt. "This is her." I showed the pic to David. "Or should that be 'she'? This is she?" I suspected my focus on grammar was my brain's way of distracting me from the hurt I was going to cause Uncle Bob. Necessary hurt, I reminded myself. He was in danger. "She's wearing a black blazer over a black and silver leopard print top and black pants," I told David. "She's probably with a big guy who looks like a rancher. I saw her about ten minutes ago by the Charles Dickens statue."

"Got it. Any message?"

"No. Please don't say it's from me, and it'd be best if you disappeared pretty quickly so you won't have to answer any questions."

David looked at me. I couldn't read his face.

"Oh." I pulled out a ten from my skirt pocket and handed it to him.

He pushed it away. "Just buy me a beer sometime. And Ivy," David regarded me with his fathomless black eyes, "I'm doing this because I like you and you seem cool, but I hope I'm not aiding and abetting or anything."

"I just want to talk to this woman in private, without the man she's with knowing about it."

I always felt better telling the truth, even if it wasn't the whole truth.

"All right." David tipped his ratty Dodger top hat and turned to go.

"Wait," I said. "Speaking of aiding and abetting." David's normally placid face began to cloud over. "No, nothing like that. It's just..." I told him how Ada had helped Oliver by letting him into our room to scare me. "I don't get her," I said. "Why does she hate me so much? Just because she wanted to play Nancy and I got the role?"

"That role was really important to her, but...Ada hates everyone. Women most of all. She's just...I don't know," he shrugged, "really unhappy, I guess."

"Was she mean to Harley too?" This was my way in.

"Yeah." David said it with a little chuff, as if it was a given. "She was horrible, spreading rumors about Harley."

"Like Harley was...easy?"

"Like she was a prostitute," said David. "Really bad stuff."

"But since Ada said things like that all the time, why would it matter? Why would anyone believe what she had to say?"

"Well, the prostitute thing happens, though it's usually men."

"Really?"

"Some single women like to have 'escorts.'" He shrugged. "But Ada's bitchiness, it was mostly because Harley was an easy target. She had a hard time speaking up, even if..." David shut his lips tight, as if to keep from saying anything more.

I needed to keep him talking. "Ada told me Harley was deranged."

"She was not." David's hands curled into fists. "She just had epilepsy. Is this the Middle Ages or something? God, Ada. She was just pissed off that Harley didn't have to have a roommate."

"Harley had that room because of her epilepsy?"

"Because her roommate complained, then started spreading rumors. The stupid bitch made it sound like drugs or something, so *Get Lit!* called Harley in. She told management what was really happening. They ended up giving her a room to herself for privacy. Probably also because they wanted to stop the drug rumors." David's hands relaxed, his anger spent. "I miss her."

"I'm sorry."

He shrugged off my sympathy. "I've got to go. Besides delivering this note, I've got stuff to do before the show tonight." He ran off.

A thought dropped into the pit of my stomach like a falling stage weight. The show tonight. I wasn't actually nervous about the play itself. It wasn't high art, I had my part down, and all my nerves had been around *Fagin's Magic Show* and the silks. Which someone had tampered with last night. Aye, there was the rub. I took a deep breath and shook off the heavy feeling. After all, I was just singing and dancing tonight on the nice safe stage in front of hundreds of people. No one would dare try anything. Right?

CHAPTER 54

Two Sister-Women

Bette looked more hunter than prey in her animal-print outfit. She strode into the bar, eyes darting around, hair swinging in a blonde curtain thanks to that expensive haircut. Which she probably got some man to pay for, one way or another.

Oh, c'mon, Ivy, I thought. You really have to stop this. Detectives need to be objective.

Screw that. She wasn't who she said she was, and she was after my uncle.

Bette caught sight of me as she made her way to the corner booth. Her eyes narrowed. "It's you," she said as she slid into the booth.

Seeing this was an assignation, I tried to channel 007. "It's me," I said, "but it's not you."

Bette's eyebrows drew together.

"I mean, you're not you. You're...someone else." Bette rolled her eyes. So much for Ivy Bond.

"Where did you find my phone?" Bette's rural accent was gone.

"It's not important."

"It is to me."

How did she get control of the conversation so quickly? "What's important is that you're pretending to be someone else. I bet there are lots of people onboard who would be interested to learn that information."

"I'm traveling under my real name, Bernadette Woodward—that's what's on my passport and on the ship's manifest—so I'm not doing anything illegal. And there's a good reason I'm Bette Foxberry during this cruise."

"Anything to do with Theo?"

Her face took on a calm look. It felt practiced, like "this is my not giving anything away" face. "Why would you say that?"

"Because you worked for him for years before he fired you for embezzlement."

"If you know that, you know the allegation was never proven." Bette's lips were set in a tight line. "And just why did you decide to Google me, or whatever you did?"

"I heard you arguing with Theo that morning when you said he ruined your life. Then when he was murdered—"

"Murdered?" Bette's face blanched under her bronzer. Her reaction looked real. But she was good. She even had my uncle fooled. I needed to remember that.

"Theo was poisoned," I said.

She sat back in the booth for a minute, taking it in. "I can't say I'm not happy he's gone," she said slowly. "He was a horrible man."

"That's what Madalina said."

"Madalina?" Bette's face grew even paler.

"Tell me. What was it about Theo's money?"

Bette kept quiet, but stretched her neck and rolled her head from side to side, as if she was trying to release some tension.

"You asked a question about it at Theo's book signing."

She still didn't say anything.

"Do you want your phone back or not?"

"Do you promise not to tell anyone about my two identities?"

I crossed my fingers under the table. "I won't, as long as you tell me why you need an alias." Of course I'd tell Uncle Bob. "And if you buy me a beer."

Although people think that actors can say anything, lying never came easily to me. The beer might help.

Plus I liked free drinks.

Bette flagged a waiter. "A Jack Daniels on the rocks for me, and a..."

"Guinness."

"For her. Make mine a double, please."

We didn't say anything for a moment. I was determined to make her speak first. But when she did, she said, "Did you steal my phone?"

"Maybe. But this conversation isn't about that." I mentally patted myself on the back for switching subjects fairly smoothly. "It's about your duplicity."

Bette sighed. "There are two reasons I used another name. I can tell you one of them."

"But—"

"This is the one that has to do with Theo."

I nodded my assent. I'd find out the other reason later.

"I used the name Bette Foxberry because I didn't want Theo to know I was onboard until we set sail. This was the perfect opportunity to confront him. He'd have to talk to me—there's nowhere to go. If he found out I was on the cruise before we sailed, I was afraid he might cancel his reservations."

"How would he have found that out?"

"Money greases every wheel." Bette stopped talking as the waiter arrived with our drinks. She took a big swallow of hers, then swirled the amber liquid. We both listened to her ice cubes clink for a moment. Then she said, "I grew up in a trailer in the desert just outside of Yuma. Dropped out of high school at sixteen when I got pregnant. It was probably good I lost the baby. I was pretty heavy into drugs then." She set down her glass. I took a big drink of my beer, mainly to keep my mouth occupied so I wouldn't say anything that would stop Bette from talking.

"I held minimum wage jobs 'til I was in my early thirties," said Bette. "Then I discovered Powerful Positivity. It turned my life around. First I just worked at imagining my potential, then I came to believe in it. I got my GED, went to community college, got my BA from Arizona State, and I did it all while working forty hours a week. When I graduated, I sent a photo of myself in cap and gown along with a note of thanks to Theo.

"He wrote me back and offered me a job working with his company in California. Can you imagine how I felt?" She looked at me for the first time since beginning her story. "I had nothing until this man's work turned my life around. Now he'd given me the opportunity of a lifetime. I was his biggest fan.

"I was also one of his biggest success stories. He liked to trot me out at conferences, that sort of thing. I didn't mind. After all, everything he said was true. Theo had changed my life. Plus he gave his Powerful Positivity workshops in fabulous cities all over the world. I got to travel to places I'd never even dreamed of.

"One day we were on a European tour when I was cc'ed on an email from one of our Eastern European colleagues. The message was innocuous enough, just details about our next stop in Dubrovnik, but it was part of a string of emails. I didn't remember receiving the others, so I read down the string."

She pulled her glass of whiskey back toward her and took a drink.

"You weren't supposed to be cc'ed on that email," I prodded.

"No, I was not. The correspondence was vague, but it mentioned purchases and shipping and large amounts of money. It also listed a time and place for a meeting. So I went."

I was beginning to understand what Uncle Bob saw in the woman. She had balls. If she was telling the truth.

"I'd begun to wonder where Theo's money had come from," she said. "He was rich years before he started his positivity crusade." Bette's eyes became unfocused, as if she was watching a scene playing on a screen I couldn't see. "After reading that email, I figured it was drugs." Her eyes grew wet. "It wasn't. It was—"

"Olive, goddammit!" Uncle Bob stormed into the bar. "This has got to stop. Did you take Bette's phone?"

"Sort of. I took—" I was about to say "*Bernadette*'s phone," but stopped. She hadn't told me everything yet. Plus, for some reason I was beginning to believe her.

"What is it with you two?" said Bette.

Uncle Bob said, "She's my nie—"

"Niece's third cousin," I finished. Wow, he must be whipped. He nearly blew our cover. "We're close."

"Didn't you say a few days ago that he knew your uncle?" Bette looked from Uncle Bob to me.

"It's a big family," I said.

"Why didn't you tell me?" she asked Bob.

I looked pointedly at Bette. "We all have our secrets."

"And you still have her phone," said my still-angry uncle.

"Shall we continue our conversation later?" I asked Bette.

Uncle Bob glared at me. "Olive, this better not be about—"

"It's not."

"Why does he keep calling you Olive?" Bette said to me.

"Ivy's a stage name."

"So you have two names?"

"Touché." I smiled at my worthy opponent. "And our conversation?"

"Let's finish it up later. How 'bout after the show? I'll even buy you another beer."

I handed Bette her phone. "Until then."

Uncle Bob, who had been watching us openmouthed, shook his head. "I'll never understand women."

CHAPTER 55

The Blood Chilled

I got dressed for the show, grabbed a quick dinner at The Best of Days, Wurst of Days, and texted my uncle on the way to the theater. I had three whole bars. Guess the stars were aligned in my favor— or at least the ship and the satellite were.

"Think I know how H. colored her hair," I texted. The hair color bit was code for "died."

"Not Bette?"

"No. It was natural. Sort of."

Big Ben bonged. I should have been at the theater by now. "More later." I took the stairs two at a time to the Pickwick Promenade deck and walked as fast as I could toward the Royal Victoria Theater.

I made my way through a knot of people waiting for the seven-thirty show. Some of the ambient characters from other books were working the crowd in front of the theater. I spotted a familiar costume: a brown vest over a white blouse, a brick red skirt, and a mob cap. How did they find a new Madame Defarge so quickly?

"It would be easier for the weakest poltroon that lives, to erase himself from existence, than to erase one letter of his name or crimes from the knitted register of Madame Defarge," said Harley's replacement in a loud voice. A familiar voice.

Ada's voice.

I had a few questions for my roommate.

Did this mean she was also playing Madame Defarge in *Great Expectations* in the spring show?

As Little Dorrit, Ada was just an ambient character—she didn't get to perform in a play. Madame Defarge would be a big step up. It'd look better on her resume and probably pay more. And did she know about Harley's epilepsy?

Could she be insisting that Harley was being pimped out just to throw me off the trail?

I had just minutes to get ready for the show. Ada would have to wait. I pulled open the stage door and bumped into Jonas. "I've been looking for you," I said. I had a few questions for him too.

"Later. We have all the time in the world." What did that mean? Jonas kissed me on the cheek, then turned away. "Break a leg, sweet pea."

"Wait." I wanted at least one answer. "You said something earlier, when you were, ah, celebrating."

"Can you believe I don't have a hangover?" Jonas said cheerily. "Maybe I'm still drunk."

Maybe. "Anyway, it's about Val. Why did you say he was unemployable?" That particular bit of information had lodged itself in my brain, like a popcorn kernel stuck to a tooth.

"Did I say unemployable? That wasn't nice at all. After all, it's not as if it's his fault. And it's not even true. Plenty of people—"

"Is it because he's not a U.S. citizen?"

"Because he can't read. English, at least. Maybe not at all. Not sure."

"Ivy!" Timothy skidded into me. "I need to talk to you."

"Better get ready first," said Jonas as he walked away. "They called fifteen minutes to places a while ago."

I steered Timothy the few feet to my dressing room. "Did you know Val can't read? Or can't read English?" The "unemployable kernel" had been replaced by a "can't read kernel." Something wasn't right.

"Yes, but—"

"I wonder how he memorizes his lines."

"He tapes them," Timothy said as I opened the women's dressing room door. "But, Ivy, my porn magazine. It's gone. I think someone stole it."

At the mention of porn, several techies turned around.

"Did you search Oliver?" I said.

"Ivy." Timothy grabbed me by the arms. "My porn magazine? *Inches*? The one with the, um, big white centerfold?"

Omigod. Someone had stolen our whiteboard. Our whiteboard that listed all the people we thought were criminals.

"What do we do?" said Timothy. "We can't let it fall into the wrong hands."

"You're right. It could scar those kids for life," I said before Timothy's loose lips sank our ship. "I'll see what I can find out. I need to get ready." And I needed to think. I pushed Timothy out of the dressing room and shut the door. I remembered what Oliver had said about Timothy teaching him to steal. It couldn't be true, could it? Was Timothy playing with me?

"Five minutes 'til places." The stage manager's voice came over the speaker in the corner of the dressing room. Thinking would have to come later. I looked in the mirror. I could be ready in five, since I was in costume. I just needed to fix my wig, which was slightly askew, and amp up my makeup for the stage. I sat down at the dressing room counter and took a big swig from the bottle of Gatorade I'd left there. It was warm and not very good. I made a mental note to get a new bottle for every show.

Okay, makeup. I reached for my kit. Huh. A small Russian nesting doll sat on the counter in front of my makeup kit. The same doll I'd received earlier? No, that still sat on the counter close to the mirror. Besides, that one was blue. This new one was painted in gray and black.

I was the only woman in *Oliver! At Sea!* so I was the only one who used this dressing room. The doll had to be for me.

I hurriedly stuck a few bobby pins in my wig, swiped on some lipstick, and drew in bolder eyebrows. It'd have to do. Then I picked up the doll and unscrewed it by the waist, doing the same for each successively smaller doll. I carefully looked for a scrap of paper each time. Nothing, until I got to the last, tiniest doll, and the Russian winter invaded my bones.

There was no note for me, but there was a message.

The last doll was beheaded.

CHAPTER 56

The Violent Current of Her Thoughts

"Places," crackled the dressing room speaker.

Shit. I gulped some Gatorade and ran out of the dressing room. I didn't have to be onstage for a few scenes, but several of us—David, Timothy, and I—sang backup vocals in the wings. I ran to where the others were gathered around a microphone on a stand. The click track started.

"Ooooh," I crooned into the mike. "Ooooh." It was a good thing the words weren't difficult because my mind spun like a muddied whirlpool. A thought swam to the surface: Was I in danger right now? I looked around me. Here, backstage, I was surrounded by my fellow actors and half a dozen techies. Onstage, I'd be in full view of the audience. I was safe—for now.

"Ahhhh," I sang. "Ahhhh." Other thoughts joined the first one, like debris caught in the whorls of a rapidly rising river. Why did it matter to me that Val couldn't read? What did Bette have on Theo? And who stuffed poor dead Harley in the closet?

"Ahhhh." Another idea started to surface. I was just about to grab hold of it when we reached the big finale. "Ohhhhhh!" The song ended with a blackout.

My first scene was next.

Time to replace my mind's muddied muck with Nancy's thoughts about criminals, thieves, and orphans. Huh. That last slippery idea bobbed to the surface again, but disappeared before I caught it. Good thing too, because the lights came up. I slipped into character and into Victorian London.

The ship didn't begin to leak until right before my death.

There was a blackout right before the scene to give the scrim time to drop down. That's when the water began to creep across the stage floor. It looked jellied. And alive.

"Aaahh! Val!" I whispered, pointing at the floor. My entire body clenched as the watery goo crept up to our ankles. I kicked at it. Something dark rose out of the water and bared its teeth at me.

"Val, help!" I hissed. The thing—an eel?—wrapped itself around my leg, slimy and strangling. "Help me!" I bit my lip to keep from screaming. I tasted blood.

Val's brow furrowed. "What is wrong?"

"The eel." I pried the creature off my leg. It released its grip with a wet sucking sound and flashed needle teeth before disappearing into the dark water—which kept rising. "The water! Everyone's going to drown. We have to do something."

The lights came up. The stage had buckled, its floor rising and falling in waves. I hurried onstage toward a dry spot in the middle. Safe. For now.

"Olive!" My mom's voice behind me. "*Olive.*" I turned. No Mom, just Val—and gelatinous seawater pouring down the backstage walls like an enormous waterfall.

"Mama!" Was it me who cried? No, a little girl, stage right, where sticky webs now covered the wall. "Help me!" The small shrouded figure struggled against its silken bonds. Oh God. I couldn't breathe, but took a step toward the child. As I did, many-legged shapes coalesced from the shadows. They started for me.

An arm grabbed me by the shoulder, cockroaches where its nails should have been, their insect legs wriggling against my neck. I screamed and Val pushed me to the floor, into the slimy sludge that now covered the stage. He raised his snake to strike me—his snake? The goo slithered over me, the spiders grew nearer, and I screamed again. Bill Sikes lifted his snake higher and his topcoat flew open. A glint of gold from an inside pocket, a glitter of ice. A diamond necklace?

"You're one of the thieves."

The necklace turned into sharp shiny teeth that gnashed as they came for me. I cowered on the floor, protecting my neck. "But you didn't kill Harley."

Bill's face crumpled. The snake dropped to the floor. The teeth backed off.

But the spiders didn't.

They swam toward me as the lights faded to black.

CHAPTER 57

With a Degree of Wholesome Fear

I opened my eyes. A slight sheen covered the ceiling. Flickering fluorescent lights made it quiver.

"Ivy?" said a familiar voice. "Are you awake?" Someone was holding my hand. Actually, two someones were holding both of my hands, one on either side of the bed. Bed? I blinked.

Jonas held one hand. Val, still in costume, the other. Their faces were shiny. Too shiny, like they were covered in a thin layer of Vaseline. I closed my eyes again. "Are we dead?"

"You just had a bad trip," said Jonas.

"Where?"

"We're not sure, but it wasn't nice. You're safe now. They gave you something to counteract the drug."

I opened my eyes. "What drug?"

"They think it was a Dramamine overdose. They've assured us you won't have any long-term effects, but you won't feel well for a while."

"You can say that," I wanted to say. But I couldn't. My tongue was stuck to the roof of my mouth. "Water," I croaked instead.

Val poured me a cup of water from a blue plastic pitcher near my bed. "Ivy, baby, I am so glad you are okey-dokey."

I drank the water down in one gulp.

"We are all glad," he said. "Even Oliver."

I held out my glass. "Please, sir, I want some—"

"You remember what happened?" Val said. "Anything?"

I shook my head. It was heavy with seawater, which sloshed in my ears. I reminded myself not to move for a while.

"They said you'd probably have some short-term memory loss," said Jonas. "But from what I heard you screaming about, that's probably a good thing. Swimming spiders." He shuddered. "I'm going to go tell everyone you're okay." He brought my hand to his lips, kissed it, and left.

"I stay," said Val.

I closed my eyes. Val gripped my hand again tightly. "You do not remember saying anything to me?"

I began to shake my head, then remembered the seawater. "No."

"You talked about Harley. How she died."

"SUDEP." Guess my memory loss was contained.

"Soodep?"

"Sudden...Unexplained Death...in Epilepsy."

"Epilepsy?"

"I think that's how she died. She wasn't killed."

"Thank God." Val kissed me on the cheek and a familiar aftershave filled my nose. I could somehow see it, curling up like lazy smoke inside my head, beckoning me to a soft dark place. I inhaled and drifted off on the scented current.

When I woke a while later, I was relieved to see that the ceiling wasn't glistening anymore. I did still smell aftershave, but it was different, spicier. Timothy, still in his Fagin costume, sat in a chair beside my bed, snoring gently. I turned my head to the other side. A small wheeled bed table held the blue pitcher and a glass. I picked up the pitcher gratefully, then nearly dropped it. Behind it sat another Russian nesting doll. I put the pitcher down and checked on Timothy. He slept on. I reached for the doll.

This nesting doll was painted in shades of red—definitely different from the first two. I slowly unscrewed it. The first doll with its "right track" message seemed to come from a friend. The second one, meticulously beheaded, was definitely not from a friend. Who was this from? I got down to the second-to-last doll, another smiling Russian woman, this one with a blood red kerchief. I rolled the wooden figure back and forth on my palm before opening it with shaking fingers. Yes. There was a note wrapped around the tiniest crimson doll. It said, "I will tell all. Meet me onstage at one o'clock this morning."

Did whoever write this think I was completely nuts? As if I'd drag my poor poisoned self to a deserted theater in the middle of the night. I might be curious, even nosy, but I wasn't an idiot.

"Hey," said Timothy. "You're awake."

I shoved the note under the covers and smiled at him.

"Where'd you get the doll?" He pointed at the figurine in my lap.

"I guess someone left it as a get well present," I said. "You didn't see who?"

"No, but I know it wasn't your uncle. He asked me to give you a message. Said he came down to make sure you were okay, but you were sleeping. He didn't think it would look right for your third cousin's uncle—do I have that right?—to hang around watching you sleep. Anyway, he loves you, is glad you're okay, and will talk to you when he can."

I put the doll back together. "Maybe Val left this. He's Russian."

Timothy yawned. "Could be. Could be anyone. They sell them in the gift shops."

"They do?"

"Yeah. Not sure why. Maybe *Get Lit!* had some left over from the *S.S. Anna Karenina*. I heard they're quitting the Tolstoy cruise and reconfiguring the ship. Everyone got too depressed."

The male nurse I'd met earlier when looking for the morgue came over and put his fingers on my wrist. He nodded in satisfaction. "Better. How do you feel?"

"Thirsty." I poured myself another glass of water. "And like my head wants to fall off."

"You'll have a hangover for a while. Dramamine is nasty stuff."

"How do you know that's what it was?"

"We're not completely sure, but we've seen a few cases of Dramamine overdose before. Usually kids trying to get high. Did you see spiders?"

Vague dark shapes crawled at the edge of my memory. "I don't want to think about it."

"Sorry, sorry. You'll probably feel some of the effects for a while, but you're okay now." He turned to Timothy. "Why don't you take your friend back to her cabin?"

I didn't really want to go with Timothy. I didn't really want to go with anyone except my uncle. Or Cody. Or Matt. Or even my mom and dad. But Timothy was already helping me out of bed. I was surprised to see that I was still in costume. I looked at the clock on the hospital wall. Midnight. I'd only been in the hospital a few hours. I took Timothy's arm and walked gingerly toward the door.

"Wait," called the nurse. "Don't forget this." He handed me the Russian doll.

CHAPTER 58

So Troubled with Anxiety

"What exactly happened?" I hung onto Timothy's arm for balance as we walked slowly back to my cabin.

"When you went onstage for your final scene, you started talking to Val about water and eels and drowning. You didn't start screaming until Bill Sikes killed you." Timothy pursed his lips, impressed. "Even drugged, you are a consummate actor."

"Not sure I can take credit for that."

"You didn't get up during the blackout, so a couple of us carried you offstage. You were terrified, thrashing around and whimpering about spiders." He shivered. "It was scary, hearing what was going on in your head. Jonas and few others got you to the infirmary right away."

"A Dramamine overdose. But how did...oh no. My Gatorade. It didn't taste right. But who...?"

"I think it was Oliver," Timothy said.

"Oliver? Why would he poison me?" The kid was a brat, but I didn't think he was malicious.

"I think it was a practical joke gone wrong. When they took you to the ship's hospital, he seemed subdued, maybe for the first time ever. The little shit."

"And he didn't say anything? The poltroon."

Timothy opened my cabin door with a keycard. I reached into my skirt pocket. My cell phone was there, but my keycard was gone.

I didn't remember giving it to Timothy. Maybe he got it from the nurse? "Poltroon?" he said. "Where did that come from?"

"I don't know." But I was pretty sure I did know. It was just that the thought lurked somewhere back in the far reaches of my consciousness among the spiders. "Thanks for bringing me down." I hugged Timothy. "I'll see you in the morning."

"You sure you should be alone?"

"I'm sure." I was also sure that I didn't want to be with anyone who might have tried to kill me on the silks and poison my Gatorade. And that included Timothy.

"Okay." He closed the door.

I sank down on my bunk. Poltroon. I was pretty sure it meant coward, but where had I heard it? It was right before the show. Yes, Madame Defarge said it. Ada. Who now had Harley's role. That seemed awfully convenient, but then the cruise probably needed a Madame Defarge more than a Little Dorrit, and they would've had to replace Harley from among the actors already onboard. Still...

Something else bothered me. As I reached back in my memory for Ada's pre-show Madame Defarge, a spider extended a leg out of its shadowy hiding place. I sat up and grabbed my library copy of *A Tale of Two Cities*. Maybe by reading I could find out what was bugging me while keeping any spiders at bay.

It took me a good twenty minutes to find the line in the book's five hundred and forty-four pages. There it was: "It would be easier for the weakest poltroon that lives, to erase himself from existence, than to erase one letter of his name or crimes from the knitted register of Madame Defarge." The knitted register, the knitted register, the knitted...scarf. The scarf Harley had been knitting, with the symbol of Russia and Valery's name crafted into the design. A knitted register. Harley was trying to tell us that Val was a criminal. I put the book down. But why? Why not just tell someone? What had David said about her? That she was...

I couldn't grasp the thought because another one invaded my mind. Harley and Val. There was another connection. I could just...smell it? Yes. Now I knew where I smelled Val's aftershave before. It was the same scent that had been in the bottle in Harley's bathroom, the aftershave I'd doused myself with after her death.

That's why Val seemed so relieved to hear that Harley's death was an accident. He'd said they were "buddy-buddy," but I was pretty sure they were more than that. Maybe Harley discovered that he was stealing and confronted him. He must have thought he'd killed her.

It all made sense, but I had no proof. I needed solid evidence, something like...jewels. A memory crawled toward the front of my mind—a necklace made of diamonds and teeth trailing out of Bill Sikes's coat pocket. The teeth bit pointed to a hallucination, but was part of that memory based in reality? And why would Val have stolen goods on him during the show? Oh. I remembered the crush of people waiting to get into the theater. Great opportunity for a pickpocket.

I leaned back on my bunk. What could I do? I didn't think I could search Val's costume. Besides, if he were smart, he wouldn't keep the jewels on him for very long. I picked up *A Tale of Two Cities* again. Maybe there was another clue in the story.

I began speed-reading the book, looking for anything that might jump out at me. Nothing.

The poltroon quote echoed in my head. Why? I'd figured out the knitted register bit. What else was bugging me? Poltroon. A poltroon was a coward...a coward...I closed my eyes and saw a highlighted passage in a book, something about being cowardly: "I was too cowardly to do what I knew to be right." Yes. The passage Harley had highlighted in *Great Expectations*. She must have struggled with the decision to give up Val. Now David's words came back to me: "She had a hard time speaking up, even if..."

Had Harley told David about Val? Maybe gave him some evidence? Or maybe there was another clue in that quote? I tried to remember the rest of the line to no avail.

I glanced at Ada's bookshelf. No Dickens, just a couple of travel books. No matter.

I could get a copy of *Great Expectations* from the library.

Oh. Oh, oh, oh.

I knew for certain Val was a thief. And I knew where he hid the jewels.

CHAPTER 59

No Better Place of Concealment

I ran softly down the hall. Correction: I tried to run. My legs still felt rubbery from the Dramamine, and the floor didn't stay quite still. So I sort of power-walked toward my destination.

I arrived and put my ear to the door. No voices. I slowly pushed open the door, peeping around it, just in case someone was inside and not talking. I couldn't see anyone, so I stepped inside the library.

I stood still for a moment, remembering the scene that night: Val, still in his Bill Sikes costume, telling me he was getting a book to help him fall asleep. Val who couldn't read English.

I padded to the place where he pulled out a book and closed my eyes, the better to see my memories. What book had he taken? Yes. *Our Mutual Friend*.

First I pulled out all the copies of *OMF*. I checked behind them and rifled through their pages. Nothing except a tale of money and greed.

Copies of *The Pickwick Papers* filled the bookshelf below. I had only gone through two of them when something slid to the floor. A passport. I shook the book and a driver's license fell out too. I quickly pulled out all the copies and shook them. Two others gifted me with several stolen documents. Yes. But where were the phones and the jewels? They had to be here. The diamond and teeth necklace gnawed at my memory.

Wait. The papers were hidden in *The Pickwick Papers*. I had no clue where to begin looking for phones since they weren't around during the Victorian era, but jewels...damn. I really wish I'd read Dickens more thoroughly. A lot of people wore jewels—Miss Havisham in *Great Expectations* for example—and there seemed to be thieves in nearly every book, even...I turned around and pulled out a copy of *Oliver Twist* from the standalone bookshelves. I flipped through it, trying to find the scene where Oliver sees Fagin hiding his booty.

There it was: Fagin stashed the jewels in a box in a hole in the floor. My heart sank. Ship's floors were made of metal, no way to dig a hole in them. Still, I halfheartedly tapped my foot around the floor in the area, listening for a hollow sound. Nothing.

Even so, I had a hunch I was on the right track. I slid *Oliver Twist* back in its place and pulled out another copy. Its weight shifted oddly, as if it were a box with a present inside. I opened the book and flipped through the first few pages. There it was, a hollow space in the book. Someone had glued the pages in the back half of the book together, cut a hole in the middle of them, and fit a small cardboard box into the hole. I pried off the lid with a thumbnail. Gold winked at me in the low light of the library. I drew out a heavy gold chain, a real Rolex, what looked to be a gold antique locket, and...

"You discovered my secret place." Val's hand gripped my right shoulder. I turned to face him. He was too close, and his creepy colored eyes were cold. "I follow you." He put his hands on my shoulders. It would have felt like an embrace if his hands weren't so close to my throat. "I thought you might remember what you said onstage, so I follow you."

A memory swam toward me. "I said you were a thief, didn't I? Did you have a necklace made of teeth and diamonds?"

"Teeth?"

"I didn't think so, but it seemed so real." I should be more scared than I was. Was it intuition, or just the leftover drugs dulling my responses?

"You remember what else you say?" Val backed me up against the wall of books. Now I was getting scared. "About Harley?" he said.

"Harley." My head hurt with the effort of thinking. "Harley was...she had epilepsy."

"Yes."

"I'm pretty sure that's why she died. She had night seizures?"

"Yes." Val's eyes looked at me but he was somewhere else.

"And she'd stopped taking her medication?"

"She ran out. She did not want anyone to know, so she did not get more prescriptions."

"And she found out you were the thief."

"One of the thieves."

"All of that combined—the type of seizure, stopping her medication, and the stress of knowing..."

"That I am criminal."

"Maybe. They don't exactly know why it happens—it's called sudden unexplained death for a reason—but it's somehow connected to the epilepsy." I looked at Val's faraway eyes and my heart went out to him, criminal or not. "Were you with her when it happened?"

Val gripped me harder, his mind back in the here and now. "Yes. I find scarf." Of course, the coded scarf. "Though I do not read, I know about Madame Defarge's knitting. I find scarf in her cabin. I see Russian bear and recognize my name. We fight, and she...she falls down. She shakes, and then stops. I go to her, but she...she was..."

"She was dead."

"But it was not my fault?" His grip was hard enough to hurt now.

"It wasn't your fault. She just died."

Val released me. "Thank God. Thank God."

I slid sideways toward the door, just a titch.

"No." Val grabbed me again. "Now we must talk about Valery the thief."

CHAPTER 60

With Desperate Determination

"I do not want to go to jail." Val's heavy brows knit together, shading his eyes. "But I think you tell police. What to do?"

I watched the shadows roll over Val's face and stayed quiet.

"I did not do much bad. The people I steal from, they are rich. They do not have to look in garbage for food. They do not sleep under bridges." Val stiffened. "They do not have to do bad things for money."

"Is that why you did it? For money?"

"No." He seemed amazed I would think such a thing. "I have good job now, food, place to sleep. I do it for family."

Do it, present tense. Did that mean Val was going to continue with his criminal ways?

"Or I thought I did. What you said about my cousin is true, I think."

"I'm so sorry." I was. Truly.

"I help him because he sends money back to his family. My family, I think. But now I know I have no family. My 'cousin,'" he spit the word out, "used me like everyone else."

"About that police thing..."

Val's eyes narrowed.

"If you gave up your cousin and the other thieves to the police, I bet you wouldn't serve much time." I really had no idea about sentencing, but it did sound likely.

"Really?" Val's eyes searched mine.

"I think so."

But...

Oh.

Shit.

I tried to hide the look on my face but obviously failed, because Val shook me by the shoulders. Not hard, just enough to remind me that he was capable of violence. "What?" He shook me harder. "What?"

"Theo. We'll have to explain Theo."

He stopped shaking me. "I do not understand."

I didn't either. How did Theo fit into all this? "Theo found you out, didn't he?"

"I do not think so."

"You didn't steal from him?"

Val shrugged. "I did not have time." He dropped his hands from my shoulders and looked at me, his eyes no longer cold, but soft and pleading. "You help me, Ivy? So I don't go to jail for long time?"

"I'll do everything I can. But Theo..." Theo had ruined Bette's career because she found out how he made his money. She said it wasn't drugs. Maybe it was jewels and stolen identities? "But you were planning to steal from Theo?"

"Sure. He was very rich."

Val wouldn't steal from one of his compatriots, right? So Theo wasn't in on the theft ring.

"Ivy?" Val brushed my face with the back of his hand. "Will you help me?"

What was Theo selling? Just then I remembered Madalina in the bar, her beautiful face ugly with hate. I saw her wineglass shatter. I heard her say to Bette: "Children? No!"

Theo sold children.

"Omigod." I wanted to simultaneously hug Val the motherless child and back away from Val the killer. "You were one of Theo's orphans."

"I do not understand." Val tilted his head to one side, his forehead wrinkling. He really did look like he didn't understand. Then again, he was a fine actor.

"Theo bought and sold children from Eastern European countries. You were one."

"No, I was not." The head tilt was gone, replaced by a clenched jaw.

"So you didn't kill Theo?"

"No. But I want to spit on his corpse."

"Were you the one who messed with the knot on my silk?"

"No." He pursed his lips. "I forgot about that."

"Did you just poison my Gatorade?"

"No. That was Oliver. He is—"

"Did you send me a beheaded Russian doll?"

Val's face blanched. "Ivy, you are in terrible danger."

"You are the thief—"

"One of the thieves."

"Who stuffed Harley in the closet."

"Yes, that was me. But I did not kill her."

"And it wasn't you who sent me a note saying you'd tell me everything if I met you onstage at one o'clock this morning?"

"No. It was not." Val's hands moved to his throat. "And I am sorry. This is for your good." He whipped off the scarf around his neck, grabbed my hands, pulled them behind my back, and tied them together tightly. He shoved me into one of the library chairs, kissed me full on the lips, and took off running.

CHAPTER 61

Make Haste!

I couldn't untie my hands. I tried. I gave up and struggled to my feet. I nearly lost my balance (damn Dramamine), but made it across the wavery floor to my next obstacle: the library door. The heavy door opened inward. How in the world was I supposed to pull it open?

My mushy brain went to work. The door had a lever handle—easier than a knob.

I tried using my mouth (I did say my brain was still mushy) but realized pretty quickly that wouldn't work. I turned around, placed my tied-up hands on top of the handle, squatted so that my hands pushed down the lever handle, then used my free fingers to grasp the door and pull it toward me. Not that hard once I figured it out.

Now I had to get to the theater. It should've been simple, but my mental state and tied-up hands made it slow going. I even took a wrong turn and ended up in the casino. "Hi," I said to the few folks who were still up gambling. "Could someone untie me?"

An older man with silver hair leapt to his feet. "Of course," he said as he loosened my hands. "Are you okay? What happened?"

"Oh, just playing a little game." I winked at him. "And my boyfriend fell asleep. Too much vodka."

"Ah." The gent reddened, cast a glance at a white-haired woman playing Nickleby's Nickel Slots, and fingered the neckerchief he'd just untied. "Would you mind if I borrowed it for the evening?"

"Keep it. And thanks," I said as I scooted out of the room. On to the theater. I pulled my cell phone out of my skirt pocket as I race-walked down the hall (running was still not an option). I punched in Uncle Bob's number on speed dial. As soon as he picked up, I said, "Valery's one of the thieves, but he didn't kill Theo. He ran off to meet the real killer onstage. Meet me there ASAP."

"Ivy?" said a familiar voice. Not my uncle's.

"Timothy?" Shit, I dialed wrong. "I was trying to call Uncle Bob. Call him and tell him what I said, okay?"

"I don't have his number."

"Figure it out." I hung up. The theater doors were right in front of me. How should I do this? Enter backstage, to begin with. Much more discreet.

I went as quickly as I could to the backstage door and was just about to open it when a thought struck me. Val kept saying, "one of the thieves." Oliver had said Timothy taught him to steal. Had I just called the killer and told him my plans?

My seawater-and-spider-web-filled brain wasted precious seconds trying to figure out what to do, until raised voices from inside the theater prompted me to move. I quietly pushed open the stage door and slipped behind one of the black velvet curtains.

"I know how you feel." Val's voice. "I am orphan too."

Too?

"I do not think you know," said Madalina.

Shit, I was right. I just had the wrong orphan.

"I do not feel," she said. "That is why I can kill."

Even my web-filled brain knew that was a threat. What could I do? I looked around for a weapon. Everything backstage was locked up tight. I looked above me. I had it. I padded silently to the ladder that led to the catwalk and climbed up.

"Maybe I teach you to feel," said Val.

I stole onto the catwalk. The two of them faced off below me onstage. Something glittered in Madalina's hand. A knife?

"You teach me?" Madalina tried to sound cynical, but I heard the plea underneath. Then she laughed, a hard bitter sound. "No. We are not the same. Maybe it was the time I spent in dark rooms. Or the cigarette burns. Or..." Even I heard her swallow. "Or the men."

I crept to the place where my silk was looped up out of sight.

"Where there is life there is hope," said Val.

"Ha. You sound like Theo: 'Think positive and all will be good.' Do you know what he said when I told him I knew about the children? He believed he was giving them better life. And because he believed, it must be so. His power of positivity would keep them safe." She snorted. "Even as he handed little girls over to bad men."

I tugged on the knot in my silk and tried to remember how many carabiners to check.

"So you killed him?" Val said.

"I did. I did not feel bad. I hoped I would. When I heard what he did with children, my heart cracked. It hurt, but it was feeling. I thought my heart was healed, that I feel again when I kill Theo. But I did not. And I do not want to go to jail, so I must kill you. And Ivy."

I unlooped my silk.

"You are going to kill me with that knife? I am too strong for you."

"I thought you would be Ivy and I would surprise her. But do not worry. I have seen much in my life. I know other ways to kill. You and she, you are dead by morning."

"No." Valery started toward her, his hand held out. "It is over. Give me the—"

"Ivy!" Timothy flew in the backstage door. Val turned to see, Madalina lunged at his back with the knife, and I jumped off the catwalk and into the air.

CHAPTER 62

A Brief Reputation for Undaunted Courage

"Did so," Timothy said.

"Did not," I said.

"Did so."

"Kids, could you stop arguing about whether Ivy yelled like Tarzan and tell me exactly what happened?" Uncle Bob had arrived with Bette just seconds after Timothy's entrance. We were all still onstage waiting for security to take Madalina and Val to the brig.

"I swung down on my silk," I said.

"And she gave a Tarzan yell."

"Did not."

"Did so."

"Are you guys like five years old?" said Uncle Bob. "Cut it out."

Mr. Brick Bungalow from security walked in. His eyes got big when he saw me.

I said to Uncle Bob, "So I swung down and hit Madalina."

"It hurt." Madalina rubbed her neck.

"Hello? You were going to kill me and Val."

"Yes. Okay." She shrugged.

"And when Madalina fell, the knife flew out of her hands," I continued.

"Nice work," said Val.

"Thank you."

Uncle Bob sighed.

"And then Timothy charged onstage—"

"Charged. Has a nice manly sound to it," said Timothy.

"And wrapped up Madalina in duck tape."

He'd done a pretty decent job of it, too. She sat on the stage like a duck tape-trussed goose.

"I keep a roll of it handy now," said Timothy. "Just like Ivy."

"You keep a roll of duck tape handy?" Brick asked me. I remembered his dog collar and declined to answer.

"Timothy tried to duck tape Val," I said. "But I stopped him."

"It was smart," said Val. "I would punch him."

"I thought I should subdue him since Ivy said he was the thief," Timothy said to Uncle Bob.

"One of the thieves," Val said.

"About that," I said.

"Later," said Uncle Bob. "So you stopped Timothy from subduing Val because..."

"Because Val was trying to protect me," I said. "And because except for maybe wanting to punch Timothy, Val isn't dangerous."

"What about Harley?"

"Pretty sure she died because of her epilepsy."

"Sudden unexplained death in epilepsy." Val sounded as if he'd committed the words to memory.

Bette, who had been silent up to now, said, "And Valery didn't kill Theo." It didn't sound like a question.

"No. I am not killer. I am thief. Also lover." Val slid closer to me.

"I am killer," said Madalina. "But I do not care. Theo deserved to die."

"You used the vaping liquid, didn't you?" I asked.

"Yes. I put some in his drink and pour some on his mask."

"Were you one of Theo's orphans?" Bette asked gently.

"I do not think so."

"But you killed him because of the children?" said Bette.

"I kill him *for* the children. Now maybe more can feel."

I nodded. Bob and Brick looked at me.

"I'll explain later," I said.

"Me too," Bette said.

"I will explain now," Val said. He told everyone about how he'd been duped by his fake cousin. "I thought I steal to help my family. But I have no family." He shook his head sadly.

"You kept saying you were 'one of the thieves.' What did you mean?" I glanced at Timothy, who was twirling his roll of duck tape around his finger and looking as unlike a thief as you could get.

"There are ten, maybe more, on this ship," said Val.

"You know who they are?" asked Uncle Bob. Timothy still looked innocent. Pretty sure I had that one wrong.

Val shrugged. "Sure."

"You willing to give them up?" said Uncle Bob.

Val's eyes traveled the darkness above the stage. "I think they know Nikolay is not my cousin. Some even tell him about my eyes. They let me think I steal for family, when I do not have any." He brought his gaze down to meet mine. "I give them up. "

"Time to go then," said Brick, hauling Madalina to her feet.

"One more question," I said. "Val, the rest of the booty is hidden in the library, right?"

"Booty. Ha." Val slapped my ass.

"I'm serious."

"Yes. Look for the ugliest books."

Ah. The books where I found the stash were dog-eared with scarred covers. "Is that why you thought no one would find the stuff? Because people only check out the best-looking books?"

"No one likes ugly books. Also," he said as he followed Brick out the backstage door, "most guests don't check out Dickens's books. They like BBC DVDs."

CHAPTER 63

The Foulest and Most Cruel

I was quiet as I followed Uncle Bob and Bette down the hall, partly because I was distracted by the way my feet sank underneath the surface of the carpet (was this Dramamine stuff ever going to wear off?), but mostly because life felt particularly unfair. Madalina and Val had nightmare childhoods and now they were going to prison.

My companions were quiet too, but right before we came to Bette's cabin, Uncle Bob stopped and turned to her. "I guess you've figured out that Olive isn't my niece's third cousin." Bette nodded. "She's my niece." Another nod. "And my employee." Bette didn't nod this time, but raised her chin in a question. Uncle Bob sighed. "I'm not Bob Stalwart and I'm not a rancher. I'm Bob Duda, private investigator. Olive and I were hired to find out the story behind all the thefts onboard this line." He looked at Bette, whose eyes were downcast. "I'm really sorry I lied to you. Please. Say something."

He'd just given Bette the perfect opportunity to come clean about her real identity. But she kept her eyes averted as she swiped her keycard in the cabin door lock. "Come in." She opened the door.

Bette guided us to the cabin's loveseat and sat in an armchair across from us. No one said anything for a minute. We needed to talk, but how to start the conversation without putting any of us on the spot? I began by telling them about Madalina, what she meant when she said she wanted to help the children feel, about how she shut down her emotions in order to survive.

"It's not just her," said Bette. "Many children raised in orphanages grow up without the ability to form emotional bonds." Bette had dropped her accent. Uncle Bob didn't seem to notice. All his attention was focused on her face. "Those who grew up in the really awful places in Romania and Eastern Europe had it especially bad," she continued. "A lot of them have severe reactive attachment disorder. Some never learned to function outside an institution." This vocabulary didn't belong to the Bette we knew, but my uncle seemed unfazed. "Many grew up without a sense of right and wrong. They were often beaten, and whoever was strongest was the 'winner.' I should have thought more carefully about all that before I talked to Madalina, but I was so angry with Theo."

"What exactly did you tell her?" I asked.

"That Theo was selling children. He had been for years. Called himself an adoption broker. Pretended he was giving children better lives. Or maybe he convinced himself, I don't know. He started with the Rumanian orphanages. Moved on to a wider area. Then he started buying children from their parents."

"You found this out when you were on that trip with Theo? When you thought he was selling drugs?"

She nodded. "Remember when I said I found out about a meeting? I followed Theo to the poorest section of town. His contact met him in a tavern, then took him to an apartment building, a horrible bleak place, concrete blocks held together by mold. I watched from a hiding place below. The building's doors all opened onto outside walkways, so I saw Theo and his contact go into several apartments. Each time they came out, they emerged with a child, who was handed off to another person who led her— they were mostly girls—to a white van. Six children in all. And that was just that one apartment building."

Bette stood up and paced. "It took years before I had enough evidence to expose Theo. I came on this cruise to give him one more chance to repent before I exposed him. After all, he was rich. He could start to fix some of the damage he'd done, maybe fund a foundation or give the money to legit adoption agencies. But when I told him I was going to tell the world about his dirty secret, he just laughed at me. 'Who's going to believe you?' he said.

"He was wrong about that, but I couldn't wait. So I started poisoning the well close to home. I told Madalina first." She shook her head angrily. "I'm not sorry Theo's dead, but I am sorry it was her who killed him."

She sat down. I waited. Nothing. What was up with this woman? She sounded like some sort of avenging angel, but how could we trust anything she said if she was pretending to be someone else? I couldn't stand it any longer. "Don't you have something else to tell us? About your name?"

She looked at her lap. "Yeah. Um. I'm not really Bette Foxberry."

The color went out of Uncle Bob's face.

"I'm Bernadette Woodward, but you might know me better under another name."

"Wait," I said. "You have *three* names?"

"Sometimes I need to go undercover."

"Don't tell me you're a PI too," said Uncle Bob.

"When Theo fired me, I finally knew what I really wanted to do, to make sure that creeps like him didn't get away with murder. I'm not the cop type, and I didn't want to study law, so I went back to school and became an investigative journalist. Then I started my own online news site, 'All Bets Are Off.'"

I was speechless. "All Bets Are Off" was huge—the biggest investigative news website in the country, if not the world. They broke big stories about corruption in government and corporate misdeeds and hushed-up environmental disasters.

"I write under the name Bernie Woodard. Sort of a nod to the real guy." Bette turned to me. "You know, from Watergate? Woodward and—"

I gave her an "I'm young but I'm not stupid" look. She shut her mouth.

"So you're not really an oil widow," said my uncle, shaking his head in wonder. "Had me fooled."

She shook her head. "Bob, I'm really sorry."

Suddenly Uncle Bob laughed. "Bette. *Bette.* From 'All Bets Are Off.'"

"Gotta love a little pun." She smiled hesitantly.

"This is great!" Uncle Bob jumped up and grabbed both of us. "See, Olive was right. You *were* suspicious. I mean, this whole time you were pretending to be somebody else. Sort of like an actor." He slid a look at me. "And I was right, because you are a good person. A good woman." The top of his cheeks flushed light pink as he looked at Bette.

"And a member of the media." I wasn't willing to give up the fight just yet.

"An investigative journalist," said Bette. "Note the adjective. It's not unlike—"

"Yeah, yeah, I get it," I said. "You're like an actor and a PI." Now I gave up the fight. I had to. I had a grudging respect for the woman. And Uncle Bob was looking at her like she was his favorite sandwich *and* a beer.

CHAPTER 64

Restored to Pleasant Company

I met the two lovebirds for a late breakfast the next morning. I'd just sat down at their table with a blood pudding-free breakfast (I was still out of sorts) when my cell rang. I looked at the display.

"My parents," I said to Bob and Bette. Wait, my parents? They never called. "Oh crap." I picked up, putting the phone on speakerphone so Uncle Bob could hear too. "Is everything okay?"

"Hello to you too. Everything's fine," said my dad. "Just wanted to call and let you know that. And to thank you for helping Cody."

I hadn't really helped Cody, but a "thank you" from my parents was so rare that I wanted to keep it. "Thank *you* for going down there. Matt said you were the ones who got Cody into Costco."

"Cody called us from there. They wouldn't let him in after hours, so we explained the situation and they let him in. So, you're on a ship?"

Another one for the books. My parents never took an interest in what I was doing. "Yeah. But I think Uncle Bob and I are wrapping up this job."

"Good," said my dad. "We'd like to take you to dinner when you get back."

"Me too," said Cody's voice behind him.

"You too," said my dad. "See you soon, Olive. Love you."

I stared at the phone.

I hadn't heard that since...since before Cody's accident. My throat felt thick.

"Olive-y!" Cody had picked up the phone. "Are you coming home soon? I miss you. And we get to go to the Old Spaghetti Factory when you get here. When are you coming?"

"In just a few days." We'd arrive in Honolulu today, cruise the islands, and then fly home.

"Good. I love you. Hey, did you want to talk to Olive-y?" he said to someone there.

"I love you too," I said before I realized Cody was off the line. It didn't matter. What did matter was the way my heart warmed at the thought of him.

Val and Madalina never had this, never felt this rush of love. Yeah, my parents had been horrible to me since the accident, but they had also given me Cody. And to be fair, they'd given us a good childhood. I hadn't realized how good until now. I suddenly wanted to be off the ship and back in Phoenix right away, to see my beautiful brother and maybe hear "I love you" from my dad again.

"Ivy?" It was Matt. "I've been worried about you."

"You have?"

"Last time we talked, you said something about a murder. And you haven't been answering your calls."

"Bad cell connection." I'd tell him about getting overdosed, catching a thief, and clonking a killer later.

"Okay. Glad you're all right. Enjoy Hawaii."

"You don't sound like you mean that."

"I am very glad you're all right."

"About Hawaii, I mean."

"Busted. I'd rather have you back here."

"I'll let you know as soon as I'm in town. It'll be good to be home. See you soon." I hung up to find Uncle Bob and Bette sharing a smile. "What?" I said.

"That guy on the phone," said Bette. "Sounds like a real nice guy."

"One of the best," said Uncle Bob.

My cell bleeped: a text from Jonas. Reception had stayed surprisingly good, probably because we were nearing port in Hawaii. "Need to talk to Val about our future plans. Meet me at the brig in an hour?"

"Sure." Needed to squelch that whole our-future-plans thing. "See you guys later," I said to Bob and Bette. "I need to freshen up before I meet Jonas at the brig."

"I'll probably see you down there," said Bette. "I want to talk to Madalina." Bette was going to release Madalina's story in a few days *and* she was putting together a defense fund for her. I guess Uncle Bob was a pretty good judge of character after all.

"Brig," he said. "Did you know that's not just an onboard jail? It's also a type of two-masted ship."

"Did you know," said Bette, "that our ship's brig, the Marshalsea Prison, was named after the debtor's prison in *Little Dorrit?*"

"Which was based on the one that Dickens's family was sent to," said Uncle Bob. They grinned at each other. A match made in heaven.

I went back to my cabin. I'd only slept about five hours, so my idea of freshening up included closing my eyes for a few minutes. But as soon as I opened the door, I knew that wasn't going to happen. Ada filled the cabin, both literally (her clothes were everywhere) and figuratively (her anger bounced off the walls).

"What's going on?" I asked.

"Like you don't know. They're putting me off in Honolulu." She balled up a dress and stuffed it into a suitcase. "Oliver can get away with anything, but I play one—maybe two—harmless pranks, and that's it. Good riddance, Ada."

"Harmless pranks?"

"Come on. You know that knot would've never come untied. It was just meant to slip."

"The silk knot."

"Duh. And stupid old Harley would never have even sprained her wrist if she'd used good technique." Ada grabbed a duffle bag and swung it up to my top bunk, missing my head by inches.

"Alrighty then. Good luck," I said, backing out of the cabin. "Guess I'll head down to the crew bar." I closed the door just before Ada's suitcase hit it.

I did go to the bar, just because I could, but had a cup of coffee at the counter. I'd just stirred some sugar into my cup when a hand placed a Russian nesting doll in front of me. I turned to see David. "For you," he said. I unscrewed the yellow doll until I found a scrap of paper wrapped around the tiniest doll. It read, "Nice work."

"Thanks. So the first doll was from you?"

Madalina had told me the other two nesting dolls were from her. She got the idea when she went to my dressing room to leave me a "back off" note and saw the first doll. "I come up with doll with no head by myself," she'd said with misplaced pride "Scary, yes?"

David sat down on a barstool. "Yeah, it was me. I wanted to encourage you to find out what happened to Harley. I really liked her—she was one of my best friends onboard—but things changed when she started going out with Val. He didn't kill her?"

"No," I said. "Sudden Unexplained Death in Epilepsy,"

David was quiet for a moment. "Val didn't seem like a killer, but from watching him, I was pretty sure he was in on the theft ring. I didn't have any proof though. It seemed like you were getting close to the truth, so I sent the nesting doll as a sort of clue."

"That I was on the right track with the Russian thing."

"Yeah. I had no idea it would be so dangerous. I'm glad you're okay."

"Just part of the job," I said in a tough guy voice.

"About that. I'm confused. Are you an actor or a detective?"

"Both," I said. "I'm both."

CHAPTER 65

How Things Come About!

A little while later, I made my way to the bowels of the ship and the onboard jail. I really hoped Jonas hadn't put too much stock in any kind of future with me. Sure, he was sweet, good-looking, and now incredibly rich, but he just wasn't for me.

I slowly pushed open the door of the Marshalsea Prison. Jonas talked quietly with Val, who stood behind the iron bars of a Victorian-looking jail cell.

A similar scene played out a few yards away, where Bette huddled outside Madalina's cell.

"Ivy!" said Jonas and Val, almost in unison as I walked toward them.

"Perfect timing." Jonas put an arm around my shoulder, while Val looked longingly at us throughout the barred wall that separated the free from the imprisoned. "I have something to say that concerns you both. Ivy, you know how I've been talking to you about our future?"

"Actually, I wanted to ask you about—"

"I mean, since you helped me get Theo's money, it's only fair that—"

"*I* helped you get Theo's money?"

"You certainly did. That kiss on deck during the captain's dinner? It was just what I needed to convince Theo I'd been cured of my 'moral weakness.'"

"Gluhh," I said, not because I was disappointed that Jonas was gay—au contraire—but because, once again I was wrong about someone.

"Oh, Ivy." Jonas squeezed my shoulders. "You never thought I was interested in you, did you? Romantically, I mean? I just assumed you knew."

Oliver's mom burst into the room, towing her little rat by the arm. "I want you to lock him up," she said to the security guy (thankfully not Brick this time). "He just broke the straw on the camel's back."

"It's about time," I said to her. "That Dramamine overdose could have been serious, you know." A big waterlogged spider crept out of the corner of my mind. I swept it away with a shake of my head.

"Drama-banana-meene," Oliver said.

"That's not Dickens," I pointed out.

"We're not here because of that," said Oliver's mother, who again wore horizontal stripes. This knit top was black and white. She looked like an overfed zebra.

"Maybe it's because of all the stuff he stole?" I said. "Or the vandalism?"

The security guard looked back and forth between the two of us, waiting.

"That was all in preparation for his role." His mother stood up straight.

"My poisoning too?" I said.

"Dickens's characters poisoned people," said Oliver.

"None of that. It's this." She grabbed a magazine from her bag and flung it to the floor. *Inches.* Timothy's porn magazine. The one where we'd hidden the "whiteboard."

"Lock him up." She pushed Oliver toward the security office. "I'm sure it's illegal for young children to possess pornography. And while you're at it, I think you should arrest whoever gave this to my son."

"Yes. Arrest Fagin," said Oliver. "He's a criminal."

I grabbed the little bugger by the arm and wrangled him to a corner. "I won't press charges for the Dramamine overdose if you're straight with me about one thing," I whispered fiercely.

"Press charges?" Oliver's face puckered in perturbation. It would have been cute if he wasn't such a snot.

"Even though you're a minor, and even if you didn't mean your prank to go as far as it did, it's still assault, and enough to send you to juvie." I sounded sure even though I had no idea.

"Okay. What one thing?"

"Is Timothy a thief? Did he really teach you how to steal?"

A smarmy smile spread across Oliver's face. "I never said that."

"Yes, you did. When we were talking on deck, right after—"

"I said *Fagin* taught me to steal. Can't you tell when an actor's in character?"

I pushed him back toward the jailer. "Lock him up."

Oliver whined. "But you said—"

"I lied. They do that in Dickens."

The security guy pursed his lips. I winked at him and he looked to Oliver's mom, who nodded.

"Good thing we've got one place left." He led Oliver to a cell. "You can come get him in an hour, ma'am," he said quietly to Oliver's mom.

"I'm not sure I will." She swept out of the brig.

"Wait, what?" Oliver's face turned red as the jailer locked him behind bars. The entire jail erupted in a cheer.

I turned back to Val and Jonas. "Boy, that felt good."

"Yes, very nice. Can we talk about our future?" said Val. "I want to know I have one."

"Right," said Jonas. "Now that I have Theo's money, I can produce my play."

"*Oliver! At Sea!?*" I said.

"Lord, no. Haven't I told you about it?" Jonas said. "I could have sworn I did."

I shook my head.

"For the last year, I've been working on a farce-slash-murder-mystery called, wait for it..." Jonas held his hands with a flourish. "*Grave Expectations.*"

"Wow," I said.

"I know. I think it'll be big." Jonas twiddled his fingers in excitement. "And there are perfect roles for you both. Val would play Pep, and Ivy, you'd be Esmella."

Maybe I could talk him out of that later.

"I had planned to workshop the show in L.A., but..." Jonas turned to Val. "I suspect the judge will go easy on you, but you'll probably serve some time. And I know how hard prison is, especially on creative types."

Val hung his head.

"*But,*" Jonas bounced on his toes, "you've heard about Shakespeare Behind Bars? I'm going to mount *Grave Expectations* in prison. Starring you, of course." Val's mouth dropped open. "It'll give you something to hang onto while you're inside," he said to Val. "It'll look great to the parole board, and who knows, maybe you'll even be famous by the time you get out."

"Why?" Val backed up, like a child who was afraid to take a present for fear it'd be yanked away. "Why you do this for me?"

Jonas stopped bouncing. "I understand you better than you know. I didn't know my father. My mother was stoned for most of my childhood. I haven't heard from her in years. The only other family I had was my stepfather, and you saw how he was. After everything I've gone through with my relations, I decided that my friends are my family. 'Family not only need to consist of merely those whom we share blood, but also for those whom we'd give blood.'"

"It's Dickens," Oliver whispered from his cell.

Val pressed his lips together, his Adam's apple working.

Jonas wrapped his hands around the bars that separated Val from him. "Sound good, brother?"

Val swallowed. "Yes. Okey-dokey." He smiled. "Brother."

*   *   *

Later, I waved to Jonas as he zipped away on the back of a Harley, his arms around the big bearish guy in front of him. "My Hawaii husband," Jonas had said. "I don't dally onboard, but I do have a man in every port."

I wove through the chattering tourists and joined Timothy, Bob, and Bette at a table under a thatched umbrella. I listened to them debate the best way to get sand out of your shorts. I sipped a cold slushy Blue Hawaiian, complete with a slice of fresh pineapple and a pink cocktail umbrella. I breathed in the warm humid air, perfumed with salt spray and flowers and a whiff of coconut tanning lotion. I watched happy bronzed people run across the white sand and splash in the surf. It was truly a tropical paradise. And it was all wrong.

After two deaths and sending two people I liked to jail, I wasn't in the mood for sand and surf and drinks with little umbrellas. "I want to go home."

"You're kidding, right?" said Timothy. "The islands are the best part of the cruise."

"Nah. I don't really like cruising. All that water." I felt like I'd worked through my phobia, but still, dry land felt wonderful. "We're done here, right?" I asked Uncle Bob. "Job-wise?"

"Yeah. And there'll be a nice bonus waiting for us."

"Great. Then I want to go see my family." I smiled at Bette, leaned down and kissed Timothy on his hairy cheek, then bussed my uncle on the top of the head. "Besides you guys, I mean."

CHAPTER 66

Home Again Straight

After eight hours of traveling and stops in San Francisco, L.A., and Yuma, I finally arrived at Sky Harbor and dragged myself to baggage claim. Staring at the carousel in a daze, I felt a tap on the shoulder.

"Olive-y?"

I turned around. "If it isn't Brad Pitt," I said as I hugged Cody. He did look like the film star—tall and blonde and handsome. Plus open-mouthed.

"I wasn't sure it was you," he said, still gawping after our hug. "Your hair. It's...it's..."

"It's sexy hair," I said.

"I think so." Matt, a few inches shorter than my brother, smiled at me over his shoulder. "Welcome home."

I felt it then, when Matt smiled. Home.

"But how did you know when I was getting in?"

"Uncle Bob told us," said Cody.

"Those are my suitcases." I pointed at two bags now customized with gold polka dots, courtesy of a metallic Sharpie.

Matt grabbed the bags off the carousel. "A matched set. Nice."

On the way home, I sat with Cody in the backseat. "Since it's almost midnight, I'm going to drop Cody off first." Matt met my eyes in the rearview mirror. "Then I'll take you to your apartment. Sound good?"

"Sounds wonderful." I leaned back against the seat and closed my eyes.

Cody punched my arm. "No way. You can't go to sleep before you tell us about your case."

I gave the two of them the shortened version of my adventures, ending with Jonas's idea about a prison theater production. "Cool," Cody said. Matt didn't say anything, but then again, he was driving. He turned into the Coronado neighborhood. Cody's group home was just a few blocks away.

"Now it's your turn," I said to Cody. "I want to know everything about Stu and—"

"I already told you everything."

"Nuh-uh." I could finally ask Cody the question that had plagued me ever since he had disappeared. "Where did you sleep all those nights when you were gone?"

"In Uncle Bob's garage."

Phew. Uncle Bob's nice safe garage.

But wait. "How did you get in? Didn't he lock the doors?"

"Yeah." Cody managed to swagger, even sitting down. "But I remembered that video you showed me. 'How to Break into a Garage in Sixty Seconds.'"

Research for a case, I swear. "You remembered that?"

"I watched it on the computer at our house a couple of times. Stu too. He helped me practice."

"On our garage?" said Matt, pulling in front of the group home.

"Cody." I hugged my brother. "You may be shaping up to be a criminal, but you're a hero to me."

"And Stu," Matt said. "And me."

"I'm not a hero. Or a criminal." Cody let me go, done hugging. "I'm a detective."

Must run in the family.

I switched to the front passenger seat for the ride to my apartment, leaning back against the headrest and watching the streetlights flicker across Matt's face like moonlight on a lake. We rode in companionable silence until he parked in my lot. "I'll walk you to your door."

"That'd be nice."

We got out and he grabbed my suitcases out of the trunk. Matt was quiet as we climbed the Astroturf-covered stairs to my second-floor apartment. When we got to my place, I unlocked the door and turned to thank him.

He put down my bags. "Ivy." The porch light glinted off his glasses, so I couldn't see his eyes, but his voice sounded serious. "This prison theater thing sounds like a great project, but it's not here in Arizona, is it? You'd have to leave, right?"

"It's not in Arizona," I said, "but I don't think I'll take it. I want to stick around here for a while."

"Good." Matt stepped closer, but he didn't pick up my bags.

The air was suddenly filled with electricity, like before a thunderstorm, but I went on, "In fact, I think I'm going to recommend Candy. She's not the same type as me, but she's a great actress and—"

I couldn't say any more because Matt's lips were on mine and his arms were around me and he was *kissing* me and I was kissing him back and oh. Oh. *Oh.*

We finally stopped to breathe. Matt's face, that face I'd known but never really seen, was just inches from mine. Heat and joy flooded my body. Matt cupped my face in his hands. "Ivy, should we—"

I placed a finger on his lips, opened the door to my apartment, and took him by the hand. "Please, sir," I said. "I want some more."

Reader's Discussion Guide

In *Oliver Twisted*, author Cindy Brown takes readers on a literature-themed cruise filled with characters influenced by Dickens's famous novels. Ivy Meadows, actress and part-time PI, has to navigate this new world of thieves and orphans while working with her detective uncle to expose a theft ring. The job is tougher than she expected: in her undercover role as an actress, she has just days to learn to perform on the aerial silks; her uncle is sidetracked by a suspicious blonde; and her brother in Phoenix has given her a long-distance mystery to worry about. As always, Ivy's world is slightly screwball, but in *Oliver Twisted* she also explores the definition of family, and of criminal behavior.

Topics and Questions for Discussion

Would you like to take a literature-themed cruise? What book or author would you choose to cruise with? What details would you like to see included—which characters, what types of food, what types of activities?

Why do you think the author chose a cruise ship as the setting for *Oliver Twisted*? What other settings might reflect the world Dickens wrote about?

Jonas uses a Dickens quote to explain his feelings for Val: "Family not only need to consist of merely those whom we share blood, but also for those whom we'd give blood." Are there people not related to you whom you consider family? Who are they? Why do you feel so close to them?

Ivy thinks she'll never be able to perform aerial dance in such a short time, but she manages to do it. Have you ever accomplished something you once felt impossible?

In the original *Oliver Twist*, Oliver's half-brother Monks is a greedy, sinister man who has seizures. How do you think our view of epilepsy has changed since Dickens's time?

If you attended the costume ball onboard the *S.S. David Copperfield*, which Dickens character would you want to dress as? Why?

What do you think of Theo's "Positively Powerful" philosophy? Has positive thinking influenced your life? What are its benefits? Its downsides?

There are several famous Dickens lines parodied throughout the book. Can you find them?

Dickens had famously evocative names for his characters. Can you think of any names in *Oliver Twisted* that pay homage to this trait? If you could choose a Dickensian name for yourself, what would it be?

Did you catch the Dickens reference in the opening line of the book?

Some of the screwball antics in Ivy's books have been inspired by true stories (like the scene where Ivy's trapped in the shower). Do you have any wacky true-life experiences that might fit into Ivy Meadows's madcap world? (If so, the author would love to hear about them).

Enhance Your Book Club or Class Discussion

Read Dickens's *Oliver Twist*, or watch the miniseries and/or the musical *Oliver!*

Create your own Dickens-themed meal. You can have a simple ploughman's lunch (Ivy eats a version on pgs. 120-121), enjoy traditional tea and scones, or create a Victorian feast with recipes from *What Shall We Have For Dinner?*, a cookbook by Charles Dickens's wife, Catherine.

Catch an aerial dance performance, or even take a class. If you can't find an aerial dance troupe in your town, watch the "Maiden Light" performance online.

See if you can fit inside a restroom stall while wearing a hoopskirt (just kidding).

Visit www.cindybrownwriter.com to learn more about the author, and to sign up for her Slightly Silly Newsletter, an irreverent look at mystery and drama (with a smidgen of book news).

Cindy Brown

Cindy Brown has been a theater geek (musician, actor, director, producer, and playwright) since her first professional gig at age 14. Now a full-time writer, she's lucky enough to have garnered several awards (including 3rd place in the 2013 international *Words With Jam* First Page Competition, judged by Sue Grafton!) and is an alumnus of the Squaw Valley Writers Workshop. The first Ivy Meadows mystery, *Macdeath*, was an Agatha Award nominee for Best First Novel.

Though Cindy and her husband now live in Portland, Oregon, she made her home in Phoenix, Arizona, for more than 25 years and knows all the good places to hide dead bodies in both cities.

The Ivy Meadows Mystery Series
By Cindy Brown

MACDEATH (#1)
THE SOUND OF MURDER (#2)
OLIVER TWISTED (#3)

Available at booksellers nationwide and online

Visit www.henerypress.com for details

Henery Press Mystery Books

And finally, before you go...
Here are a few other mysteries
you might enjoy:

MURDER ON A SILVER PLATTER

Shawn Reilly Simmons

A Red Carpet Catering Mystery (#1)

Penelope Sutherland and her Red Carpet Catering company just got their big break as the on-set caterer for an upcoming blockbuster. But when she discovers a dead body outside her house, Penelope finds herself in hot water. Things start to boil over when serious accidents threaten the lives of the cast and crew. And when the film's star, who happens to be Penelope's best friend, is poisoned, the entire production is nearly shut down.

Threats and accusations send Penelope out of the frying pan and into the fire as she struggles to keep her company afloat. Before Penelope can dish up dessert, she must find the killer or she'll be the one served up on a silver platter.

Available at booksellers nationwide and online

Visit www.henerypress.com for details

FATAL BRUSHSTROKE

Sybil Johnson

An Aurora Anderson Mystery (#1)

A dead body in her garden and a homicide detective on her doorstep...

Computer programmer and tole-painting enthusiast Aurora (Rory) Anderson doesn't envision finding either when she steps outside to investigate the frenzied yipping coming from her own back yard. After all, she lives in Vista Beach, a quiet California beach community where violent crime is rare and murder even rarer.

Suspicion falls on Rory when the body buried in her flowerbed turns out to be someone she knows—her tole-painting teacher, Hester Bouquet. Just two weeks before, Rory attended one of Hester's weekend seminars, an unpleasant experience she vowed never to repeat. As evidence piles up against Rory, she embarks on a quest to identify the killer and clear her name. Can Rory unearth the truth before she encounters her own brush with death?

Available at booksellers nationwide and online

Visit www.henerypress.com for details

A MUDDIED MURDER

Wendy Tyson

A Greenhouse Mystery (#1)

When Megan Sawyer gives up her big-city law career to care for her grandmother and run the family's organic farm and café, she expects to find peace and tranquility in her scenic hometown of Winsome, Pennsylvania. Instead, her goat goes missing, rain muddies her fields, the town denies her business permits, and her family's Colonial-era farm sucks up the remains of her savings.

Just when she thinks she's reached the bottom of the rain barrel, Megan and the town's hunky veterinarian discover the local zoning commissioner's battered body in her barn. Now Megan is thrust into the middle of a murder investigation—and she's the chief suspect. Can Megan dig through small-town secrets, local politics, and old grievances in time to find a killer before that killer strikes again?

Available at booksellers nationwide and online

Visit www.henerypress.com for details

FIXIN' TO DIE

Tonya Kappes

A Kenni Lowry Mystery (#1)

Kenni Lowry likes to think the zero crime rate in Cottonwood, Kentucky is due to her being sheriff, but she quickly discovers the ghost of her grandfather, the town's previous sheriff, has been scaring off any would-be criminals since she was elected. When the town's most beloved doctor is found murdered on the very same day as a jewelry store robbery, and a mysterious symbol ties the crime scenes together, Kenni must satisfy her hankerin' for justice by nabbing the culprits.

With the help of her Poppa, a lone deputy, and an annoyingly cute, too-big-for-his-britches State Reserve officer, Kenni must solve both cases and prove to the whole town, and herself, that she's worth her salt before time runs out.

Available at booksellers nationwide and online

Visit www.henerypress.com for details

CPSIA information can be obtained
at www.ICGtesting.com
Printed in the USA
LVOW01s0115110716
495801LV00015B/107/P